A
LANCASHIRE
STORY

Ged Melia

Grosvenor House
Publishing Limited

The right of Ged Melia to be identified as the author of this
work has been asserted in accordance with Section 78
of the Copyright, Designs and Patents Act 1988

The book cover is copyright to Ged Melia
Book cover design by Claire Marsden

This book is published by
Grosvenor House Publishing Ltd
Link House
140 The Broadway, Tolworth, Surrey, KT6 7HT.
www.grosvenorhousepublishing.co.uk

This book is a work of fiction. Any resemblance to
people or events, past or present, is purely coincidental.

A CIP record for this book
is available from the British Library

Paperback ISBN 978-1-80381-009-6
Hardback ISBN 978-1-80381-010-2
Ebook ISBN 978-1-80381-011-9

Website: http://www.dmsltd.co/alancashirestory/

This novel is based on actual events but some characters, scenes and
incidents have been created, or changed, for dramatic purposes.

To my family

"The life of the dead is placed in the memory of the living."

Marcus Tullius Cicero
106BC – 43BC

ACKNOWLEDGEMENTS

Readers of my first novel, *Family Business*, suggested I write a sequel, bringing it 'up to date', or at least into the last quarter of the twentieth century. Perhaps in time I will, but my recent preference has very much been to delve further into the past, assembling the increasingly scarce fragments of family history into a credible narrative. Thus, *A Lancashire Story* was born. As with *Family Business*, it is a family story, perhaps typical of aspirational descendants of Irish Catholics, perhaps not; I cannot say for sure. What I can say, is that although it is anchored on fact, I have necessarily had to embellish what details there are with family anecdote and originality. Situations have been created and characters introduced to assist with the narrative flow. Characterisations of people are largely down to supposition and guesswork; there has been very little to actually work with. I trust that you, the reader, will forgive the approach. Although facts and events are used as cornerstones, the book is predominantly a work of fiction.

Although there was scant verifiable information to work with, there have been events, newspaper cuttings, photographs and family anecdotes which have helped structure the story. I am indebted to family members, many no longer with us, for leaving me this material. Much of it would clearly have been lost to memory without their kind help many years ago.

The usual suspects have tolerated my requests for comment and narrative review. Oliver, your help in identifying the far too many typos and errors in the early drafts is very much appreciated. As with previous scripts, my immediate family were enlisted for proofing help and content critique. Enthusiasm for undertaking these tasks has been mixed, but for those that have managed to find the time, thank you.

Thank you also to my great grandfather, Austin Melia. The more I learned about his life the more it becomes obvious that he and Emma, his wife, were responsible for the lives we currently have. Austin was the son of an illiterate coal miner. Notwithstanding this rather exacting impoverished start in life, he managed to qualify as a steam engineer, ascend a career ladder, and provide the pecuniary seed for his children's road haulage business. We, several generations later, perhaps don't realise how much we owe him.

Thank you, Austin.

Entwistle, Turton, December 2021

PROLOGUE

'Ouch!'

The boy had tripped over some unseen obstacle, a loose coal or stone.

A transient pain to his right hip, caused by the fall, soon gave way to sheer horror. In trying to steady himself, the naked candle he was holding had flown out of his hand and landed at the foot of a dusty cloth brattice. It was aflame in an instant; caked in coal dust it was a natural fire accelerant.

What should he do? Try and put it out, or call for help?

The choice had been made for him. In the space of thinking about his next action, the rest of the thin barrier had become a wall of fiery light; its angry sulphurous fingers had already reached out across the floor, and even further along the seam's ceiling, carried by the now uncontrolled flow of air. A life-preserving ventilation screen no longer.

He shouted and then ran.

'Fire!' 'Fire!' 'Fire!'

Hundreds of yards deeper into the cannel seam, still well beyond the source of the threat, a look of concern had appeared on Joseph Bye's face. He turned to his nearest companion, George Gerrard.

'Can tha smell it?'

George Gerrard turned his head towards the route out.

'Smoke.'

Concern turned to horror on both men's faces. Having dropped their tools, they could now hear the vague sounds of a commotion in the distance. The tunnel carried the noise but also acted to muffle its sounds.

There was no time to waste. They had to act.

'Quickly!' said Bye.

No explanation was needed. Gerrard followed his work mate, both moving as fast as they could in the dark, and increasingly smoke-filled tunnel. It was unsaid, but they knew already that their very lives were at stake.

Minutes later they joined others who had also been working beyond the flames, deep in the pit. Some were coughing, others praying, and yet others were shouting for help.

Bye dropped to the floor, where the air was marginally better than at standing height.

'We can't stay 'ere!' shouted Bye.

He was addressing everyone within earshot, but only his mate seemed to pay any attention. The others, both men and boys, seemed frozen in fear. All could hear the sounds of a possible rescue, an unknown number of yards away, and had seemingly already decided that to wait was their only choice.

Not Bye. He knew that the smoke was as much of a threat as the fire itself.

"We shan make a run for it," he shouted.

Gerrard nodded.

'Now!'

About the only luck they had was that it was January and he had worn an old coat as protection from the snow that morning. Holding it over his head, and bent low, he started to move as briskly as the flames would allow. George Gerrard followed in like manner. Within the space of a minute Bye cried out.

'Men on't floor!'

There wasn't enough time to undertake anything other than a cursory check, but all looked like life had already passed. Bye counted at least eight bodies in all.

Sixty or so yards into their ordeal and both men had to drop from a crouch into a crawl. They coughed uncontrollably as the heat became unbearable, scorching through their thin garments and searing any exposed skin. But to survive both knew that they had to carry on.

Another twenty or so yards and men's voices could clearly be heard.

Bye cried out.

'Elp! Help!'

'Where is thee!' came the reply.

'Eer, eer, me an' another,' replied Bye.

Bye kept crawling, leaving Gerrard some yards behind him.

'I can sithee!' cried out one of the would-be rescuers.

Two unknown men had covered themselves in wet cloths and had entered the conflagration. Upon reaching them, only a matter of yards away from sanctuary, each had grabbed an evacuee and dragged them to rescue.

Bye tearfully accepted the water offered by his saviour. He started, almost incoherently, an uncharacteristic prayer of thanks. Overcome by the experience and clearly in pain from the burns, it would be some hours before he became aware that his friend, George Gerrard, had been less lucky. He had almost made it, only succumbing a matter of yards from safety.

Tuesday 23 January 1877 had been a day Stone Hill Colliery would never forget.

Chapter 1

CHRISTMAS 1891

The rail journey from Bury to Farnworth was not a long one, and the only decision Austin had to make was whether to take the Bolton route, changing at Bolton's Trinity Street station, or the Manchester route, changing at Clifton. It made little difference in time, leaving the principle criteria for a choice – variety. Today that choice had been via Bolton, stopping at Radcliffe, Bradley Fold and Darcy Lever, before a change in Bolton. For most people it would have mattered little but Austin had the mind of a technician. He liked detail, and would often savour consideration of the minutiae of daily living and how things worked.

He was a collier like his father but he was also a militia man in the Lancashire Fusiliers. As he wasn't a regular, Austin was not subject to the full rigours of army life. He might have earned less than a full-time serviceman but his pay was still a useful supplement to the subsistence wages paid to miners. All he needed to do to earn it was to undertake a few weeks of training per year, and to undertake short service or instruction when required. And the army had also helped him achieve his ambition of working with engines; obtaining a few skills that would soon be useful in his regular work. For most of December he had been training with his army pals at the Wellington Barracks in Bury, but Christmas had brought a welcome respite from the oftentimes drudging routines of military life. His last posting, earlier in 1891, had been in Glasgow, Maryhill to be exact, towards the north of the city. In late spring he returned to civilian life but in November he had been told that his unit would be posted to Belfast soon in 1892, and that some preparatory training would be required. It would be a few short weeks back in the barracks and then over the Irish Sea to Northern Ireland for a few more weeks.

He thought that he would enjoy a change despite the inevitable disruption it thrust upon family life.

Time with his family would be precious, as would a planned liaison with Emma, the woman he struggled to meet privately even when he was in Farnworth. Ironically, when he was serving, he often felt closer to her. She would write on a weekly basis proffering news of home, her family, and sometimes his. It had become as much a romance by pen and ink, but no less of a romance for that. A sometimes distant life in the British Army, tempered by the mellifluously toned strokes of italic script telling of news 'back home', always fuelled a yearning to see her again. She even wrote when he was posted in barracks in Bury.

As the train passed over the Darcy Lever Viaduct, the rhythmic clatter of engine wheels against track, steel on steel, increased in volume, mirroring a similar increase in his sense of excitement and anticipation; every inch brought him closer to home.

'Pheeeep! Pheeeep!'

The steel beast carrying Austin and a hundred other passengers had exclaimed its arrival at Trinity Street in Bolton. His motley travelling companions, like Austin, who would have also paid threepence or so for a cheap ticket to the heart of Lancashire's cotton industry, began readying themselves for escape. A minute later and the train's brakes were fully applied; its wheels squealed, and engine and carriages shuddered to an abrupt halt. A whistle from the platform, and the doors of each carriage opened and started disgorging its now animated passengers. Austin recovered his travelling bag from the rack and followed others out of the train. Momentarily disorientated, he soon recovered and then spotted his connection, another engine exuding steam on an adjacent platform. To Austin, steam engines seemed to be like a set of excitable carriage horses in need of restraint. An engine was like that. It was a battle between master and steel, with steel always seeking liberation, and master imposing restraint until permission was granted.

Slightly in fear of his connection leaving without him, he advanced briskly towards one of the still open carriage doors on an adjacent platform. It was only then that he realised how chilled the December air had become, crisp even. Breathing was usually a subliminal autonomic function of his being, but the cold air promoted it into awareness. Each exhalation of breath generated a white cloud of carbon dioxide, before instantly evaporating into the slightly smoky atmosphere of Trinity Street Station.

Two minutes after stepping on to the platform he was sitting in a carriage of the 17.35pm train to Manchester. Two more minutes and the engine's master released its power. The cortege jerked and shuddered into life with a 'chuff' and a 'hiss'; his carriage started to move.

In a matter of minutes, he would be back in Farnworth.

Expectations and plans for his time at home echoed around his brain, distracted somewhat by thoughts and reflections of the past, of how he had come to be in this position. Austin remembered little of his early childhood life in St. Helens and considered himself a Bolton, or more accurately, a Farnworth lad.

He allowed his mind to drift again.

Neither of his parents wanted him to 'go down't pit' like his father but necessity demanded that he yield to the requirements of earning a living. It was pragmatism that drove him into the colliery, but Austin remained determined that it would not be the end of it. One day he would be out of colliery work, and the army would be at least a part of the solution. From an early age he had been interested in steam engines, and like many youngsters had dreamt of working on the railways as an engineman. But the world wasn't going to hand him his dreams on a platter, and there were also practical aspects to address. Like bringing home a wage. His father was also a collier and didn't earn nearly enough to feed all the hungry mouths in his growing family. Shortly after their move to Farnworth in 1878, and at the age of eleven, Austin was working as a 'little piecer' in a cotton mill on Lorne Street. Even at that age he knew it wasn't what he wanted, but he had no choice but to make his contribution towards the family purse.

But Austin also knew he was lucky. Well liked and intelligent, it wasn't long before opportunity, and ultimately escape, presented itself in the form of education and service. His family were Catholic and impoverished, two apparently insurmountable social constraints on the ability of the working poor to scale a rigid Victorian class structure. But his natural acumen and appealing personality soon attracted the attention of, and beneficence, of a parish priest who recognised scholarly potential. Fortunately for Austin, the priest wasn't of the 'spare the rod and spoil the child' variety. Not for him were sermons of punishment and damnation that seemed to culture working class behaviour towards children. Most likely this kindly priest had an influence on his own father's approach towards discipline. While his home retained the preferred instrument of chastisement, a leather thonged strap, it was rarely on display, and even more rarely used.

Austin remembered his early years, sitting in an anteroom in Lowe House Chapel with a handful of others. He pondered over how fate could have dealt a different hand; he could have been in a mine at age eight like others. But no, his enigmatic father wanted his son to read and write, and allowed him the time, even if it did mean they had to learn the Bible in studious detail. Perhaps the cleric thought he might become a priest himself, mused Austin, just as his thoughts were interrupted by a passing train thundering past in the opposite direction.

The engine and its cavalcade of carriages rattled on, but then gradually started to slow as it approached Moses Gate, the penultimate stop before Farnworth. Within minutes he would be on home territory; in perhaps less than half an hour he would be greeting his family. Austin took only a passive interest in the characters leaving and boarding the train at Moses Gate, then drifted back into reflection.

Those early sacrifices by his parents had to be repaid somehow, and after arriving in Farnworth, Austin and his older sisters obtained employment in a cotton mill. But that would not be the end of his education. With this support of his father he had been able to occasionally attend Bolton Mechanics Institute, and use its facilities to pursue an increasingly active interest in science and engineering matters. There were lectures, yes, but much of what he had learned had been self-taught. The family's move from St. Helens had been something of a blessing in that he felt released from any obligations he might have felt towards the parish priest. Farnworth was a clean slate; unshackled, he could pursue his true interests. He would always be a Catholic but never a priest.

The train whistled again, signalling its impending arrival in Farnworth. Austin and another passenger in his carriage stood up to retrieve their belongings. There was less than a minute to go before its doors would be flung open and he would be away from the rolling stock.

The brakes squealed and hissed as the engine again shuddered to a halt. In an instant the doors were opened and Austin was on the platform. There were only a handful of other passengers leaving and boarding, so he took a minute to survey train and station. He had little time to notice in Bolton, but the locomotive he had just left looked like a new one. Elegantly painted in black and with its panels outlined in a thick red and thin white lines, it proudly displayed an L&Y logo and crests. 'L&Y', thought Austin. That must have been a new innovation. He already knew it was a Lancashire and Yorkshire engine, but now so did everyone else.

His gaze moved across the rest of the station. It was unchanged from his last visit. The Rawson Arms still towered over Farnworth and Halshaw Moor's small but still impressive station. Its three-storey stone administration building still welded to another on the opposite platform via a soot tarnished covered footbridge, and the passenger slipway still invited travellers to cross a sister bridge, joining Bridge Street to the cemetery road.

He left the platform and started the gentle ascent up the footway to the bridge. After sitting for the best part of an hour a walk would be refreshing, though very cold. He was thankful for the heavy coat he was wearing. At the centre of the bridge, Austin looked back along his arrival route towards Bolton. Within the straight line of the track the station's covered footbridge blocked much of the view, but he knew what was there. He could not see it, but still chuckled as he thought of the appropriately named 'Squeezebelly Entry', a footbridge near Ash Street, that as children they would use to cross the railway to fish in the reservoirs near Rock Hall. Not that they ever caught much.

Austin shivered. It felt like it was getting colder, perhaps thirty degrees. It was time to get home.

He decided that the quickest way back would be to walk up Peel Street, signalled by the elevated Rawson Arms Hotel. Peel Street was like most other streets in Farnworth. Its two rows of Daubhill brick housing, 'Dobble' as they say in Bolton, each topped off with Clamerclough fire-brick chimney pots, faced each other, cliff-like, guiding entry to an inescapable destination. A few commercial buildings littered his path, including the town's Reform Club building. The Reform Club had once been Farnworth and Kearsley Mechanics Institute. Had it still been operating when he was younger, perhaps he would not have needed to go into Bolton. And now even that was gone. Whatever, he couldn't regret an opportunity he was never presented with. Besides, Bolton's would have been a lot bigger and better.

Austin turned left at the Peel Street and Market Street junction, just as Farnworth's leaden grey sky began to release its weary load. It had started to snow. Light at first, it soon became a more challenging onslaught. He was lucky he had not got far to go. A horsecar appeared, pulled by two giant draft horses. It halted outside Farnworth's now familiar Cooperative building, a regular stopover for his mother. As its sole passenger descended from the open deck at the top of the vehicle, the wind picked up and gusted snow directly into the eyes of both horses, momentarily disturbing them. It also caught the driver unaware, and he was unable to stop the two creatures pulling the horsecar forward a few feet just as the passenger stepped off. The movement threw its poor victim off balance; there was a shriek as the unfortunate man fell to the floor. For a few seconds he just lay there.

Austin called across.

'ist thee alreet?'

The man either couldn't hear him, or was ignoring him.

Austin repeated, but louder.

'Alreet?'

The former passenger twisted to face him, waving as he returned to his feet. His coat was covered in fine white snow which he proceeded to brush off. He looked more embarrassed than injured, the almost instant all-encompassing thin blanket of white powder had perhaps softened his fall.

Oblivious to what had transpired at the rear of his vehicle, the horsecar driver gently coaxed the equine giants back into motion.

Austin quickened his pace to the maximum speed the weather would allow, but was forced to stop on the footpath directly opposite his parent's home street. Increasingly violent snow gusts had slowed the progress of the vehicle; he needed to wait for it to pass by. Notwithstanding the horsecar's slow progress, he didn't want to risk an accident by crossing ahead in what was clearly becoming a full snowstorm. Eventually, the less than sure-footed horses and car slithered past revealing the Queens Hotel. Its many stone lintel windows, all encased in a deep red brick, and its two floors confidently marked out the junction of Market Street and Bridgewater Street.

He crossed the road diagonally, towards the confectioner on the corner opposite the 'Queens'. As he did so, he caught sight of public house's gable end and read its sign. It was still Sharman & Sons public house, the Bolton brewer which had recently been expanding out of its home town. Careful not to lose his footing, Austin continued a brisk pace towards what he fully expected would be a warm reception. He was really looking forward to seeing his family and enjoying Christmas celebrations.

Austin trudged past the sentry-free arched doorways of the monobloc terraced housing of Bridgewater Street before finally reaching 118. By which time the gentle snowfall he had experienced less than ten minutes earlier had transformed into a full blizzard. He knew the front door would not be locked. No one seemed to bother carrying the heavy, jailer type, cast iron keys that would probably unlock more than one door on the street. And there was, after all, little that many would deem worth taking. Without knocking, he simply opened the door and walked straight in, taking care to gently close it behind him - the icy gust of winter accompanying his entry would not be a welcome companion. In the space of a few seconds he attempted a survey of the space he had just entered. There was no one present; the sitting room was almost pitch black, lit only by an attenuated ribbon of orange light penetrating the darkness via a wafer-thin gap at the bottom of the kitchen door. He removed his coat and waited a few seconds to let his eyes adjust to the dimness. A smile crossed his face as he listened to the many voices chattering about nothingness in the other room; all could be heard except his father and the baby, his now youngest sister.

Surprised that no one had heard him, he walked across the sitting room to the kitchen door, opened it, and announced his arrival.

'I'm home.'

Multiple pairs of eyes turned towards him. In an instant Margaret, his next youngest sister, leapt up and hugged him. He wasn't surprised that everyone was there. He knew that his older sisters worked from 8.30am to 6.15pm, and that they would have been at home, and probably have eaten, by the time he arrived.

'You're early,' said Edward, Austin's collier father. Despite being born in Liverpool his accent still carried the hint of Irish twang, an early influence of his own father. He must surely have had a hard day, thought Austin, familiar with the backbreaking toils of a collier's day.

Edward remained seated, glued to one of only two armchairs strategically placed by the open coal fire. Neither Austin's father nor his mother had many rules but one he did have was on the use and placement of 'his' armchair. Everyone knew they had to respect their father's right to the seat by the fire. And woe betide anyone who had the temerity to sit in it while he was at home. Above the fireplace his mother's favourite motto still hung, as it always had: 'East West, Home's Best'. A testament to 'fortress home', a sanctuary from a hostile world. Glancing around the rest of the room revealed nothing else new. It remained spartan and utility oriented, a few chairs, a table, some storage, washing materials, and some clothing drying on a makeshift maiden adjacent to the other armchair. It was austere, and yet strangely comforting.

Sitting on the other armchair was Ellen, Austin's grandmother. This would usually be occupied by his mother, Mary, but Ellen was visiting for the Christmas period. She attempted a smile, but in doing so exposed the two of the handful of remaining teeth she still had. Her appearance had deteriorated since his last visit. A failed attempt to neatly comb her unkempt grey hair, and her increasing gaunt facial expression momentarily tugged at Austin's heart. But this was not a time for sadness. He smiled back, then turned to his mother, younger brother, and other sisters.

Catherine, Ellen, or 'Nell', and Annie, were now all working at the same mill on Lorne Street in Moses Gate, the same one that had employed Austin in the years before he joined the army militia and worked as a collier. They just called it 'Horrockses' now, but when he was younger it was Crewdson, Crosses and Co, or simply 'The Mill.' All three of his adult sisters were sitting at the family's general-purpose wooden kitchen table with John, Austin's school age brother, sitting at one end with a book in hand. Austin mentally approved. Education was everything.

His mother stood up after tending to the baby.

'Are you hungry, Austin?'

'I am, Ma. Nothing special though.'

Austin knew that there would be more food than usual in the larder but also knew that his mother would want to make Christmas Day as special as she possibly could. Supper would probably be a bit of bread, butter and cheese. It would be enough.

'I'll make thee something.'

'I'll do it,' interjected Nell, as she stood up.

All three sisters appeared to be sewing some garment or other. Nell obviously wanted a break, surmised Austin.

His mother acknowledged her daughter's help before addressing him again.

'We missed you, Austin.'

'I know, Ma. I'm glad to be home.'

'How long will you be here?' interjected Catherine, Austin's eldest step-sister.

'We're off to Belfast early January. I'm using all the leave I have left.' replied Austin.

He did not want to talk about his leaving day only minutes after arriving.

'Will you be seeing Emma?' asked Catherine.

It was direct question from one of his sisters, perhaps not entirely unexpected, though very soon in the family reunion. With the exception of his brother everyone seemed interested in his answer.

'I might,' lied Austin. He had every intention to.

'You might?' interjected Nell, before adding, 'That's not what she said to me,'

Austin was a little taken aback. Only minutes at home and he was already being interrogated about his growing fondness for Emma. He searched both of his sisters' faces for clues about what she might know about the two of them. It seemed like the whole family knew a lot more about his business than they really should.

'We've become quite good friends while you've been away, Austin. We meet quite often now,' said Nell.

It was true that Emma's letters had mentioned seeing Nell, but she hadn't given much away about a growing 'friendship'. And he had only been away a matter of weeks.

Austin looked for a way out of this particular subject.

'She said that she often writes to you,' said Nell.

This was sometimes a sensitive subject at home. Neither Austin's father, mother, nor grandmother could read or write, so any letters home would be read out loud by one of his sisters. And there were some things he wanted to keep private, rather than share for family discussion. This was definitely one of them.

Austin shrugged.

'Everyone knows she's not Catholic,' added Nell.

He started to feel uncomfortable. From his perspective it was still too early in the relationship for even thinking that her religious denomination might be a problem. Why was she probing so much? he wondered.

Austin ignored the comment and attempted to change the subject.

'Did she tell you I've been promoted?'

'She did,' said Nell.

'We know its Corporal Melia,' added his mother.

'Yes. I was an acting corporal for a week or two but its official now. I get more money as well,' replied Austin.

'I bet you could afford to wed Emma now, Austin,' added Nell rather mischievously.

'It's only just been confirmed,' said Austin, pointedly ignoring his sister's teasing. It was time to ask one of his other sisters a few questions. He scrabbled around for something to talk about.

'Are you still a drawer-in at mill, Annie?'

Austin knew it was a rather limp question to ask, but it served its purpose.

'I am,' replied Annie.

Annie had injured herself a few years earlier. After the incident she found it easier to sit down rather than stand up for long periods, and the bosses at the mill had been good to her in finding employment that avoided having to constantly negotiate moving spinning machinery. Her nimble fingers were employed in taking the threads from many bobbins fixed to a frame; she would help to form the required patterns. It was a job that lent itself to sitting down. Fortunately, she was reputedly very good at it. At least, according to her sisters.

'They give me ten shillin' a week now,' Annie proudly added.

Money, or the lack of it, was always an open discussion in the Melia household. With the exception of himself, it all went into the family pot, often literally. It was an open secret that his mother kept an old teapot with 'savings' in it, in what she regarded as a 'safe place'. Some now went to the Farnworth and Kersley Cooperative Society after his mother had finally been persuaded that it would be just as safe, and that she might even earn a bit of interest. Even his father gave his wages to his mother, most of it, after keeping a little back for some beer and a little tobacco.

Austin acknowledged Annie's 'achievement', though quietly thinking that the mill would soon drop her wage if times became more difficult.

'You'll be sleeping in the sitting room with John,' said his mother.

Austin nodded; he was used to it. Bridgewater Street was typical of the terraced housing in Lancashire, and so was his household. Recently built of the now ubiquitous red brick, the family had been pleased to be able to afford to move into it.

Two rooms downstairs and two upstairs, it was an improvement on their last accommodation but was still small given the number of people in the house. The girls, or women, would share a bedroom, as would his parents with the baby. With his grandmother staying, she would have to sleep in the kitchen, and he and John in the sitting room. Every room occupied. It was true that he was used to it, but he longed for the day when he would have his own space. There was no privacy in the army either.

Nell placed a plate with some bread, butter, cheese and a slice of pork pie and mustard in front of him. The pie was unexpected and welcome. He started to tuck into it as a tin mug of lemonade was added to the feast.

'Thank you.'

'How's working at the mine, Dad?'

'Better,' replied Edward.

'How so?' asked Austin.

Edward paused before answering, taking the time to replenish his pipe with some tobacco retrieved from a pocket.

'They still talk 'bout it,' he finally replied.

Austin knew what his father was referring to. It was the reason, or catalyst, the family had come to Farnworth in 1878, some thirteen years earlier. His father worked in the Stone Hill Colliery on the Walkden road for most of those years. In 1877 eighteen men and boys lost their lives, mostly through suffocation from a fire. It was a black day for Farnworth and Walkden. But it wasn't the only disaster. A matter of weeks later, fate dealt another blow against the local mining community. Barely had the funerals taken place for the victims of Stone Hill, when Foggs Colliery in Darcy Lever suffered an explosion, killing ten men and boys, and pit ponies. The mines had lost dozens of experienced men in the space of a couple of months, injured many others, and caused more than a few with families to seek employment elsewhere. Farnworth needed replacements, and Austin's father eventually answered the call. The promise of higher wages ultimately made it an easy choice for him. He joined others from the St. Helen's pits, uprooted his growing family and moved to Farnworth.

The rest of the family also knew about it, and no one wanted to talk about the risks their father took in pursuit of a wage, a daily descent into the horrors of the Lancashire pits.

Catherine rescued the discussion before it became one of death and disaster.

'You'll be coming to Midnight Mass tomorrow, Austin? It is Christmas Eve.'

'Of course,' replied Austin.

'I'm glad you've not lost yer faith since being in the British Army,' said Mary.

'No, Ma,' replied Austin.

Attending services was expected in the Army, and Roman Catholic chaplains had been appointed for decades. Still, perhaps he had not been as diligent as he could have been, but there was no need for his mother to know that. He side-stepped providing the detail she was probably interested in, with an obfuscation.

'I know who the chaplain is, Ma. He's a good man.'

His mother looked at him with approval, but also for the subliminal signs body language divulges, typically without conscious thought. Austin knew this. He knew his mother could read him in a way only a mother can. She nodded and turned her attention back to the fire. It needed replenishing.

Soon lulled into unconsciousness by the gentle warmth of the fire and the somniferous tones of family conversation, his mother picked up the baby and removed her to their parent's bedroom. The act seemed to trigger his dozing father into action.

'Another half hour, then bed.'

Was it an announcement, an instruction, or a suggestion? Obeisance towards the head of the household had been ingrained into the behavioural patterns of all his children, though Austin's father rarely lifted a hand in anger. In response, each of his sisters stopped what they were doing. Catherine then collected the textiles and sewing materials, and placed them in one of the few pieces of furniture the family owned, a rustic pine chest of drawers. It was barely nine o' clock, and yet preparations for sleep were already underway.

'I'm tired as well, Dad. I was awake very early too,' replied Austin.

His father nodded, before spitting into a metal jug to the left of his armchair. Austin had not even noticed, but Edward had finished his smoke and had commenced chewing some tobacco. He had forgotten about this rather unpleasant habit of his father. 'Baccy', as his father called it, unlike drinking, had not been a lifelong habit, but he had taken to it only a year or two before Austin had started in the army. No one in the house liked it, but they had to accept it as a fact of life. Austin pitied his mother who had to empty the contents on a regular basis.

'John, can you get the bedding,' requested Austin of his younger brother.

His brother closed his book before leaping to his feet to comply.

Tomorrow was Christmas Eve. Austin knew he would be woken at 5.30 am by the 'knocker-up', but he also knew that unlike his father and sisters he would not have to work. He could do what he wanted with the day, perhaps go for a stroll, chat with his mother, or maybe take a trip over to a certain slate merchants in Little Lever.

By half past nine the flames of the kitchen fire had retreated into orange embers. As the rest of the family retired to their bedrooms, Austin and John made their own way into the sitting room, and to a makeshift bed that was usually the sole domain of his brother. The door to the kitchen had been left open to let a little of the residual heat into the sitting room. After the lamp had been turned down, all that remained was a little light from the dimming embers casting ambiguous shadows, and the quiet solitude of the world outside, its sounds now heavily muffled by hours of snowfall.

* * *

From an early age Emma had proven to be an asset to her father's slate business. It wasn't a full-time occupation, but he certainly found her administrative skills useful, especially given her father and mother's inability to read, or write. They had tried to of course, but daily demands of life inevitably led to failure – there was only so much time available. Emma believed she had been lucky. Unlike her parent's generation she had been provided with a rudimentary education while also learning a 'trade'. By day she was a cotton weaver, tending two looms in the deafeningly loud weaving shed of one of

Farnworth's largest mills. She might have taken on a third, and been paid even more, but preferred to keep a little of her energy in reserve to help her father. Not that it would have made much difference in hours worked, but certainly in her strength. Besides, she actually enjoyed being involved; it was a change from her usual working routines.

The Christmas period meant a deviation to the predictable daily rhythm of home and work. It was Christmas Eve and the completion of Emma's usual endeavour had allowed an early finish. As a favour to her father she had agreed to bank a little cash he had been given the previous day. He did not really like banks but had been persuaded by a business associate to open an account at the Manchester and Salford Bank a couple of years earlier. It had just opened a branch on Little Lever's High Street, a short walk away from where they lived on Church Street. Edward Kay, Emma's father, thought that its proximity meant that he could keep an eye on them and his money. And yet he still preferred that his daughter dealt with the bank as much as possible; perhaps his illiteracy forced his diffidence, or perhaps he simply felt intimidated by the experience of dealing with bank clerks. Emma was not entirely sure, but simply accepted that her father needed help and she was able and willing to give it.

She hadn't been entirely honest with her father. Unknown to her family, a month earlier, Emma had secretly agreed to meet Austin at what they believed would be a 'quiet' location. By letter they had agreed a time, date and place. It was a calculated risk. Anything could have happened in the intervening weeks, the weather, work, or her father could have twisted fate in a direction not in her favour. But she was determined. One way or another she would find a way to meet him, even if it meant lying.

Emma's father knew that she had a soft spot for Austin, but he clearly didn't realise that it was now growing to be more than that. While her father had not forbidden her from seeing him it was obvious that he did not approve. Why, Emma wasn't certain of. She loved her father but he could be frustrating at times. She cared little about his lack of an education, but she did care about his approval. And at this time, she was not ready to engage in discussion about Austin, the man she had already decided to marry. Not even Austin knew that yet; nor even did her mother.

Her father's request for her to go to the bank had been a stroke of luck. It provided a genuine excuse to leave the house, thus avoiding a lie. Nonetheless, her careful planning had stretched into arranging for a friend to provide a cover story. They would accidently 'bump into each other', then go for a walk near the locks at Nob End. Given the recent snowfall there would not be many people around and little risk of being recognised. Her father might not like her tardiness in returning home, but Emma felt sure he would accept it.

After completing her task at the bank, she started the walk to the canal towpath, carefully choosing a route which avoided Church Street. It wasn't really the weather for this kind of thing but what else could she do? The journey provided some time for reminisce, while the cold seemed to equally fuel an increased longing to see him. Her heart started to beat in excitement with each step.

Emma's first meeting with Austin was unplanned, as many are. Both were children, and both were earning a wage at Crewdson, Crosses & Co at the Moses Gate end of Farnworth. Her father's status as a businessman had afforded his children a little more time than many to pursue study, but even she had to eventually earn a living. Emma was thirteen and learning a weaver's trade while he, of a similar age, worked as a little piecer.

At that age Austin was still a cocky imp, full of confidence, fun and adventure. Indeed, he was undoubtedly a show-off. He worked in a different part of the building to Emma but would often take an opportunity to explore during the infrequent breaks mill work afforded. As was both need and custom, most workers, adult and child, would be barefoot when tending machinery, and Austin was no different. Typical of Austin at that age, and for reasons only known to him, one day he had decided to 'walk' the area Emma was still working in, on his hands. She could not help but notice and had to smile at his apparent talent for the absurd.

Then he fell.

And then she laughed.

And that was it. Austin noticed her and repeated his antics on the following days. It then wasn't long before they were on first name terms and occasionally meeting outside of mill work. They became firm friends for a time, until the dictates of hormonal maturity presented something more complex and compelling. She started to have 'feelings' for him.

But there was more to Austin than his sense of fun. Most half-timers, and almost every working child was one, would initially benefit from school in the morning and work in the afternoons. They would start their working life quick and alert, but the dull repetition of work soon retarded their development and mental acuity into dullness and lethargy. But not Austin. He was ambitious. Underneath a playful character was a steely determination to progress beyond the factory floor to something better. Unlike many of his companions he was able to apply himself to study, nurturing an early interest in railways and trains into a passion for engines and engineering. As he grew older that inner self also began to display. The childish Austin matured into something even more appealing to Emma. A more serious, thoughtful and attentive Austin appeared, someone perhaps she might spend her life with.

'Emma!'

A man waved, interrupting her thoughts and clearly intending to attract her attention. It could only be Austin.

She returned the wave without making a noise.

'I'll meet you at the bridge,' shouted Austin.

It had been pre-agreed that they would meet near the Nob Inn, a popular canal tavern. Austin had walked the Manchester, Bolton and Bury Canal towpath from the Moses Gate end to get to her. A little precarious in the snow, thought Emma, but she soon dismissed any concerns as he edged towards her.

Somewhat coyly, Emma checked her surroundings. An untended 'Bastard' size boat lay moored nearby, and there appeared to be no one else about. Dim light escaped from the lower windows of the nearby red brick public house but that was about it. Other than her own, she could see no footsteps in the recently fallen snow cloaking the cobblestoned road over Nob Bridge. They were alone.

Emma threw her arms around him as they met, literally, at the centre of the narrow bridge. He responded in like manner.

'I've missed you.'

'And I you.'

Emma's heart raced as their embrace extended to a full minute.

'I'm cold,' said Emma.

She had just realised that her feet had become numbed by walking in the snow for nearly an hour. Dressed in a thick shawl covering her head, her attire was typical for Lancashire mill women, even down to her clogs. It wasn't Sunday and she didn't have to wear her best. She just needed to keep warm.

'We could go for a drink,' suggested Austin, nodding in the direction of the public house. 'It will be warm inside.'

'I'm not sure. I don't really want to be seen. Not yet,' replied Emma, also concerned about breaching the male preserve of a public house. It wasn't something she would usually look forward to.

'I'm sure it will be fine,' replied Austin, while releasing his arms from around her.

Emma acquiesced, allowing Austin to take her hand and lead her towards the slightly elevated tavern fifty or so yards away.

Inside the tavern Austin found a quiet corner, out of sight of most except the landlord. He need not have worried. There were only two others inside, and neither were known to either Austin or Emma. After seating Emma, Austin went to the bar and ordered a pint of Wilson's Best for himself, and a half-pint for Emma.

'I can't stay too long, Austin. Father will start to worry. I'll tell him I met Rose on the way back from the bank," said Emma.

Austin also knew Rose from his days at the mill.

'I know,' replied Austin, before adding, 'How are you?'

'I'm well, and so is the family,' replied Emma

'I hear you have become friends with Nell while I have been away. She's talked about seeing you,' said Austin.

'Yes. After the time you introduced us in Farnworth Park, I saw her at the market a few weeks later. We agreed to meet again and, well…, we just started seeing each other more often. She's been over to Little Lever you know. I did mention that in my letters,' replied Emma, a little defensively. 'Have I done something wrong?'

'No. It's just that she started teasing me about us last night. I had only just got home,' said Austin.

'I'm, errr, sorry. She should not be doing that,' replied Emma.

'We need to keep us quiet, perhaps even until I come out of the army,' said Austin.

'I know. I know–,' repeated Emma. 'And there is my father as well.'

Austin knew about Emma's father's disapproval of him. He had thought that becoming a serviceman might influence his views, but up until now he had not budged an inch. Like many times before, Austin wondered what his problem actually was.

'He will change, Austin,' Emma added. She had tried to appear reassuring but still emitted a lack of confidence.

'We can't go on ignoring the fact that your dad doesn't approve of me, Emma. We'll have to do something about it if we are to be together,' replied Austin.

'Now is not the time, Austin. You know it isn't,' said Emma.

'We have been courting for nearly two years now, Emma. My family are starting to expect something to happen. What shall I say to them?' said Austin.

'I'll speak to Nell. I'll ask her to stop. Now can we talk about something else? I can't stay for long. What are your family's plans for Christmas Day?' enquired Emma.

'It will be the usual custom. Midnight Mass tonight at St. Gregory's and a feast tomorrow. I expect the Waits will be carolling in Farnworth and Little Lever this evening,' replied Austin.

'Yes. We all look forward to hearing them. They always mark the start of Christmas for me,' said Emma.

Austin looked down at his new treasure, a pocket watch.

'It's time.'

'I know, but it's been so short,' replied Emma.

Their conversation had lasted less than a half hour. Weeks of waiting for such a fleeting encounter, but it could not be helped. It would be the only occasion when they could meet on Austin's latest visit to Farnworth. While his Catholic family were more insouciant towards Emma, almost to the point of approval, Emma's father, a strict Anglican businessman, would certainly not have permitted this meeting, or any other. Austin continued to wonder what he would have to do to earn his respect and blessing. Without it, his growing fondness for Emma would be doomed before it had a chance to flourish.

* * *

Christmas Day.

There was no work today, and therefore no violation of collective slumber by the 'knocker-up'. And yet Austin knew that his mother would be up and about at seven to prepare for this special day. He also knew that she would leave Austin and John undisturbed, at least for a time, while she conducted her morning wash, started a fire and arranged breakfast. By seven thirty all would be awake, hungry, and probably buzzing with excitement in anticipation of what the day might bring.

His family were not wealthy but nor were they impoverished. With several wage earners, and some careful planning, Mary had the means and ability to provide a memorable feast for all. Its highlight in recent years had been a cooked goose for dinner, a rare treat for the family, typically only provided once a year, during Christmas. Some years earlier his mother had joined the 'Farnworth Goose Club', organised by two local pub landlords, paying a few pennies a week so that the family could enjoy a traditional Christmas meal. It was now almost a family custom, and it would no doubt also be Austin's role to collect the cooked treat from a local baker later in the day, as he had in previous years. It was all very organised, and much better than the beef and rabbit adorning the Christmas dinner table of his childhood.

Austin yawned.

The gentle but muffled chatter of his mother and sisters preparing a family breakfast had penetrated the closed door, and brought both him and John into consciousness.

'Mornin,' announced Austin.

John grunted, apparently still unwilling to rise from his makeshift sleeping arrangement.

He needed the closet. Austin quickly dressed in the shirt and trousers he had worn the previous day, before leaving John to enter the kitchen area. A large pot cooking an oatmeal porridge had already been erected over the range sitting adjacent to the open fire, and his sister Nell had started cutting some stoneground bread on the kitchen table. And there was something different today; he saw fish, eggs and bacon. It would be a breakfast feast indeed.

'Mornin, Ma,' said Austin.

'Sleep well?' replied his mother.

'I did, Ma,' said Austin before proceeding to the back door.

There was no need to announce his intentions. It would be clear to all. The brick ash privy stood far enough away from house to prevent the unpleasant smells of 'dejections' from permeating living areas. Everyone knew what went on there but no one wanted to talk about it, ever. As an aspirational engineer Austin would have been more than happy to talk about the relative benefits of the latest technology, the pail or tub closet system, versus traditional ash pits, but he knew that there would be no one willing to take him on. It would be a subject as interesting or appealing to his family as the privations of the 'nightmen', without whose services the system would simply not work. Having happily distracted himself for a few minutes with these thoughts, Austin finished his business and returned to the house to wash.

The kitchen had filled with the whole family by the time he returned, even John, who had no doubt been encouraged by the sizzling sounds and enticing smells of frying bacon.

'It will be half an hour,' announced his mother, who was now directing Austin's sisters in their breakfast tasks.

'Tea?' asked his mother, Mary.

'Yes please,' replied Austin.

His mother then proceeded with the established ritual of emptying the teapot of hot water. After checking that it was satisfactorily warmed, she then partially filled it with tea leaves, and then re-filled it with boiling water. Austin knew exactly what she would say next.

'It will need to steep for five minutes.'

'Yes, Ma,' replied Austin.

'You were out late last night, Austin,' said Mary.

'Not that late. I went out with John Aucutt' for a pint,' replied Austin.

'Just the two of you?' said Mary.

'Why do you ask, Ma?' replied Austin.

'I was just wondering...' said Mary.

'You're not going to bring up Emma again, are you?' questioned Austin.

Austin suddenly became the centre of attention again. All three of his sisters seemed to pause in their chores to stare at him, seemingly with a mix of curiosity and mischief. He had no wish to tell a lie but nor was he willing to share the truth.

'Of course not,' replied Mary.

His mother had probably sensed that she had not been given the whole story, but she did not know for sure and was clearly unwilling to provoke her son. There would be another time. His sisters, meanwhile, were naturally disappointed at the missed opportunity for some gossip over the breakfast table. But then again, they also realised that it simply meant a little bit of a delay. They would get to the bottom of it soon enough, and then what would happen? A Catholic and an Anglican. How could that work? Nell in particular salivated over the intrigue.

Christmas Day instructions and tasks were allocated at the end of breakfast, with Austin being expected to collect the cooked goose from the baker. His sisters were each directed to undertake various food preparation and cooking duties, while Edward's sole contribution seemed to consist of keeping out of the way, and John was allowed to sit and read. Perhaps it wasn't a fair allocation of work but it was simply the way it was.

* * *

Dinner had been a success and a feast indeed. In addition to the centrepiece, a goose, traditional fare had been on offer, home cooked beef, rabbit pie, a variety of fresh vegetables, and a new innovation, sweet mince pies. With the meal over, each member of the family sought a quiet spot, as close to the fire as possible, so that they could digest, and perhaps be entertained. Parlour games, as the rich called them, were not popular within the Melia family, but there was one which did seem to appeal to the men of the family, 'snapdragon'. Participating in it was not without an element of danger.

'Bring the bowl from the parlour, Mary,' directed Edward.

Lubricated with a quantity of beer that he had drunk with his food, Austin's father was looking for a bit of fun. The bowl he was referring to was still half-filled with some wassail punch that had been left in case carollers came to the door. They hadn't of course, which meant that there was a vigorous mix of rum and cider, fruit, and a mix of spices, nutmeg, cinnamon, and cloves, all waiting to be consumed.

It was Nell who recovered the bowl from the front room and left it on the range to warm. It was always better hot.

'Give it twenty minutes, Nell,' said Mary.

'Yes, Ma,' replied Nell.

'Austin. You first,' instructed Edward, his cheeks now well ruddied by the warmth of the fire and the effects of alcohol.

Austin knew what was coming next. It was indeed fun, but then again, he had lost a few hairs in the past when playing the game, much to his father's amusement.

'What about you, Dad?' said Austin.

'Maybe later. You first,' replied Edward.

His father had little intention of joining in, thought Austin. He just wanted to see what happened.

'I'll have a go,' said John.

Edward laughed.

'Of course, you will.'

After testing the bowl for its warmth, Nell took it off the stove and placed it on the table.

Showing only slight trepidation, Austin stood up and moved towards the bowl.

'Put some more rum in and throw in a few raisins,' said Edward.

Nell complied.

'Now light it. And turn the lamp down' added Edward.

Nell again complied. The bowl was aflame, with only that and the fireplace illuminating the faces of excited family members, each now gathered around the kitchen table.

'Go on,' said a grinning Edward, directing his instruction towards Austin.

Austin rolled his sleeve up. The object of the game was to remove by hand each raisin from the bowl, and extinguish it by eating. If he was quick, he could avoid the sharp, and not exactly pleasant, sensation of singed hairs on his arm. If not, well that would be unfortunate for him, but fun for his father.

Austin dived in, quickly retrieving a fiery raisin and consuming it, all within the space of a few seconds. Uninjured it was then the turn of John.

John tried to emulate his older brother's example but failed to find a raisin in time. He screamed, delighting Edward, again showing his mercurial character.

'I'll go again,' said John.

'No,' replied Mary, now alarmed that her son could do himself a real injury in his persistence.

'Let the girls have a go,' said Edward.

'No,' said Mary, before adding. 'I think Austin should read something to us.'

'I'll show you how it's done,' said Edward.

Mary shrugged. Her husband had been drinking and she had no wish to argue on Christmas Day.

Edward then proceeded to show off. With both hands in the bowl and an almost demonic expression on his face, accentuated by the low-level flickering lights of the fire and snapdragon bowl, he chased the raisins for longer than common sense dictated.

Removing two flaming raisins, one in each hand, he placed both in his mouth and doused them, failing to notice how the flaring bowl had singed the hairs on both his arms.

'Edward, your arms,' said Mary, clearly alarmed.

'Be quiet woman,' snapped Edward.

Mary complied. It was Christmas, and her husband's reasoning had obviously been affected by the copious quantities of alcohol he had been consuming. It wouldn't do to take any risks.

'I'll recite a story from that book I bought, 'Comic Lancashire Tales.' It will be a funny one, Dad,' suggested Austin, intervening to appease and distract his father from any intentions he might have had towards his mother.

Edward appeared mollified by the suggestion and turned to refill his mug from the now rapidly depleting punch bowl.

'Do it,' said Edward.

Austin went into the front parlour to retrieve J.T. Staton's volume of comic tales. He returned to the kitchen with a suggestion.

'What about this one?

He had opened the volume, a mix of stories and 'funnies', and suggested one he thought would entertain his family.

'It's called 'PADDY UN TH' COLLIERS,' he added.

In the absence of comments or objections from the gathering, he proceeded to read its contents as was intended, in thick local dialect.

'A short time back an Irishman who had come to Bowton to tak up his querters for a short time, that he met look after hervest work ith nayburhood, sterted off early ith mornin to seetch a job ith vicinity o Horridge. After inquirin at several ferms, meeting wi various sorts o luck, un getting promises un invitashuns regerdin th' future, he plodded his way back tort Bowtun. On arroivin ith naybourhood o Doffcocker, feelin a little bit teighurt, he sat hissel deawn on a hedge side, un in a very toothrey minnits dropt off into seawnd sleep.'

Austin had already got the attention of his family. Local references and a sleeping Irishman; it had to be fun. The effects of the consumed liquor and the prospect of humour would soon have them laughing. And Austin was a practised and competent storyteller. He took a breath before setting out the next part of the scene, a dozing man and the three or four young colliers who had tripped over the scene. Edward, in particular, started to chuckle at what would inevitably come next.

He proceeded to tell the tale.

'Aw say, he says, by George, chaps, let's have a mank wi this felly. He's as fast asleep as a cob o coal.

Well, says another, wot mun we do wi him?

Waw, says the fust speiker, let's tak him deawn th' coal pit, un leov him there till he wakens.'

Austin continued, telling how the colliers had picked up the man and lowered him into a nearby coal pit, following him down to see what happened when he awoke. Upon waking, disorientated in pitch blackness, the man would hear a collier pretending to be Satan, 'Emporer oth Sulphur Regions, un King oth Fiery Mountains.'

Edward burst into laughter at the masquerade, fully empathising with his new collier friends.

'Tis a good story, Austin. Go on,' said Edward, his involuntary laughter being the cause of the interruption.

'…his Imperial Majesty says – Give Paddy summat to eit un drink. Fot him a salamander pasty, un a little beighlin leod to season it wi; un let him have some sulphur broth to wash it deawn wi.'

Initially unwilling to eat the unappetising feast, the Irishman eventually yielded to 'Satan's commands', and proceeded to eat and drink the perfectly normal fare of beef on bread, and ale and whiskey, that had been presented by the disguised colliers. His initial circumspection gave way to enjoyment, and it wasn't long before the whiskey and the 'gibberish' chanting of the colliers sent the man back to sleep. After returning the sleeping man to the hedge where they had initially removed him, the colliers sat down opposite to watch what would happen.

Austin paused, to help to build expectation of the outcome.

'Well, what happened?' asked Ellen, impatient to hear the rest of the tale.

Austin took another breath and resumed reading.

'By the powers! he says, rubbin his eein, so it's not in hell that I am, after all. Hettin up, he lookt reawnd, to be shure that he wur on earth, un lookt o'er th' hedge to see if his Satanic Majesty or his imps wur anywhere abeawt. On th' opposite side oth road, th' colliers sat smookin their pipes, watchin him, un grinnin at his evident confushun.

By dad! he says, but I feel part drunk yet; I'm sartin the salamander pasty un the sulphur broth was no drame anyhow.

Takkin up his bundle, he hurried forrud, un, gooin straight to his lodgins ith town, towd his landlady un fellow-lodgers what a quare dreom he'd had.

If it be railly hell that I've been in, he says, by dad! Un it's not meeself that would object to goin again, for, for quantity un quality of the mate un drink, never did I see the likes of.'

With that final remark Austin closed the book and looked up. It was clear that they had enjoyed the story, and predictable that his younger brother would ask for another.

'It's getting late,' said Mary.

'Just one more,' said John appealing to his mother's softheartedness, before adding, 'It is Christmas.'

'One more then,' replied Mary.

'What about a ghost story?' suggested Austin.

'Not Dickens again. We have it every year.' said Edward.

'No. I have another short one from the same book. It will only take a quarter of an hour.' said Austin, addressing his mother.

Mary nodded in assent.

Austin started. 'It wur seven o'clock at neet, just before Kesmus; the snow wur fawin i' flakes as big as little poncakes...'

As the dimming light from the embers of the barely flickering fire faded, the younger members of the family, Margaret and John, cosied up to their mother. Slightly in fear of the story, and slightly in awe of their elder brother's storytelling, it was soon obvious that the evening's festivities and fun was having a toll. Margaret started to doze on a chair, leaning against her mother who was still listening attentively. Meanwhile, John fought to keep alert, the family having indulged him in the rare treat of some alcohol-laced punch. It was after all, Christmas.

By the end of Austin's second recital it wasn't just the younger ones ready for their beds. There was little complaint as some collective yawning marked the end of what most agreed had been one of the best Christmases ever.

Chapter 2

MARRIAGE

'We can't keep it a secret forever,' said Austin.

Emma studied his expression for further clues on intentions. It was true that they could not keep it a secret for much longer. Both his and her own family had become more than suspicious over the preceding months, as the 'coincidences' of their meetings had increased. Farnworth was a growing town, yes, and Little Lever was more than a village, but it remained difficult to meet without the threat of prying eyes and gossiping tongues. It was inevitable that they would be seen from time to time.

Austin had proposed to Emma the previous summer and of course she had accepted. Even if he had not, Emma had already resolved to marry him; she would have proposed to him! But they had both agreed to keep it a secret 'for now' until such time as they had developed a plan to negotiate the path of parental approval, and the even more problematic area of religious persuasion. Austin was a Catholic, Emma was an Anglican, and Emma's father would not seem to be too keen on Catholics. Emma was not the sort of woman who had a shy, retiring character, and would usually get her own way. But the question of her father's approval would need some careful handling.

'I know Austin, but I need a little more time,' replied Emma.

'We've been engaged over nine months, Emma. I'm ready to tell mine; as if I need to. I think they have long since guessed that something is afoot,' said Austin.

Emma squirmed at the suggestion that their news was already in the air. It would not do. Tradition called for Austin to seek her father's permission before marrying, yet she knew that he was nowhere near prepared to receive such a request.

'I know. I will say something, Austin. I'll get mother to invite you round for tea, not to say anything of course, but just to get to know father,' replied Emma, hoping her answer would mollify him.

It was strange. Her father had already met Austin on two or three occasions but the meetings were fleeting. Once at Farnworth Carnival, once when out for a stroll near the canal locks, and once while out on a shopping trip with both her parents. None were planned, and none afforded much more than an exchange of pleasantries. On each occasion her father had been cordial and polite, but also rather frosty towards Austin. Austin's diffidence in her father's presence also didn't help. How could he be so confident with others, and yet seem to shrink in the presence of her father? She had yet to work that out.

Austin started to respond but was interrupted by the sudden onset of an April shower. The Lancashire weather expressed its mercurial character in its usual manner. It was after all April, and he supposed sudden rain was to be expected.

Distracted, Austin grabbed Emma by the arm, 'Let's shelter under the bandstand. I doubt it will last,' exclaimed Austin, attempting prescience.

Two minutes later they were both standing under Farnworth Park's recently opened, and already locally iconic, bandstand.

Fortunately, the threat of rain had thinned out the usually popular park. There had been a handful of fellow locals 'out for a stroll', mostly couples, but almost all had either disappeared or found cover elsewhere.

Austin had been right. The shower had lasted less than the time it had taken them to find cover. They could have stayed under a tree and would perhaps have stayed drier.

'When shall you do it?' asked Austin, returning to the unresolved question of what the next step would be.

'I'll sort something out by the weekend,' replied Emma.

Austin nodded. There was little else to say on the subject and plenty to think about. How was he going to soften Emma's father, Edward's, position towards him? Was there really going to be a problem? Were perhaps both Emma and Austin reading too much into the apparently standoffish behaviour of her father? Austin was uncertain and somewhat intimidated. He was used to being well liked, so some apprehension would be inevitable. He decided to change the subject.

'I hear that the new public baths in Farnworth will be opening on the 29th,' said Austin.

Emma looked at him, slightly amused at the complete change of subject.

'Yes. Father has said as much. He's looking forward to the time when he won't have to bathe in our old tin bath next to fire,' replied Emma.

'I'll have to go, Austin. I'll be expected back before dark and it's getting late already. You don't need to walk me.'

Austin knew that Emma often preferred to walk herself. He now knew better than to insist. She often had her own reasons.

They both stepped down from the pyramid shaped, canopied bandstand, and headed for its small iron gate. As they passed the half dozen wooden slatted benches, they noticed a lone man sitting on the one nearest to the entrance. He held an umbrella up in the air, and had apparently not even bothered to move during the last shower. Emma smiled at him, while Austin had to contain his amusement. It was not a usual sight.

On reaching the entrance, Emma and Austin agreed on their next meeting and then walked together for a time towards Moses Gate. They parted at the Bridgewater Arms in the Gravel Hole end of Farnworth, Emma continuing her half hour walk back to Little Lever, and Austin heading inside for a drink. It was after all a Saturday night.

* * *

What kind of reception was he to expect, thought Austin, as he continued to progress along Church Street in Little Lever. Emma had been true to her word and had arranged for Austin to visit the following weekend. For most of the half hour walk from Farnworth he had managed to distract himself with thoughts of work, the army, and other domestic matters, but the sight of St. Matthews Church tower and roof in the distance signalled a change of mood. Apprehension. The church was only a matter of a minute or two's walk from Emma's family home; he would be standing outside 55 Church Street in a little more than five minutes. For a second, he was tempted by the dim glow of light emanating from the window of the Jolly Carter; perhaps a little Dutch courage was needed. But he thought better of it. Barlow & Fogg, the locally famous mineral water manufacturer, also came into view. It reminded Austin that he didn't even know if Emma's father was teetotal.

It would not be wise to appear smelling of beer; especially not on his first actual visit.

Austin collected his thoughts. So, what did he know of Emma's father? Endeavouring to answer this rhetorical question, he attempted a mental summary. Well, he knew that he was a slate merchant, and before that he had been a slater. He was also apparently a devout Anglican, at least that's the impression Emma had given him. Although in not so many words, Emma had also given him reason to believe he did not think too much of Catholics. All of which meant that this was not going to be an easy meeting. How was he going to tackle the subject of marriage, when even the rather delicate subject of his religion might be inflammatory? Austin had not got a plan or a solution. He would have to hope that Emma would seize the initiative, and that she had helped prepare her father in some way.

Austin paused outside his destination. Emma's family home was much the same as most of the others on the street. A small simply designed iron fence sat on a low six-course brick wall that protected a tiny garden area. It could not have been much more than six feet, thought Austin, surveying the space. The area was flagged, though there were three neatly tended shrubs sitting in pots, closer to the wall than the window. He could not determine their variety; gardening was not one of his strong points. The front door and upper and lower windows were painted a deep mahogany colour. Well maintained but a little plain. The overall impression was that of a better house than that of his own family. The presentation did not help his mood as another thought entered his mind. Might Emma's father think that Austin was a social climber? Perhaps his disposition towards him was not about religion but about class.

He gently knocked using a recently polished brass knocker, the door's most noticeable feature. It would not do to rap it too hard.

Within less than thirty seconds he was facing Emma.

'We've been expecting you, Austin. You are a little late,' said Emma, registering some soft disapproval.

'I'm sorry. I was delayed at home,' replied Austin. It was not true. The truth was his pocket watch was broken and he had lost track of the time. But in Austin's view that sounded too feeble. Better to let Emma think there had been important matters to deal with at home.

Austin followed her into the empty front room parlour.

'I'll go and fetch mother and father,' said Emma.

Austin nodded, then proceeded to sit down on the soft cushioned furniture. He looked around the room. Everything was of a better quality than his own home. It even housed some decorated ornaments and pottery. Perhaps unsurprising, given that Emma's father was a well-respected local businessman. Austin was thankful that he had elected to dress in his Sunday best. It would not have been fitting to wear his usual day clothes.

Emma returned to the parlour followed by her mother, and then her father.

'Father, you remember Austin, don't you?' said Emma.

'I do,' replied Edward, Emma's father.

Austin held out his hand as if to shake.

'I'm honoured to meet you, sir; properly this time.'

Emma's father hesitated before taking Austin's hand and briefly shaking it. There was no invitation to use his Christian name. Austin would have to continue to use 'sir'.

'And my mother,' said Emma.

'You can call me Ann,' volunteered Emma's mother.

'Thank you,' replied Austin, grateful for her inviting tone.

The four of them sat down.

'Edward', thought Austin. That could become confusing. His own father was 'Edward', and so was Emma's. Emma's father appeared to be about the age of sixty. He still had a full head of hair but it was distinctly greying. His facial features were, Austin couldn't initially think of the word, 'rugged'. The skin was not that of the ruddy complexion of an innkeeper, or the overfed master of a local shop. It was worn and weather-beaten, as if having faced a lifetime facing the elements. Austin supposed his possible future father-in-law had not always had it so easy.

By contrast, Emma's mother presented a far softer appearance. Her face was not at all weathered or work-worn; her skin was a little whiter than most, smooth and soft. Time had been kind to Ann, perhaps it was nature's way of providing some sort of recompense for the premature loss of some of her children. It was a strange thought, but how could Austin see into the mind of God.

'Tea?' Austin's thoughts were interrupted by Anne's question.

'Yes. Of course. Thank you,' replied Austin.

'I'll make a full pot,' said Ann, scurrying out of the room.

'Emma tells me you want to become an engineer,' said Edward.

It was a statement that required an answer. Emma's father did not seem to have a lot of time for small talk. Austin thought that he might be asked about his family first but that would clearly not be the case.

'Yes. That is my ambition, sir. As Emma might have said, I am presently a collier but have also the rank of corporal in the British Army, the 7th Royal Lancashire Fusiliers Militia, Third Battalion,' replied Austin, hoping that an armed services rank might help impress.

'Aye. I know. Tell me more about being an engineer,' said Edward, brushing aside Austin's military designation.

'Well sir. The army have helped a little there. I signed-up to be an engine driver but the army made me a fireman. I've worked the supply trains and have learned something of tending steam engines,' replied Austin. He tried to gauge Edward's response while Emma remained discretely silent.

Austin continued.

'The family call me a collier, but I'm really a tenter for the boilers that run an engine winder. I work at Foggs on Hall Lane,' he added.

'I didn't know that. What's an engine winder?' interjected Emma.

'Well. You know the big wheels you see at the pithead at Foggs?' replied Austin.

Emma nodded in assent.

'The power that enables the cages, or skips, to go up and down a shaft is provided by a steam engine. The engine winding man controls the winding engine and we provide the power. Our steam engine and boiler is similar to those used in the cotton factories,' added Austin, before addressing Edward again.

'I also go to the Mawdsley Street Technical in Bolton, the one that opened in March last year. It used to be called the Mechanics Institute. Mr Berry holds Applied Mechanics and Technical Engineering classes on most evenings and Saturday afternoons. I like to go there as often as I can.'

Emma's father appeared to be listening, but his demeaner still suggested a lack of interest or focus. It was as if he was still passing time.

Ann returned to the parlour carrying a tray with a pot, biscuits, cups and saucers. She asked Emma to retrieve a small oak table from under the window, and proceeded to put down the tray and lay out the cups and saucers. The conversation had momentarily stopped as she entered the room.

'Emma, you should pour. Leave it a minute or two,' instructed Ann.

'And how are your family, Austin?' asked Ann.

'Very well indeed, Mrs Kay, Ann. All are working and in good health,' replied Austin, correcting himself as he did so.

'Good health is always a blessing,' said Ann.

Emma interpreted the comment and reacted before her father could say anything.

'Mother, Austin knows little of my brothers and sisters.'

'I have met Sarah, the dressmaker,' said Austin, before Emma had finished.

Emma looked intently at Austin. It was clear to him that she wanted him to say nothing more.

'My mother is referring to... I'll use their names; John, Mary, Edith, Edward and Schofield. I will speak to you about them another time, Austin. Let us talk about something else,' said Emma.

'Of course. I believe you have been seeing Emma with Sarah these past few months,' said Ann.

'Yes,' replied Austin. He was not sure what to say.

Emma interjected.

'We have met in Farnworth Park, and for walks on the towpath. Martha sometimes joins us as well,' said Emma.

Austin was a little bemused but kept quiet. Emma, Sarah, Ann, and possibly Emma's cousin Martha had created a story. It could only be for the benefit of Emma's father, who would surely disapprove if he knew of the true extent of their private liaisons. Austin would have to go along with the tale.

Emma poured out the tea, offered biscuits, and passed the cups and saucers to each of them before taking one herself.

'Where are Sarah and Martha today?' asked Austin.

'They are both out visiting cousins. Perhaps they will return before you leave,' replied Ann.

Emma's father sipped his tea before asking the question Austin had been fearing most.

'Which is your parish?'

Emma looked at her mother.

Austin hesitated for a second or two, but he knew that he could not lie or obfuscate.

'St Gregory the Great in Farnworth, sir.'

Edward looked at him disapprovingly.

'You're a Catholic, a papist?'

Austin recoiled somewhat. He had hoped that Emma had prepared her father in some way. He knew already that this would not be the occasion when he could ask for Emma's hand.

'Father! I told you Austin was Catholic. Why do you embarrass him?' said Emma.

Her father smirked. Clearly enjoying the situation. Perhaps he thought it was a joke, thought Austin.

'I was baptised a Catholic, sir. I was born in St. Helens and baptised into the Catholic faith at Lowe House Chapel, but I now attend Mass at St. Gregory's on Presto Street. Fr. Boulaye is the rector there. They call him "The Apostle of Farnworth". He's a good man,' replied Austin.

'He doesn't sound Irish or English. A foreigner then?' challenged Edward.

'French, sir,' replied Edward. This was not going well.

'Edward, please,' said Ann.

'Yes father. Please don't make this unpleasant. Austin is a Christian just like you and I,' added Emma.

'Huh. Popery,' said Edward dismissively.

Austin was surprised at him using what was already considered an antiquated term, but thought better than to say something. However, it was clear he needed to either change the subject or bring the meeting to an end if he wanted to avoid any more difficult conversation.

'Perhaps it is time I went,' said Austin.

'No. I will leave the three of you to talk. I have agreed to meet Ned Jones at St. Matthews at six,' said Edward, as he lifted himself off the chair. He had spent barely forty minutes with them.

Five minutes later they heard the front door close.

'I am sorry, Austin. I knew it would be difficult but not quite like that. I think he's known for months that you were Catholic,' said Emma.

'Does your mother know?' said Emma.

'I do,' answered Ann.

'Yes. She knows we are engaged and does not care about you being a Catholic,' said Emma.

'I will help wherever I can,' offered Ann.

Satisfied that their secret was no longer a secret, conversation reverted to family and community gossip. Today would not be the day to cement their relationship with a date but at least they were a step further ahead.

* * *

There were limits to where they could meet in private in Little Lever and Farnworth, but Bolton offered greater scope. Bolton had a fine indoor market on Knowsley Street, and a wonderful fish market in an adjacent building. Before leaving Emma's house the previous weekend, the two of them had agreed to meet in the centre of Bolton, and take tea at one of the town's increasingly popular team rooms. The plan was that Austin would meet Emma and her mother at the Moses Gate horsecar stop, and they would then travel together into Bolton town centre. Edward, Emma's father, would be told that it would be a shopping trip; he was to know nothing of Austin's presence. Their last meeting did not go so well so this would be an opportunity to work out how to manoeuvre him into a more compliant state. How they would do this was not at all clear to Austin. He would have to rely on Emma, and her apparently supportive mother for ideas.

The journey from Moses Gate, on the edge of Farnworth, to the Trinity Street horsecar hub in Bolton had taken about half an hour. They could perhaps have taken a train, but Ann seemed to prefer the gentler, and more sedate, motion of pure horsepower, to that of a noisy, exuberant steam engine. Austin sensed that Emma's mother might be yearning for the slower pace of life of her youth, rather than the hectic pace modern living demanded.

At the Trinity Street stop the entire horsecar emptied, spilling people onto the paved area. Austin followed Emma, who in turn followed her mother off the vehicle. The two women waited for Austin to disembark, seemingly waiting for his lead.

'We should probably go straight down Newport Street to the Market Hall,' suggested Austin, sensing what was expected of him.

The journey would not be complicated, nor would it be long. It was almost a straight line to the Market, passing the Town

Hall on Victoria Square, and then on to Oxford Street and Knowsley Street. They could have taken another horsecar but it was hardly worth it, especially as the weather remained clement. A pair of rails in the centre of the cobblestoned street marked the unwavering, linear path of the street's horsecar route. The cobbles themselves had already lost the sheen afforded by a shower earlier in day, soon drying in the spring sunshine. Bolton was far larger than Farnworth and the streets showed as much. Dozens of people, generally well dressed, thronged the busy streets. Mothers, typically with daughters, traders and men turned out for business. Although traffic could not be compared to Manchester, thought Austin, it was certainly busier than Farnworth. At least a dozen horses and carts could be seen making their way up and down Newport Street, through the square in front of the town Hall, and to and from Oxford Street.

One of the faces of Bolton Town Hall clock, a landmark visible from most parts of the town centre, could be clearly seen in the distance. It was twenty past ten. Gas lamps set into the flagged pavements were situated at regular intervals, and seemed to mark progress points on their walk, not than anyone counted them. Most of the buildings were built of local brick, and were of three storeys, with the lower floor typically a shop selling its wares, many of which used lowered blinds to protect goods and customers from the elements.

Austin, Emma and Ann paused on the edge of Victoria Square, outside the Exchange Building which housed the public library, to admire Bolton's Town Hall.

'Look at it. And Farnworth still doesn't have one. The councillors still meet in that room in Darley Street,' said Ann.

Austin nodded. It was true. Until Farnworth had its own town hall it would always be seen as an upstart by Bolton people.

Bolton Town Hall was impressive, at least when compared to Farnworth and Little Lever, although having seen Manchester he knew that the city's monuments were even more so. The days when Bolton vied with Manchester for supremacy in the cotton industry were now long gone. A pair of stone lions placed on either side of centrally placed steps, guided the eyes towards the large ceremonial doors, inset into the building behind six Corinthian type columns holding up a sculptured pediment. The building's neoclassical clock tower subliminally announced that the town and its people were something to be reckoned with. A statue in honour of a well-respected local doctor and philanthropist, Samuel Taylor Chadwick, had been erected two decades earlier on the square's cobblestones to the left of the square. As he looked towards the left, Austin was distracted by some firemen who appeared to be undertaking some maintenance work outside of the station house at the end of Corporation Street. There were no horses, just the engine itself, and several men busily cleaning and polishing the machine's brass metalware. A large advertising hoarding promoting 'Harvest Home Food' stood unduly prominent behind the Town Hall. Whatever the distractions, the overall effect of the building and its square was that of an imposing monument to the town's prominence in the cotton industry. Manchester may have won Lancashire's battle for cotton industry supremacy, but Bolton was a close second.

'It's extraordinary, but it is also dirty,' added Ann.

She was referring to the colour of the stone, thought Austin, the effects of many years of Bolton's thousands of domestic and mill chimneys belching out the residue of burning coal.

'Let's walk on. It will be as well to walk down Oxford Street, that is unless you want to go to the fish market first,' asked Austin.

'No. Later,' replied Ann.

Crossing Hotel Street, they passed another local landmark, 'The Commercial Hotel', locally famous for being one of the town's principal inns. Upon reaching Knowsley Street Emma had a suggestion.

'We could take tea at Black and Green's tea shop or the new tea tasting room in Liptons on the corner of the Market Hall.'

'Black and Green's,' replied Ann, Austin not having a preference.

'I'll take tea with you and then leave the two of you while I shop,' said Ann.

It was not really protocol but none of the group cared too much. After Ann left them, Austin ordered another pot and asked the question they both needed an answer to.

'What about your father?'

It needed no explanation.

'I'm over 21. We could just get married, Austin. We don't need his permission for the banns to be read,' replied Emma.

'Without your father's consent? I'm surprised you would even think of such a thing,' said Austin, visibly shocked at Emma's statement.

'It is not what I want, but if father is awkward...'

Emma's statement tailed off into silence, leaving a slightly uncomfortable pause as they both thought about the implications of rejecting tradition.

'We could not elope, Emma. There is also the question of money. To set up a new household we would need your father's support until I become time served as an engineer. It could be another two or three years. I don't want you to work but it will be needed, with or without the help of our families,' said Austin, stating what Emma probably already knew.

'And there is the question of my religion,' he added.

'What of it?' questioned Emma.

'There are, er, obligations,' replied Austin.

'Obligations?' queried Emma.

'Your father might have some difficulties with our marriage, but so might the Catholic Church. I don't want to say too much in case I have it wrong. We should see our priest, together, so that he can explain it to you himself,' said Austin.

'You can't say that, Austin. What do you mean?' said Emma, unsatisfied with Austin's remark.

'There are certain commitments that a man and woman have to make before the Catholic Church will sanction a marriage between a Catholic and someone not of the faith, even between Christians. I have been told certain things, but I want to hear it from our priest. There may be allowances for Christians who are high church. I really cannot say any more,' said Austin.

'This could make matters worse, Austin. You must know that. We should see him soon,' replied Emma, unsatisfied with Austin's comments, and increasingly alarmed at the possible implications.

'Next week. I'll try and arrange a meeting for one evening next week. It would be best if you did not say anything to your father, and perhaps your mother,' said Austin.

'I will sort something out with mother. She knows my feelings for you, and knows that one way or another we will be married,' replied Emma.

'Right then. I'll get word to you as soon as I know. I don't think there is much more to be said. We should go and meet your mother. I think she said the Fish Market on Bridge Street,' said Austin, as they both prepared to leave.

* * *

Austin had arranged a meeting for 7.00pm the following Thursday. It was to be just the three of them, Austin, Emma and the priest.

Three minutes before the hour, Emma had followed Austin into St. Gregory the Great. As he reached the alter, Austin knelt, made a sign of the cross, and then proceeded to sit down next to one of the transepts. Emma mimicked the ritual, taking in the inside features of the building as she did so. It was a fairly new building; Austin had said it was only fifteen years old. Above the nave of the church, deep brown coloured timber beams and trusses stood proud against its finely whitewashed walls. The evening sunlight shone through on one side of the paired lancet windows, highlighting dust fragments floating in the still warm spring air. An alter sat on a raised sanctuary but the wall behind was plain, as if unfinished. Austin seemed to anticipate her thoughts.

'It is still not finished. The reredos and pulpit will be installed later this year. It is coming from Germany, Munich,' said Austin, taking pride in both his knowledge and church.

Less than a minute later, the sound of footsteps caused them both to turn from the alter and towards its entrance. The priest was on time.

'Thank you for seeing us, Fr. Boulaye,' said Austin.

The priest nodded.

'So, you wanted to see me about getting married,' said Fr. Boulaye. It was almost a question.

Emma noticed straight away. The priest had an accent; it sounded French to her.

'Yes, Father. This is Emma Kay, my intended wife,' said Austin.

Emma experienced a pang of doubt. Was she supposed to call him 'Father'? It seemed a little odd. She thought it best to.

'Hello, Father,' added Emma.

Austin resumed.

'Father, I don't know if you are aware but Emma is not of the Catholic faith. She is an Anglican, which is high church as you know. We want to marry and would like to understand what we need to do. I am uncertain as to the steps we must take.'

'Marrying outside the faith is not encouraged, Austin. I am sorry Emma but it is not so simple as arranging a wedding. It would be better if you converted to the faith,' said Fr. Boulaye.

Emma noticed a slight lisp that the priest encountered when pronouncing the letter 'r'. She ignored it, more interested in what he had to say. She had already suspected that the priest might expect a conversion but hoped that there might be another way. And she wanted to hear the rest of it. Nonetheless, it was still a shock to hear it in such a blunt way, almost as a demand. This could make further conversation with her own father very difficult indeed.

'I understand, Father,' she replied, somewhat meekly. Emma needed time to process her situation.

'There are other matters to consider as well. There is the question of children.'

The priest opened a booklet he had been holding. Emma could just about see the title: 'A Full Catechism of the Catholic Religion'.

'These are the rules by which we must live, Emma. Austin, you know about this,' said Fr. Boulaye.

Austin nodded.

'I'll read part of it. As I said the Church disapproves of marriages outside the Faith and may only permit them under certain conditions.'

The priest paused as he turned a page, while Emma waited, expecting something impossible to comply with.

'There are three conditions, and I will read them as they are written. 1. That the Catholic party be allowed the free exercise of religion.'

Emma breathed a sigh of relief. That would not be at all a problem, although her father might have something to say about it.

'2. That he or she earnestly endeavour to gain by persuasion the non-Catholic consort to the true Church.'

Again, thought Emma, this was not something that would be a great problem. It was not as if she would definitely have to convert before getting married.

'And 3. That all the children be brought up in the Catholic religion.'

Emma needed some time to think. Her father would certainly not approve of that one, at least she thought so.

'Thank you for explaining this, Father,' said Austin.

'Yes, thank you,' repeated Emma.

'Have you any questions?'

'Would you marry us, Father?' asked Emma.

'I would need to consult with Bishop Bilsborrow, and you must first agree to comply with the Catechism. It is hard, I know, but we have to protect our faith,' replied Fr. Boulaye, turning towards Austin.

Emma nodded, more in understanding than in acquiescence to his requirements.

'I have no questions. We will both need to talk about it,' said Austin, not wishing to hint about any problems those commitments might create.

'We will need to meet many times before any wedding, Austin and Emma. There is a path we have to follow. Now I must go. I have to see some of the sick of the parish this evening.'

The priest rose, along with Emma and Austin, who followed him back along the nave towards the entrance.

'This is not going to be easy,' said Emma, after the priest had left their sight.

'I know,' acknowledged Austin.

* * *

May yielded to June. The Lancastrian showers of spring had receded, and the warmth of early summer had penetrated what had temporarily been a malaise of indecision. But there had been some progress. Austin had now been a guest of the Kay household on several occasions, a strategy agreed by Ann and Emma to get Edward 'used' to the idea of Austin. To a degree it had worked. Edward's earlier hostility towards Austin had begun to soften as he got to know his future son-in-law as a man, rather than as a second or third generation Catholic immigrant, a 'papist', follower of the Catholic Pope.

The solution to their problem was not only simple, but came from an unexpected and unlikely source.

Emma had been far more readily accepted into the Melia household than Austin had been into the Kays. His sister's friendship with Emma had more than helped. Ellen's teasing of Austin over his own 'friendship' with Emma had long since given way to an almost conspiratorial friendship. Ellen had been aware of her brother's ever deepening relationship with Emma for well over a year, and unknown to him had decided to help her friend cement the bond. Ellen loved her brother dearly, and would very much like to have Emma as a sister-in-law. They got on well.

Austin had not asked his sister for help with meeting Emma. To some degree his awareness of his family's knowledge of his relationship with Emma was somewhat limited. He knew that the family were aware that he liked Emma, but was oblivious to the fact that all the older females in the house had worked out what was going on not long after Ellen had. Austin had not directly shared his intentions to marry Emma, but his mother and sisters already speculated about its inevitability amongst themselves.

Since spring of the previous year, inviting Emma around for a meal had almost become a matter of routine. There were no set days but for reasons of habit, Thursdays had become the day Emma would come round for tea. Ellen would typically be the one to invite her, although with increased familiarity it was not unknown for Catherine to encourage a visit, usually coincidental with bumping in to her in Farnworth's market.

'Ma, I've asked Emma round for dinner this evening. Is that alright with you?' asked Austin.

It was an unusual request on two counts. It was Wednesday, not a Thursday, and the request was from Austin. Mary suspected immediately, but decided to maintain a pretence that it was not unusual.

'Of course, I'll get something extra in,' replied Mary, clearly referring to food.

'We have something to tell everyone, but I'll tell you now. Emma and I have got engaged.'

Mary saw little point in feigning too much surprise and responded accordingly.

'I thought as much. We all have, Austin,' said Mary.

'I suppose Nell has said something. Neither of us told her but we both think she had already guessed,' said Austin.

'She has said nothing, Austin. We all knew it was coming, except your father and brother of course,' replied Mary, with more than the hint of a twinkle in her eye.

'Things are not quite as we would like them to be, but I'll tell you more tonight. I don't think Emma's father approves of me.

Look, I'll have to get off to work or I'll be late,' said Austin, unwilling to say too much more. At least he had told his mother before the rest of the family. He knew he could rely on her support.

* * *

Austin would be home later than usual. He had agreed to meet Emma at the gates of Farnworth Park and proceed to Bridgewater Street together. Emma had shared the plan with her own mother, although as far her father was concerned it was just another dinner invite from her friend Ellen.

Dinner was a typical affair, some fish and seasonal vegetables followed by apple pie. Simple but filling and satisfying. Conversation during the meal was also rather ordinary; some gossip about friends, work, talk of the new baths on King Street, and some common speculation about the town getting an electricity supply the following year. Coincidentally, it was also summer solstice, June 21st 1893. It would be daylight until late and the moon was still almost full. Perhaps Austin would walk Emma all the way back to Little Lever after the meal this evening. As the table was cleared, Austin was finally ready to share the news with the rest of his family. He saw little point in shrouding it in mystery and decided to blurt it out.

'Emma and I are engaged to be married.'

Austin's mother, Catherine, Ellen and Annie showed little surprise. His brother John simply looked at him, showing neither interest nor disinterest, while Margaret clapped, and Elizabeth started to sing and dance: 'Austin's getting mar-ried'. None of the adults immediately responded; each seemed to be waiting for another to say something. It was Edward who spoke first.

'When did this happen, Austin?'

Austin hesitated. This was going to require an explanation.

'Autumn last year, Dad. I...'

Edward cut-in before Austin had a chance to finish.

'Why now?'

'I was going to explain,' replied Austin, looking towards Emma for some possible support.

'We, er... We've been trying to work something out with Emma's family,' said Austin.

'What. You told them before us?' questioned Edward.

Emma intervened.

'No. It's not like that. Her mother knows, yes, but not father. We need to work something out before telling him.'

'And what might that be?' said Edward.

Austin and Emma exchanged uneasy glances.

'They'll have to know before long,' said Austin, addressing the comment towards Emma.

Emma nodded in assent.

'As you know, Emma is Anglican and we are Catholic. We think this might mean Emma's father might object to our union.' said Austin.

'Christians from different denominations do get married,' interjected Mary.

'We know that, Ma. But...' Austin hesitated before resuming.

'It's just that... Well, Emma's father seems to be very traditional in his views, and is not very keen on Catholics. I think he's getting used to me, and Ann, Emma's mother, is helping with that. She's not concerned in the least. I'm sure it will work out in time but...'

Edward finished his sentence:

'But it doesn't explain why you didn't tell us before now.'

Austin had not got an answer and simply shrugged.

'Well, you'll be marrying at St. Gregory's,' said Edward.

'That's just it, Dad. We have seen Fr. Boulaye and he's told us what needs to be done. At least from a Catholic view. But Emma's father will expect her marriage to take place in his parish, St. Matthews in Little Lever. He won't like what the priest has to say about bringing up any children as Catholics,' replied Austin.

'And what do you say, Emma?' asked Edward.

'Austin and I love each other. We will get married one way or the other. It's just a question of where we get married. Neither of us want to leave town to do it,' replied Emma.

Looks of both horror and shock were returned on the faces of the older females.

'Never,' said Mary.

'To even think such a thought,' she added, clearly reflecting more than her own concerns.

'So, what are you going to do? Abandon your faith, Austin, or abandon yours, Emma?' said Edward, not really expecting an answer to an obviously difficult situation.

'Well. We are starting to think that perhaps we should marry in Little Lever and ask Fr. Boulaye to give a blessing,' suggested Austin.

'You know he won't do that, Austin. The Bishop would have to agree as well,' said Mary.

'I know, Ma. Well, I just hope he might make an exception. He might you know,' replied Austin.

'He's a good man, Austin. But I doubt he will budge on this one. It might even make it worse asking him,' said Mary.

Austin felt cornered and increasingly disaffected with the situation. There was no right, or for that matter, easy answer to it. What could he say?

Margaret and John had maintained a silence during the discussion. This was adult stuff after all, and their contribution to the subject might not be appreciated. They had both realised this soon after Austin had started his explanation. The pregnant silence that followed Mary's last statement was broken by Catherine, who had seemingly remembered that there were still younger children present.

'John, Margaret and you too, Elizabeth. You are not to say a word to anyone about this. It's our business and nobody else's,' said Catherine.

The three younger siblings each nodded. Elizabeth, obviously not understanding the ramifications of the situation, mimicking her brother and sister's responses. Having been brought into the discussion by Catherine, it was down to ten-year-old Elizabeth to provide some hope:

'Why don't you get married in both churches. We could have two weddings.'

Everyone stared at her after her comment, unsure how to respond. At least initially. What at first seemed to be silly soon evolved into a discussion about its feasibility. It was Emma who broke the silence.

'I don't know of anyone who has done it before, but it must have happened somewhere. Do you know of anyone who has got married in both churches, Austin?'

Elizabeth looked pleased with herself. Her suggestion had not been dismissed out of hand and was being taken seriously. Emma's response had provided her thoughts with some credibility. She liked Emma.

'I don't. But then I don't know of any rules against it. There must be some, although I don't think I would want to ask. I think we should talk about it. This has gone on long enough already, and if Bessie's idea is the answer, we should just get on with it,' replied Austin.

'You'll have to make those commitments about children,' said Mary.

'I know, Ma,' replied Austin.

'You might be asked to convert,' said Mary, directing her gaze towards Emma.

'I know. But that might be just too much for my father. Perhaps in time it might change but I just want to make sure he consents to our marriage. I don't really want to talk about the possibility with him. I just want to get married,' replied Emma.

'It's getting late,' said Austin. 'I am going to walk Emma back to Little Lever. It's a lovely night and we have lots to think and talk about. You know everything now, all of you. But as Catherine said earlier, let's keep it to ourselves until we have worked it all out. We don't want any gossip.'

Austin turned towards Elizabeth.

'Bessie, thank you. Now give me a hug.'

Elizabeth ran over and wrapped her arms around her brother:

'I love you, Austin.'

* * *

'My father doesn't need to know the full details, Austin,' said Emma.

They had both been enjoying the walk back to Little Lever, enhanced by the still pleasantly warm air, and the slowly ebbing light of a midsummer sun. Neither had felt the need to immediately immerse themselves in the previous conversation, preferring thought and reflection for a time.

'Let's walk by the canal. We can sit and talk about how to deal with your father. It will be light for ages yet,' replied Austin.

A canal walk was not the quickest way back to Emma's home, but it was certainly a more interesting route. It was also not uncommon to catch water traffic negotiating the locks, which provided something of a spectacle to an otherwise uneventful journey. They agreed to sit down within sight of the Prestolee locks to take in the view of the nearby aqueduct, and the more industrial landscape further away. A pleasant midsummer evening or not, many of Bolton's textile factory chimneys were still emitting the waste product of their captive steam engine's efforts to power their looms. The lack of a breeze seemed to lure fingers of smoke into an otherwise clear sky in an almost perpendicular direction. Beneath those testamentary columns of industry Bolton remained at work.

'I think I shall tell him that your church will simply provide a blessing to our marriage. It would not help to share your Catechism with him, especially the talk about bringing up children. I want him to give us his blessing. He seems to be getting used to you; I just don't want to upset him,' said Emma.

'I know. Whatever you feel is best, Emma. I'm sure your mother will help. Though we mustn't delay telling him about our engagement. My family are sworn to secrecy but these things have a habit of getting out,' replied Austin.

'Mother and I will tell him this week,' said Emma.

'But I need to ask him for your hand. I will have to be there. Why not get your mother to suggest the idea rather than tell him outright?' replied Austin.

'I'll talk to her. You are right. He's getting used to you. He also needs to get used to the idea of our marriage. Mother will help, I'm sure. And I also want to marry soon. We've been engaged for so long already. No one knows quite how long, and I'm sure they will think it quick, but I want to marry this summer,' said Emma.

'That's only weeks away, Emma,' replied Austin, a little surprised at Emma's expectations.

'I don't care,' said Emma.

'Well, if that's what you want. I just thought we would need more time to plan it, and... perhaps more time for your father,' replied Austin.

'Father will agree. He has to. I want his blessing but I'm not afraid of him. We will marry, Austin,' said Emma, exuding an air of confidence and assertiveness.

Austin knew better than to argue with her. He edged closer and kissed her on the lips, apparently sealing the arrangements.

'We had better get you home,' said Austin.

'Yes. I'll get a message to you over the weekend once mother and I have worked out the how and when,' replied Emma.

* * *

Austin's trepidation about meeting Emma's father and asking for her hand had been allayed by some careful preparatory work by both Emma and her mother. He was not entirely sure what they had said to him, but when the long-anticipated day arrived the welcome mat had been rolled out.

Emma had set out some clear instructions for Austin, instructions which she made clear he had to follow:

'Say nothing about the Catholic Church, priests or even blessings. He's not well versed on the details of Catholic ritual, or your church's expectations in marriage. As far as he is concerned you have agreed to marry me in our church so don't give anything away. Nothing!'

Emma was insistent, and by now Austin had already learned that it was not a good idea to argue with her about this sort of thing.

It was a short meeting. Emma had contrived to arrange something on an evening where she had 'previously' arranged to see another relative. By doing so she had ensured that any risks of something going wrong were significantly reduced. A lack of time would manage the situation. It was almost transactional when it happened. Austin had barely had time to drink his tea before Emma and her mother had left the room, citing the unlikely need to find some knitting pattern, leaving Emma's father and him in the room. Knowing what was expected he hesitated, a little uncomfortable, embarrassed even, at the situation. Edward, Emma's father seized control of the situation.

'So, Emma tells me you have something to ask me.'

'I have, sir' replied Austin. With his heart now beating a little faster than usual, Austin took another breath. He froze for second. How should he ask? His mind had gone temporarily blank, leaving a second uncomfortable pause in the exchange.

'Well then?' interjected Edward.

Austin knew that he could put it off no longer.

'Can I marry your daughter, Emma?'

It was not quite how he wanted to present the request. It felt clumsy and banal. When rehearsing it, the question included 'asking for her hand', and slightly more romantic phraseology. But it was too late now. The request had been made.

Edward responded with surprisingly little hesitation.

'I might agree to it, but first I would like to know more about how you intend to provide for her.'

Austin breathed out in what he thought might have been audible relief, before proceeding to answer.

'I have been working with steam engines at the mine...'

Before he had a chance to finish, Emma and her mother walked in, both looking expectantly at the two men.

'Austin was just telling me about steam engines, Emma...'

It was not exactly what Emma wanted to hear.

'Well Father?'

'Congratulations, Emma, I'm sure you will both be very happy. Perhaps we should start to talk about the arrangements,' replied Edward.

'Thank you. You know I am to see Ruth Gilbert in Bolton this evening. Austin will walk me to the tram at Moses Gate. Mother and I have already been talking about it, as you might have expected. Let's talk again about it when I get back,' replied Emma.

With the essential part of the discussion ending, Emma whisked Austin out of the house before he could say anything that might antagonise her father. The whole operation had been carefully managed by mother and daughter. Emma had achieved what she wanted, without her father realising how he had been expertly moulded into delivering the right outcome. Austin and Emma would now marry, and sooner rather than later as far as she was concerned.

* * *

Some would have called it luck. Emma preferred to think of it as providence:

'It was meant to happen.'

It was July, and arrangements were already underway for a wedding in the autumn of 1893. For the rest of the Melia and Kay entourage, it would have appeared to be inordinately quick, a matter of a few months, but for Emma and Austin the engagement had already been well over a year. Emma may well have appeared impatient but she didn't really care. It was time. Austin remained compliant to her wishes and basically supported her desire to expedite preparations. She remained in control of the wedding arrangements; all Austin had to do was to find them somewhere to live.

And then caprice intervened. A wedding had been cancelled due to 'unforeseen circumstances' – Emma never discovered what those circumstances were – and Austin and Emma were offered an opportunity to marry earlier than they had been planning, August 9th. It was a Wednesday, but that mattered little to either of them. They seized it with little hesitation and accelerated their plans. It would be a modest affair, not quite as grand as some she had seen at St. Matthews, but it would be adequate. They would also have to consider the matter of the 'blessing' or 'second wedding' at St. Gregory's in Farnworth as well, so both events in fact should not be too ostentatious.

Both families were naturally surprised at this change in circumstance but understood the situation. With two mothers now enlisted to help, Emma and Austin started to consider what their new life together might bring. Austin was still regarded as a collier, but had for some time been working in the winding room at Foggs. It would still be many months before he could call himself an engineer, but at least he had made a solid start. For Emma, the prospect of setting up a home was exciting, perhaps children in time. Farnworth or Little Lever would have to do for now, but who could know what might be next?

As planned, Austin Melia married Emma Kay at St. Matthew's in Little Lever, attended by only close family from each household. The permissions for a second 'wedding', in Austin's parish of St. Gregory the Great, were more of a challenge than first thought, and the couple settled for a Catholic blessing. For Emma this worked out even better; there would be little prospect of paternal objection. What of course Emma's father would never know, is that in return for that blessing, Emma had agreed that any children they might have would be brought up in accordance with Catholic tradition rather than in her own faith. It was a compromise facilitated by Austin's parish priest. He never needed to involve his bishop with any permissions; after all it was not a wedding as such. The parish priest had managed to extract a lifelong commitment. He believed he had achieved something, and yet Emma would always feel gratitude towards him by circumventing the 'rules' to address a difficult situation. She would remain true to her word, and her father would never need to know the full details.

Chapter 3

LIFE STARTS

The 14th of January.

Austin knew the house would have a sombre atmosphere when he got back that evening. It took about twenty minutes to reach home from a day at Foggs, so there was enough time to prepare himself for Emma's inevitably disconsolate mood. As he walked up Lorne Street, one of Farnworth's longer thoroughfares, and past its dozens of identical red brick dwellings, he reflected on what the last two years had brought; both sadness and happiness. Within weeks of their wedding, they had found a house on Georgiana Street and had set up home. Alas, the joy and excitement of starting their life journey together became tainted with a sudden and unexpected illness of Anne, Emma's mother. At first the family thought it might just be a cold, but her health soon deteriorated into what everyone believed to be some sort of pneumonia. Fevers, chills and a loss of appetite. Not even Christmas provided much solace to the Kay household, and by the early New Year 1894 everyone feared the worst. Anne showed few signs of a potential recovery. She lived for barely two weeks more in yet another harsh and very cold winter.

Emma was distraught. She had a very good relationship with her mother and took her passing with difficulty. Austin had tried to cheer her in the weeks after the funeral, but he soon realised that she needed the time to grieve. He couldn't force it; he had to wait until she was ready to fully resume their life together. Emma's early reaction to her mother's death was to pay more attention to her father. Like Emma, her father had also taken his wife's loss badly. They seemed to find comfort in time together, and Austin didn't mind the extra visits she had been making to Little Lever in the months after her death. By late spring both Emma and her father were over the worst of it, and Emma reduced her visits. Edward started to visit them for the occasional meal, and by the end of the year life had reverted to some sort of normality, only without the counsel and support of Anne.

Emma announced her pregnancy to a visiting Melia family member in the summer of that same year. It was a bittersweet occasion. The happiness of a future addition to the family impaired by the knowledge that Anne would never meet her grandchild. The first anniversary of Anne's death passed quietly, with Edward and Emma choosing to attend a service at St. Matthews, where remembrance prayers were to be said. Strangely, thought Austin, he had not been invited but it was not a concern. If that was what she wanted then so be it. On April 3rd of 1895 Emma brought their daughter into the world. Attended by Austin's mother, and Sarah, Emma's elder sister, the birth was reassuringly uneventful, with both mother and child healthy and well. Tradition dictated that she be named after Emma's mother, Anne, or Annie as they had already started to call her.

After passing the Lorne Street mills and the paper works, Austin turned left down Georgiana Street reaching number 37, just as Emma had walked over to the window. She had Annie in her arms and was obviously looking out for him, thought Austin. After opening the door and walking in, he hung his coat and turned towards the two of them.

'I'll take her.'

'Wash up first, Austin. I can still see the dirt on your hands,' replied Emma.

Austin always had a quick wash at Foggs before he left, but he knew that more would be expected at home. Working in the engine room was not as dirty endeavour as working in the mine, but grease, oil, and the coal dust in the boiler room took its toll on his hands and working clothes. He nodded in agreement; he should have known better, really.

He walked through into the back room. Emma had a good fire going and had prepared some hot water as she always did. Austin took off his shirt, poured out some hot water into a waiting bowl and started to wash.

'Father is not well again. Sarah came round and said so. It's just like mother, Austin. I know it is,' said Emma.

Austin knew that Edward had been ill but had dismissed the thought that January 1896 would be a repeat of 1894. Surely, he would get better?

'I'm sure it's just a cold, Emma,' replied Austin.

'That's what we thought with my mother, Austin,' said Emma.

Austin shrugged. There was no point speculating. It was probably Emma reacting badly to the second anniversary of her mother's passing. Sarah had obviously visited after seeing her father, but it clearly had the unfortunate effect of worrying Emma more than he would like. Austin wasn't sure what to say. A change of subject, perhaps.

'How's my beautiful daughter been today?'

'Still some colic but she did sleep for a couple of hours. How was your day? replied Emma.

'Nothing much of interest today. We've got a new stoker; nice lad, I'm sure he will settle in. He went to St. Gregory's and knows Fr. Moran, the new priest,' said Austin.

Another Catholic, thought Emma. That would have helped with her husband. Fr. Moran had baptised Annie into the Catholic faith the previous May. Emma had decided at the time not to mention it to her father. She loved him but there were some things that it was better he should not discover. Emma nodded.

'I'm going to have to visit him, Austin, but I don't want to take Annie lest she catch something,' replied Emma.

'You know there is always my mother and sisters to help in these situations, Emma. We can ask at the weekend, or tomorrow evening if you like,' said Austin.

'I'll go myself tomorrow. I'm worried about him,' replied Emma.

Austin chose not to argue. It was cold January weather, not ideal for the baby, but Emma would no doubt wrap her up well.

'As you wish,' said Austin.

* * *

By the weekend his father-in-law's health had deteriorated even further. It was almost a carbon copy of the Emma's mother's circumstances. A cold had developed into flu like symptoms, with fevers and a general loss of appetite. It did not look good at all.

There was little else that Emma seemed to want to discuss over the dinner table the following Sunday evening. Austin could read his wife's mood; there was little benefit in trying to distract her. Annie had been fed and put to bed.

'Is that new infectious diseases hospital on Cawdor Street open yet?' asked Emma.

'It will be weeks, probably months, Emma. And we don't know for sure if it is what your mother had,' replied Austin.

'I know it was. I just feel I have to do something. I can't leave it all to Sarah. And she's started courting,' said Emma.

This was news, thought Austin.

'Courting?'

'Yes. He's called Frederick, a watchmaker who lives up in Deane in Bolton. She'll have no time to see him if I don't help,' said Emma.

'I know,' replied Austin. Emma would have to do what she felt she needed to do.

'Your ma is good with Annie. I am so grateful to have her,' said Emma.

Austin nodded.

'You know she will help wherever she can. And my sisters love having Annie in the house,' added Austin.

'I know,' replied Emma.

In the ensuing weeks Edward's febrile condition deteriorated further. In the last week of January Emma had taken to visiting her family home in Church street daily, even staying overnight to help Sarah. Austin was in Georgiana Street on his own in the closing days of January. Annie had been staying at his own parents, and he had resumed taking evening meals with them before going home to sleep. He still had to earn a wage, whatever the problems in the Kay household. His father-in-law's death on the last day of the month was not such a surprise when it did happen. He was 61, and his age was probably a factor in his death, and his heart had been broken when Anne passed two years earlier. He had apparently lost his purpose in life. At least that's what Emma had started to believe. Perhaps it was for the best. Emma might now be able to look forward to bringing up her own young family rather than worry about her parents. It was a hard thought, but as some people had taken to saying: life must go on.

* * *

Emma showed much more resilience than she had shown with her mother's death. Spring had been particularly warm and May had been one of the driest on record. Annie's progress and the fine weather had lifted Emma's spirits. That, and the prospect of her sister getting married. Frederick had proposed to Sarah and she had accepted, with a wedding planned for the following year. Life's cycle had turned and the losses of the last couple of years were being replaced with something more joyous. It was in these happier times that Austin had some news to share. He waited until the week of their anniversary before sharing it, on one of their now routine summer walks with Annie in Farnworth Park.

'I've got some news to share, Emma. I've been waiting for the right time to tell you,' said Austin.

He hesitated, gathering his thoughts before launching into something that would likely disrupt their lives in Farnworth.

'Well, you know I want to leave the Foggs and get some experience in a mill. There are more opportunities and a bit more money than working at the colliery.'

'We have talked about it,' replied Emma.

'I heard about just such an opportunity and have made an enquiry about it,' said Austin.

Emma stopped to sit on a free bench, beckoning Austin to sit with her.

'Go on,' said Emma.

'There is a job there but it would mean that we would need to leave Farnworth. It's not that far away, but as an engineer I'm required to live near the mill. They would rent us a house,' said Austin.

'Where is it?' said Emma.

Austin knew he had to tell her but remained a little afraid of the response he might get.

'Hindley,' replied Austin.

'What, Wigan?' said Emma.

'It's not so far. Close enough to visit family at the weekends,' replied Austin.

Emma knew that already and nodded in agreement.

'I suppose it could be a fresh start. I'm still grieving for the both of them, Austin, but I know we have a life to live. You should take the job if it's offered. A better wage?' enquired Emma.

'A little. But it's as much the experience in a cotton mill that I'm after as well. I'm hoping to see them in early September,' replied Austin.

Emma could not help experiencing a tinge of excitement, not unlike the weeks after their wedding three years earlier. Hindley may not have the attraction of a larger town like Bolton, or a city like Manchester, but a new home, and new surroundings, had lots of appeal. She just hoped Austin would achieve his wish.

* * *

'Did you hear about the walk up in Bolton?' said Stan, one of his engineering colleagues at Foggs.

Austin was still waiting to hear about the job in Hindley so no one was any the wiser about what his intentions were. It was a day like any other.

'No. What are you talking about?' replied Austin.

'They are calling it a trespass,' said Stan.

'That sounds illegal to me,' replied Austin.

'It probably is but we don't care. We are all going. You should come along too. That is if you enjoy a walk,' said Stan.

'I like a walk as much as the next man. What are you talking about? You had better explain,' replied Austin.

'Well, it started...' said Stan.

Stan began a long, and a little rambling, story about the moors in Bolton. It involved the Ainsworths, a well-known local family owning bleachworks, and the Smithills Hall estate in Bolton. Richard Ainsworth, the latest scion of the family, had attracted the ire of many in the recently formed socialist movement in the area.

'He's closed Coalpit Road.'

'Coalpit Road?' questioned Austin. He wasn't so sure where it was.

'It's at top of Smithills. You know Smithills don't you?' replied Stan

'I do,' replied Austin. He was used to walking Farnworth, Little Lever, and the Outwood areas, and rarely got up on the moors, but he did know Smithills.

'Well, it's all down to Ainsworth. He hates us, the unions; any organised labour,' said Stan.

'I don't get involved in anything like that. You know I don't, Stan,' replied Austin. He knew Stan was a socialist and didn't mind him for that. But he did not have to become one himself. For Austin, family life would always be more important than politics. He could look after himself.

'I know. But this is different. The SDF and Socialists; I'm a member you know,' said Stan.

'I know, Stan,' interjected Austin.

'Well, I don't see it as politics. Besides, I know you would be no knobstick if it came to that. So far as I'm concerned, it's the right of the working man to roam wherever he wants. Ainsworth is trying to stop us. He's put 'Trespassers Will Be Prosecuted' sign and a gate on Winter Hill. He's no right. People have been using that road for generations. We have to defend our rights, or we won't be able to go anywhere without some toff telling us what and where we can and can't go,' continued Stan, becoming increasingly animated.

'Is it his property? Doesn't he have a right to do what he wants with it?' enquired Austin, somewhat tactlessly.

'No. It's just Ainsworth making trouble. He just wants the land for shooting God's creatures. He's a typical rich Tory. Exploits his workers, wants to keep everyone in their place. You know he was against opening the libraries on Sundays? The Party believes he's like a feudal landlord and that he shouldn't be able to get away with it. There is a long-established right of way and he's no right to do what he's done,' replied Stan.

'Well, I don't know. What am I supposed to do about it?' asked Austin.

'Join us. This affects you just the same as me. There's a lot of colliers from around Bolton going; the more the better,' replied Stan.

'When is it? asked Austin.

'Sunday. September 6th,' replied Stan.

'I'll have a think about it,' said Austin.

'You do that. But don't take long about it. It's this weekend,' replied Stan.

With that the conversation ended with the two of them resuming their duties. It was a lot to think about.

* * *

Austin had plenty of time to reflect on his conversation with Stan, and on balance decided that he wanted to support his socialist friends on this occasion. There were risks, yes, but Stan had a point. While he did not want to be seen as a troublemaker, after all he had a career as an engineer and a family to provide for, he did recognise that men, and women, should have a right to roam. He enjoyed a good walk as much as the next man, and it wasn't really socialist; at least that was how he rationalised it. The upshot was that he was going to go.

'I'm going to an early Mass on Sunday, Emma; probably the 7.30 a.m.,' said Austin.

'I thought as much. You are going to go, aren't you?' replied Emma.

'I am. I've got to. We have to stand up for our rights,' said Austin.

'You sound like one of those Social Democratic Federation people I've heard give speeches, Austin,' replied Emma.

'You know I'm not political. It just feels like the right thing to do. Besides it will stand me in good stead with the lads at the colliery,' said Austin.

'But you will be leaving there soon, Austin,' replied Emma.

'That's not the point, Emma. Besides, I don't know for sure yet. I will probably hear next week. They did say it could be up to four weeks,' said Austin.

Emma nodded.

'Well, I hope you know best. I don't need to remind you what's at stake,' replied Emma.

'No, you don't. I'll be early to bed, tonight. Tomorrow will be a long day,' said Austin.

'I'll pour some tea before you go up. If you call in after St. Gregory's I'll have some breakfast ready for you. You don't want to go on nothing more than a bit of bread and butter,' said Emma.

With arrangements settled Austin retired, hoping that the night's rest would be a good one.

* * *

Encouraged by adverts in the Bolton papers in the days leading up to the protest, the rumours across the Bolton area were that hundreds were expected, perhaps a thousand. Austin felt a little reassured in this. He could express his support, perhaps without risking recognition. Colonel Ainsworth was an influential man in Bolton, and in the bleaching trade across Lancashire. It would not do to be seen to obviously cross him.

Austin was to meet Stan and some of the colliers from Foggs at Moses Gate, get a horsecar to Trinity Street in Bolton, and then catch another to the junction of Halliwell Road and Blackburn Road. They expected to get there shortly before 10 o'clock, just in time for the planned start of what many were already calling a 'mass trespass'. Stan challenged its representation, stating that you could only trespass over what is not yours.

The Halliwell tram seemed smaller than the ones to and from Farnworth. With 'Bolton & Halliwell Road' emblazoned across the side, it was already more than half full by the time the group reached it.

'It looks like we will have to go upstairs,' said Stan.

Stan seemed to have assumed leadership of the Foggs protesters. Austin didn't mind at all. After all it was Stan's initiative; he was there just to support it. Although the weather looked encouraging, rain was always a risk, which was probably why all the lower deck seats had already been taken. With luck we will see no rain, thought Austin, as he climbed up the steps to the upper deck.

On arrival at the stop near Moss Street most of horsecar disembarked, all men and lads. This was not to be a pleasant Sunday day out with the family. It was a protest. Austin looking around at the gathered mass, comprised mostly of men. There must have been at least a thousand, possibly more. It was impossible to accurately estimate with people still moving about. Within minutes after their arrival there were two speeches, both by people Austin didn't recognise.

With the speeches over with, about a dozen of what Austin believed were organisers signalled a move. The walk had started.

Clogs were noisy footwear at the best of times. The effect of a thousand or more males commencing a march was almost deafening. It was the first thing he noticed. Stan, Austin, and the Foggs group had taken a position towards the back, and it was a good few minutes before the 'comrades' started to move. Notwithstanding the fine weather, most were wearing caps and heavy coats, obviously fearing Lancashire's fickle weather. Austin's view ahead was a sea of the backs of heads and floating caps.

As the protest advanced up Halliwell Road more people appeared, apparently to join them. There were hundreds, thousands even, men, boys, and even some women. Colliers, bakers, butchers, millworkers of all kinds, domestics; even schoolchildren joined and swelled the numbers. Mill towers and multi-storey edifices of brick emerged behind the streets of terraced houses fanning out from Halliwell Road. First the Alexandra on Wolfenden Street, then Halliwell Mills on Bertha Street; Clyde Mill, Brookfield Mill, Moorlands Mill.

They were all unfamiliar names to Austin but he had taken the opportunity to strike up a conversation with a fellow marcher, a local. He was certainly in the centre of cotton country.

By the time they reached the Ainsworth Arms at the top of Halliwell Road and Smithills, the horsecar terminus, their number had reached the thousands. Looking towards the back of the march Austin realised that he was no longer so close to the end of the group, but was now in fact close to the front. Such were the numbers. There were more speeches, although it was doubtful whether those at the back could hear. And then the march moved on, down the dip past Ainsworth's bleach works, then up past Ainsworth's residence at Smithills Hall, over Scout Road, and finally on to their destination at the newly erected gate, the entrance to Coalpit Road.

There were a handful of police and Ainsworth's gamekeepers patrolling the gate. Trying to look threatening, they were no match for the thousands who had descended to demand a right of way. Austin was pleased that he was not at the front; close enough to see and hear what was going on, but not close enough to be picked on, or even recognised by the officials. He was just one in an ocean of many.

'Do you know you are rushing to eternity?'

A man had decided to address the crowd.

'It's Entwistle.'

Austin heard the name whispered throughout the crowd. He didn't know who Entwistle was, a gamekeeper perhaps?

'We are not here this morning to speak about another world, but this world,' replied one of the march leaders.

'Who's that?' asked Austin of Stan.

'He's called Joe Shufflebottom. He's SDF. Hush now,' replied Stan.

The man Austin now knew as Joe continued.

'We are here to tell Mister Ainsworth that we, the people of England, have a right to pass through, and we intend to.'

The crowd cheered, adding cries of 'hear, hear!'

Turning away from the gatekeepers, Joe addressed the crowd.

'Now I know that there will probably be legal action but take care and don't let 'em provoke you.'

The speaker seemed to take a breath, clearly ready to continue, but was interrupted by a group within the crowd. Austin could not see how many but believed that there must have been at least fifty. They rushed forward towards the wooden gate and collectively grabbed it, ripping it away from its fixings. The attending police had little chance to challenge or object. Their comparatively feeble attempts were met with mild violence. A senior officer was thrown over a nearby wall and another officer was hit on the head by a flying object, probably a stone. A young lad had a notebook he was writing something in snatched from him, and a gamekeeper using a stick was lifted by a small group of men, carried, and thrown into a pond.

The police and gamekeepers backed down, realising that taking on such a large group was futile. The march continued through the gate and over the moors towards the pubs in Belmont. Congratulating themselves with a pint in the rain outside the Black Dog in Belmont, there was no room inside, Stan had only one thing to say.

'We won,'

Austin was not so sure but put his glass up and downed half of it. He wasn't a regular drinker but it had been a long walk and he felt he deserved it.

* * *

'Teddy Ashton has written a poem about the march,' said Austin, pleased with himself. He had been told about it at Foggs the day before, and had been out to buy a copy of 'Teddy Ashton's Journal' on Saturday morning.

Emma looked at him. She knew about Teddy Ashton; everyone seemed to. All people from Bolton would know about was his 'Tum Fowt Sketches', and Bill and Bet Spriggs.

'Go on then, read it to me,' demanded Emma.

Austin nodded in assent and started to read the first few lines.

'Will Yo Come O Sunday mornin

Fo a Walk O'er Winter Hill

Ten thousand went last Sunday

But there's room for thousands still

O the moors are rare and bonny

An the heather's sweet and fine

An the road across this hill tops

Is the public's – yours and mine'

'That's good. Is that it?' said Emma.

'No. There's more but I'll leave you to read it. The post has arrived,' replied Austin, more important matters on his mind.

Austin picked up a solitary envelope that had appeared through the letterbox as he read the Journal. The sound of an envelope falling to the ground had distracted him.

'It's franked Hindley,' he added.

They exchanged nervous glances.

Carefully removing its contents, Austin unfolded the letter and began to read.

He smiled.

Emma got off her chair and hugged her husband. She was as excited as him.

'When are you to you start? Said Emma.

'November 1st,' replied Austin.

'That's not a lot of time to organise,' said Emma.

'I know, but we will manage it. They said there is a house we can move in to straight away. I'll have to give notice at Foggs on Monday,' replied Austin.

They had only a few weeks to organise themselves, but as they had little it would not be too much. Having a house to move in to would help a lot.

* * *

Hindley wasn't so bad, thought Austin. Similar in size and population to Farnworth, it had more similarities than differences. And by moving to Hindley it would not perhaps have had the shock of a move to a larger town, away from family and friends. Austin had obtained employment as what his new employer described as an 'engineman' at Robert Haworth's Castle Hill Mill on Castle Hill Road in Hindley.

Emma seemed more than pleased with their new house. It was almost opposite the mill at the road side and surrounded by open fields behind. Austin had a very short walk to his workplace, and she had the comparatively fresh air of a home on the outskirts of their new town. She expected to be happy there, especially with the news that she had been keeping from Austin until they completed their move to Hindley. She had to wait until she was sure, and decided that would be shortly after their first Mass on Sunday at their new church, St. Benedict's.

'Austin, I've got some news.'

Austin looked up. During the past year he had got into the habit of buying and reading two newspapers, a national and a local one. It was something he liked to do. It wasn't just news; it was an education as well.

Before finishing, she grabbed Annie, who was showing an unhealthy interest in the coal bucket next to the guarded fireplace. Annie resisted and needed to be distracted before Emma could continue. A rattle was found and a short negotiation with the child undertaken. It was successful, at least for a few minutes.

'Why don't you read to her. You know she likes that,' suggested Austin. Rather unhelpful, thought Emma, though she decided to remain silent on the subject.

'Well, she'll soon have someone else to play with,' replied Emma.

Austin took a second or two to process what Emma had said, initially taking it at face value but then realising the magnitude of her statement.

'You're pregnant!'

'We're having another baby, Austin,' replied Emma.

Austin smiled, put down his paper, walked over to his wife, and hugged and kissed her. They had been in Hindley barely a week, and this was news indeed. A new job and a new member of the family on the way. After that it was going to be difficult to think or talk about much else.

The newspapers would have to wait.

* * *

Castle Hill Mill was not one of the largest mills in the county, relatively small in fact. At four storeys and an attic floor, its employees numbered in the hundreds rather than the thousands, but Austin thought it a good size for his first engineering job in a cotton mill. He did not know a lot about the company, but what he did know was that it was owned by a Richard Howarth, who also owned the Albion Mill in Westhoughton a few miles away. Some said that it was an even bigger concern with mills in Manchester as well, but Austin wasn't so sure. It mattered little to him who the bosses were; his obligations were to the senior engineer in the engine room at Castle Hill. And his ambitions were to learn whatever he could about engine tending in a cotton mill; after all that was where the opportunities, and pay, were.

The engine house had surprised him a little by its similarities to the colliery. His first impressions were that it seemed slightly smaller in size than the one at Fogg's, perhaps about 40 feet long by 16 feet wide, but it nonetheless seemed more than adequate for its purpose. The room boasted what looked like a standard Corliss valve type engine, with its four rotating valves swinging from open to closed by cranks located outside the cylinder. Austin watched the large piston move backwards and forwards, controlled by the rhythmic opening and closing of the valves whose sole purpose was to let in the superheated steam created by the mill's Lancashire boilers. To a layman the action could have been seen as hypnotic, but Austin was used to it. He was used to the constant forward and reverse action as the machine's piston reached one end of the stroke and then the other.

Attached to the engine's piston was a crank, which in turn was attached to the flywheel axle, and that drove the rope drum in a constantly rotating movement. The winding engine that Austin had become used to at the colliery had more of a gear mechanism and a lot less involvement with ropes. Austin guessed that the ropes enveloping the drum must have been between two and three inches in diameter, and clearly made to last. They served to transfer the power of the engine to the pulley shafts on the various floors in the mill. He was aware of how it worked in theory but this was the first time he had seen it in action.

'Austin!'

Austin stood still, temporarily mesmerised by the interlocking action of the discrete parts of the machinery. With the noise and heat of the room he had failed to hear his new engineering supervisor call his name.

'Austin!!'

Startled, he jumped and turned.

Jim, his new supervisor, pointed at a nearby door and mouthed 'this way.'

Austin followed him into an adjacent room, the boiler room. Within a matter of a minute or two he was sweating, as excess heat radiated from one of the two Lancashire boilers built into a brick housing. Lancashire boilers were to be found pretty much wherever there was a steam engine. They consisted of a large round cylinder split into two furnaces, a left and a right, so that one could be tended without disturbing the other. The burning coal heated the water above to create the steam required to drive the engine's piston, conveyed from the boiler room to the engine room via the main steam line, and controlled by means of various valves. At the engine end, the governor, its speed regulator, controlled the speed of the engine by means of managing the flow of steam into the piston cylinder. The flue design within the boiler was such that as much heat as possible from the waste gases would be extracted before being allowed to leave through a tall chimney built next to the boiler room.

It was all in accordance with the textbooks, thought Austin.

'Well, that's the tour, Austin. Let's talk about what your responsibilities will be and what we will expect of you,' said Jim.

'Yes, sir,' replied Austin.

'I'm not a sir, Austin. You can call me Jim. If the bosses come down you can call them sir, but we are a happy bunch here. We are on first name terms,' said Jim.

'Thank you, Jim,' replied Austin.

He decided at that instant he was going to get the best out of his time here.

* * *

Life in Hindley soon settled down to a routine. For Emma, week days replicated the pattern adopted in Farnworth.

Mondays were typically washing days, Tuesdays and Fridays were used for shopping expeditions down to Market Street, with the rest of the week devoted to cleaning, cooking, tending to Annie, and generally keeping house.

Austin would not always have to work a full day on a Saturday, so it was sometimes possible to spend an afternoon together as a family. Occasionally, on a week day, he would take a drink with the men from the engine room, but he was not a great believer in alcohol. Not teetotal by any means, but also not enamoured by the effects it had on the lives of working people. Edward, his father, was far more sanguine about a visit to a public house, but then he was a miner for life. Austin had experienced a spell in a colliery and knew how hard a life it was. Coal dust permeated every nook and cranny of a miner's being, an unwelcome encroachment into a pair of healthy lungs. It was no wonder most of the colliers he knew would seek to wash away the detritus of a day in the colliery with a comparatively aseptic infusion of five or six pints of 'mild'. It was the miners favoured choice, more lightly hopped and relatively low in strength compared to other beers. It was possible to consume of five, six, or even eight pints, and yet still get up for a shift the following morning. But that was the problem, mused Austin. For his father it had become a habit years before Austin was even born; it had become a curse and his father did not realise it.

Unlike his parents, Austin had been born into a world where education had started to be seen as a social benefit. In the year of his birth, 1870, it was made compulsory for children between the ages of five and thirteen to receive an education. And now, twenty-seven years later he was reaping the benefits. Not only did he not have to follow his father's steps in working in a colliery, but he had managed to climb the first rung on a career as an engineer. His unpredictable father had resolved that none of his sons would mine, but he had still needed to contribute to the family wage. Working at Foggs had helped cement his decision to do something more with his life, and sealed a determination to pursue a career.

Austin preferred a book to a beer.

Saturday nights were family nights. He continued the Melia family custom of reading out loud to his own family, sometimes local news, but more often a book from the Leyland Free Library, or a weekly or monthly journal. Since working at the Castle Hill Mill he had got into the habit of acquiring a copy of the 'Cotton Factory Times', which, in addition to news about the Lancashire cotton industry, also included humorous tales from one of his favourite writers, Teddy Ashton. In the previous year Teddy Ashton had also launched his own journal, 'The Teddy Ashton Journal', adding to the output of his 'Northern Weekly'. Both editions were always popular with Emma.

'Is there anything in it about Tum Fowt?' enquired Emma.

It was a reference to the 'Tum Fowt Sketches' that had reached enormous popularity in the Bolton area. Tum Fowt, or Tonge Fold to a non-dialect speaker, referred to a couple of mythical characters, Bill Spriggs and his wife, Bet, and the public house they were often found in, 'The Dug an Kennel'.

'Not in this one. But I can get one of the penny editions from the drawer if you like. I'm sure there is one we haven't had in a while,' replied Austin.

Opening a nearby drawer he sifted through a small pile of loose papers, each one being examined with a grin.

'I'll light a lamp; it's getting dark,' said Emma, before going to retrieve an ornately decorated kerosine lantern from the front room.

'How about this one?' said Austin, pointing at the first line under the author's name on the cover sheet.

'Bill An Bet At Farnworth Wakes.'

'I don't remember it. Yes, that one will do,' replied Emma.

Austin proceeded to read the tale of the hapless couple, Bill and Bet Spriggs, and their tale of misunderstandings in planning and journeying to Farnworth's annual three-day fair. Emma laughed at the interactions with the ticket clerk at Bolton Station, but towards the end of what was only a short sketch she suddenly leaned forward and fell to the floor.

'Emma!'

Austin was momentarily panicked as he knelt down to help.

'I'm, I'm, I'm alright,' whispered Emma, altering her facial expression in an attempt to reassure her husband.

'It's nothing.'

'It doesn't look like nothing to me. We should call for a doctor,' said Austin.

'No. I just suddenly felt dizzy and a little sick. Help me up,' replied Emma.

'We should get you to bed,' said Austin.

'Yes. I don't think I feel very well. My ankles and feet are swollen. See look,' replied Emma pointing.

'How long have you been like this? Has it happened before?' asked Austin.

'A few weeks. I've never fainted. I didn't want to worry you. It's just being pregnant, Austin. I'm sure it will be alright,' replied Emma.

Austin seemed unsure.

'This never happened with Annie.'

'I know. I know. But I'm seven months. I'll be fine with a good night's rest,' said Emma.

'Well, I don't think you should go to Mass at St. Benedict's tomorrow, and perhaps we should send word to my family in Farnworth. I could send a postcard first thing,' replied Austin.

'That might be for the best,' said Emma.

Every two or three weeks, the three of them would go straight from Mass to Hindley Station, catch a train to Farnworth, and spend a day with Austin's family. It would have to change that particular Sunday, thought Austin. He could not take any risks with Emma or the baby.

'I'm going to ask your sister to call in. I bet she will know what to do. I'll get word to her as well tomorrow morning,' replied Austin.

'Now you're starting to fuss,' said Emma.

'That may be, but I don't care,' replied Austin, his mind clearly made up.

Emma had no wish to raise any strong objection. She was more worried than she wanted to let on to her husband, and the sight of her sister would do far more good than harm.

* * *

Sarah's visits became a regular occurrence in the warming spring weeks of April and early May. With visits to Farnworth now off the agenda, Farnworth had decided to visit Hindley, and as Emma neared term, Mary, Austin's mother, also started to call in to lend a hand. Both women had been a 'godsend'.

'It's been far more difficult than with Annie,' said Emma to Sarah.

'I can see that. But I'll be here whenever you need me. Annie has been lovely; very little trouble at all,' replied Sarah.

It was the same story with Mary. She loved playing with her granddaughter and was fully aware of Emma's circumstances. She had lost both her parents in a short space of time so it was down to the females in the Melia household to help as much as they could.

As luck would have it, Emma's waters broke around midday on a Saturday. Sarah had stayed overnight on the two previous Saturdays and had been in the house barely an hour when Emma made her announcement.

'Mary will be here later as well,' said Emma.

'I know. We had both planned to visit this weekend, and next,' replied Sarah.

Emma knew that but simply wanted to make conversation. Sarah continued.

'Let's get you to bed. I'm sure it will be a while yet. Enough time to fetch the midwife.'

'Don't leave me,' said Emma.

'Of course not. But I'll have to get word to Austin as well. I can go there. It's only five minutes away,' replied Sarah.

Emma looked doubtful but acquiesced to the suggestion.

'Ask next door to come in and mind Annie. They said they would if this happened,' said Emma.

Sarah nodded before leaving to complete her now urgent errands.

Half an hour later, Austin and Sarah were with Emma. After seeing his wife, he was immediately despatched to find the midwife, returning an hour later with her. Mary arrived an hour after that, and soon started taking instructions from the midwife. Austin and Sarah were left downstairs waiting for news.

After the challenges of the later stages of Emma's confinement, Austin dearly hoped that the birth would be relatively short and uneventful. Alas, that was not to be the case. It was nearly eleven hours before Edward finally made his entrance into the world, by which time Emma was completely exhausted. It had been a difficult birth, but in the end both mother and child had reached the end of their ordeal without harm or injury. After hugging Emma, and thanking the midwife, his mother, and sister-in-law for their assistance, he turned to have a good look at his newborn son, and spoke his first words to him.

'Well, I hope this isn't a sign of things to come, young man. You are a little rascal, aren't you?'

Emma had drifted off to sleep, so it was down to Sarah and his mother to respond. Sarah took the initiative.

'He's lovely, Austin. I'm sure he will be as good as gold. You know they often say that a difficult birth makes a lovely child.'

'I had not heard that one, Sarah,' said Mary.

Out of sight of Austin, who was still inspecting the new addition to the family, Sarah cast Mary a wry grin, and almost a wink.

'Oh yes. It's quite a common one in Little Lever.'

Mary smiled back, a little unsure of the humour but still willing to go along with it. She just had one axiomatic comment to add.

'Well. You are a family of four now, Austin.'

Austin looked back at the two women, clearly pleased with himself.

* * *

'I don't believe it, Austin. We've not been here three years. I've settled down here; I've got friends,' said Emma.

'I know. I know. But we agreed that I needed to get on and that Hindley would not be forever,' replied Austin.

Emma took a moment before answering. Austin's reply was true but a lot had happened since that discussion in Farnworth three years earlier. They had a young family and seemed to have it good. Work for Austin was only a matter of a few minutes away, and their house was on the edge of Hindley, quite a way from the smoke, dirt and grime of Wigan, Bolton, or even Farnworth. To some, Hindley was no better, but to Emma it seemed an improvement.

The family had taken a walk in Borsdane Wood on a path close to the brook. Accessed via the nearby cemetery, they often took a summer's walk there to enjoy the sensorial fruits of its ancient woodland. It was a location she thought Annie and Edward might enjoy when they got a little older. Emma clearly needed some more information from her husband. What exactly did he have in mind?

'Are you going to tell me where this new mill is? Are we going back to Farnworth?'

'Look, I've not said anything to anyone just yet. I've only made an enquiry about the job. It may not be right,' replied Austin.

He has not admitted as to where it was, thought Emma.

'Where is it?'

'It's in Stockport,' replied Austin

He did not want to leave it at that and proceeded to provide a bit more information.

'It will mean more pay and more responsibility. The mill is called the Beehive. It's in the Portwood area; there are a number of them together and I would have responsibilities across all. It's an opportunity to learn more, and on bigger engines. I want to do right by you and the children, and I think this is the way to do it. I can't promise it won't happen again, Emma, but I think It's the only way we can get on,' he added.

'Can't we just wait a while, Austin? I'm happy. And Stockport seems like such a long way,' said Emma.

'I know you are. But remember the proverb: 'It's ill waiting for dead men's shoes.' If we stay here it could be years before there is a chance to get on at Castle Hill. The Stockport trains are just as good as those from Hindley, and we could travel from Stockport to Farnworth, or Bolton, in less than an hour.

Please, Emma. I know it's hard but it really is a good opportunity. And I promise it will not be forever,' replied Austin.

'That's what I'm afraid of, Austin. I would really like to settle in one place,' said Emma.

'I know you would. But I also know that I need to get a lot of experience before I can get on. I'll be seeing them on a Saturday, the week after next,' replied Austin.

Emma acquiesced. She could have dug her heels in and raised a stronger objection but she knew that his happiness, and by implication her own, was at stake. Emma trusted Austin to make this decision, but resolved that one day she would exercise a lot more influence on the outcomes of their discussions.

The return home was largely silent, other than to remark on the beauty of a copse or the sight of a woodland creature. It was later than their usual time for Sunday walking. A cooling gentle breeze had stilled as the sun started to descend over the distant horizon, only occasionally visible between the trees. It was a time for both to reflect on where they were and what might be ahead. Emma thought about the things they had both planned to do but never seemed to get around to. That ride on a steam tram from the 'Bird i'th Hand Inn' at the crossroads in the town centre to Wigan, and, most curious of all, sight of that 'burning well' as the locals called it. Was it on Derby Lane or Dog Pool? She could not remember. And it mattered little. Perhaps there would be just as many interesting things in Stockport. She just hoped that Austin would be successful in his endeavour.

Chapter 4

THE RESCUE

Austin's first thoughts about The Beehive Mill on Marsland Street in Stockport, was that it was a bit of a misnomer. It was not really a single mill, although there was a large one of that name, but several separate buildings, ranging from two to six storeys in height. It was an impressive collection to a visitor, all owned by T & J Leigh, one of the town's best-known cotton spinners. Water Street, Marsland Street and Brewery Street were all dominated by the complex, and you did not have far to walk to see another owned by the same company, Meadow Mill. For Austin it was a world of opportunity, and he intended to make the best of it, as he always did. It would be a stepping stone to something better, of that he was sure.

Emma was a little less enamoured by her new surroundings. Austin had rented a house on Farr Street, a good walk away from his new employment, but in his mind a compromise. Emma had not seen the house before he agreed to take it, but he thought she would be happy with it. After all, there was a play area only a matter of minutes away.

'It's not like the one we had in Hindley, Austin,' said Emma.

'There's a park five minutes away. I'm sure the children will love to play there when they are older,' replied Austin.

I'm not so sure, Austin,' replied Emma.

Austin looked at her, unsure of what she was trying to tell him. Emma continued.

'I mean this whole place, Austin. It feels like we are in the centre of town. It's like Bolton and Wigan. What with the chimneys and smoke, it's just not as clean as where we were in Hindley. I'm sure all this smoke will not be good for the children. This weather we are having is not helping either, awful smoky fog.

'What can I say?' replied Austin.

'And I've not been feeling too well in the morning these past two weeks. You know what that might mean,' said Emma.

'You're pregnant?' questioned Austin.

'I don't know. It's too early to say for sure,' answered Emma.

Austin's thoughts accelerated. Two had been a handful. Were they ready for a third? Any doubts about transplanting from Hindley to Stockport rapidly dispelled. Emma might have her reservations about the place, but if there was to be an extra mouth to feed the extra money the move provided would surely prove the move to be good decision.

'You know I'll be happy if you are. When will you be certain?' asked Austin.

'Give it another couple of weeks. I want to go and see my sister next week. I'll send a postcard and let her know I'm coming, and that I would like to stay a few days. Now she's settled in Deane I doubt she will mind,' replied Emma.

'Perhaps you can buy me another watch,' suggested Austin.

He was alluding to the fact that Emma's sister had married a watchmaker, and might be able to help get a new one for a good price. The one he had was losing time.

'I'll take the one you have, Austin. Better to repair it. If I go next week, I'll know about the baby by the time I return. I'll also make some plans with Sarah about coming over here when it's due, just like we did in Hindley with Edward. This might be our last Christmas with two, Austin,' replied Emma.

Austin gave her a quizzical smile before letting Emma continue.

'I think I am, Austin. I just want to be sure.'

* * *

Occasional mill sirens echoed across the industrial landscape of Stockport's busy town centre streets. Austin's choice of career had taken him out of the bleak mining world of coal dust and dirt, almost. Of course, the boilers had to be fuelled, and the engine rooms were hot and sweaty, but he could always step outside for a minute or two for some fresh air. There was always a pretext. Life for the ordinary mill worker was perhaps a little harder, nothing like working in the pits, but nonetheless still hard. In both Hindley and Stockport he often took a little time to study their lives.

Whether winter or summer, the women wear shawls over their heads on the way to work, sometimes tartan, sometimes not. And, like the men, they all seemed to wear Lancashire's standard footwear, clogs. On his walk down to Portwood, Austin would see the daily tide of humanity tread towards its workplace, accompanied by the clatter of a thousand clogs all hitting the ground in asynchronous interval. The women, typically hiding behind shawls, carried wicker baskets containing their breakfasts, while men, often less organised, were often seen either with a lunch box, or some bread and meat wrapped in a paper bag or handkerchief. It was the same routine every day. Pasty faced wan looking women and asthmatic-looking men, all trooping towards their allocated tasks tending cotton machinery, or perhaps building it. Austin would often reflect on his situation and that of his family. In the same way that his own father did not want a miner's life for him, Austin in turn did not really want mill life for his children. Perhaps a career as an engineer, yes, but not an ordinary mill worker. He wanted them to have some choices. It was the alarming frequency of accidents that preyed on his mind more than almost anything else.

Not long after starting work at the Beehive he had been asked to 'show around' a new recruit to the mill's steam engineering group. A young lad, not unlike himself a few years earlier, still schooling in maths, science, and relevant engineering subjects, but already required to earn a wage. Austin's own supervisor had not only asked Austin to take the fellow around the steam power areas, but around one of the mills in its entirety. It was an unexpected request, but not unreasonable, and it seemed to be a very sensible course of action. Helping out with machinery power issues 'upstairs' was not a daily occurrence, but it did happen from time to time. And a mill engineer would be expected to know how a cotton mill actually worked.

After introducing the new recruit, George, Austin's supervisor left them together.

'What do you know about the production of cotton, George?' asked Austin.

'A little. I've been in one before but I'm usually in the engine room. My father had a shop so I used to help there, but when he died my mother couldn't manage it. We've both had to get work,' replied George.

Austin had been relatively lucky in this respect. His early life had been spent in a mill so he had an intimate understanding of what happened in them.

'So, you've never actually worked in a mill then. Well, I shall take you through the whole thing from one end to another,' said Austin.

As they walked towards the cotton receiving area, the start of the process, Austin talked about Lancashire's prime industry.

'There are perhaps a hundred million spindles in the world with perhaps half of them in Britain, and most of those are in Lancashire. I'm told that tens of millions of pounds are invested in spinning, perhaps fifty or sixty million. I'm also told there are nearly seventy cotton firms and two and a half million spindles at work in Stockport...'

George listened, politely nodding his head at appropriate junctures in speech. They entered an area whose purpose Austin explained was to process the raw cotton.

'This is called 'ginning'. The cotton requires cleaning. That is the seeds need to be separated from the fibre, then made up into bales, and then compressed using hydraulic presses.'

'Where is it from?' asked George.

'Mostly America, sometimes from India or Egypt. A lot comes in on the Ship Canal' replied Austin, referring to the Manchester Ship Canal. He continued.

'Nothing is wasted. The seeds are collected and crushed and made into oil cake for cattle, or other materials for paper making. And what's left is made into soap.'

George raised his eyebrows in surprise and amusement.

'Let's go to the mill,' instructed Austin.

On entering the mill room, a couple of dozen inquisitive eyes momentarily looked at them. By now, Austin's face was known to many of the mill workers, but a stranger was a curiosity. Austin ignored them, knowing that they knew better than to tease. His status was already on the rise.

'The bales are like blocks of wood when they get here. We call that machine with the many rows of teeth an 'opener'. Lumps of compressed cotton are thrown inside it and the machine quickly tears it apart. The blower you see cleans it of sand and dust. The cotton then passes through the rollers and by the time it reaches the other end it should have lost its hardness. You can also see the women over there mixing the cotton from different bales so that its quality is consistent.'

Austin pointed to half a dozen women, all dressed in aprons sorting and moving baled cotton at the other end of the room.

'We recently installed a scutching machine in. Do you know what that is?' asked Austin.

'It beats the cotton doesn't it?' replied George.

Austin nodded approvingly.

'Yes, it's that machine over there,' said Austin, pointing in a different direction.

'Pneumatic suction is now used to draw cotton from one machine to another. When the cotton passes through the scutcher it is 'lapped'. That is, it's rolled out several times so that it's easier to handle. Let's now go to the carding room,' said Austin, before leading George to another part of the mill.

'The carding engine clears any seeds that might still be remaining and also arranges the fibre in parallel formation. The three cylinders you see are called the 'main', the 'doffer' and the 'licker-in'. You can see what the licker-in does,' said Austin, pointing to the relevant part of the machine.

As the cylinder's teeth grab the cotton its fibres are loosened, while the interaction of the speedy rolling of the cylinders and the machine's wire points force it into a parallel form.

'If thread or lace is to be spun the carded cotton is 'combed'. The combining machine ensures that only thread of a certain length and strength are kept. The fibres are attenuated through that drawing frame. It's a gentle action. You can see the fibres being drawn over those leather topped fluted rollers. As the cotton passes through it is pulled a little to draw it out. Well, that's the preparation part. It's now ready for twisting, and that changes its name to yarn. Let's go up a floor.'

After climbing a couple of flights of worn stone steps in the painted brick stairwell, the two men entered a room dominated by cotton twisting machinery.

'That's called a 'slubbing frame'. The end of the yarn is attached to a bobbin, around which it is wound, layer upon layer. Not too tightly. We don't want to see it broken. Those large and small wheels over there are together called 'the sun and planet motion'. As the bobbins fill, the wheels work together to slow the speed of the move. The yarn is further twisted and rolled until it meets the required weight and length. 840 yards if I remember rightly,' said Austin.

A loud and unexpected scream from the other end of the room suddenly interrupted the tour. As Austin and George turned, half a dozen barefoot men ran to the centre of the commotion. They also followed, taking care not to slip on the greasy wooden surface upon which a number of the mill's spinning machines were mounted. By the time they both reached the group of concerned onlookers, the spinning mule had been stopped. Austin peered over the top to take a look. His heart missed a beat as he absorbed the true horror of the spectacle. He turned back towards George who was directly behind him.

'It's a lad, a little piecer. He can't be more than twelve years old. It looks like he caught his arm in the mule. There's blood everywhere. He just wasn't fast enough. You've got to be quick with a mule. If you're not, that's it; you've had it. I just hope he doesn't lose a limb. When I was a young 'un I knew a little piecer who lost an arm to one of these things......'

Austin tailed off, seemingly distracted by what had happened. It took his companion to bring him back.

'Are you alright?' said George.

Austin hesitated for a few short seconds before composing himself and replying.

'Of course. There's nothing we can do. His spinner will take him to see a doctor. I'm sorry to say this sort of thing happens all too often. I think we'll do the rest of the tour tomorrow. I'll explain what happens in the spinning, winding, frame carding, reeling, warping and weaving rooms. I'll take you through the boiler and engine rooms today. There is still so much to see.'

George nodded, also shaken by what he had just witnessed. It was not just what had happened to the little piecer but how Austin had reacted. He would not have shown it, but he had to admit to himself to a certain amount of fear. Working as a young lad in a shop had its pitfalls, but there were no dangers like the ones he had just seen. He just hoped that he would not have to observe anything like it again.

That particular day seemed longer than usual. The incident had unnerved him, more so, as it was not the first time in his life that he had the misfortune to witness an accident involving a child. When the evening siren pronounced the end of another workday, Austin made an effort to snap out of what for him was an unfamiliar mood, a reflective mix of sorrow, fear, and a little anger. He decided to walk it off.

Austin's route home was not set in stone. On a fine day in the more clement seasons, he might walk the entire route from Farr Street to Marsland Street, a journey of perhaps thirty to forty-five minutes. On the wetter days he would take a horsecar for some of the journey, walking only part of the route. Despite typical showery April weather, a walk was indeed in order. It gave him some time to think. A passing train slowing for the nearby Tiviot Dale Railway Station seemed to instruct his route. It was still passing as he headed up Marsland Street towards the tramway on Warren Street. On some days he would catch a horsecar near the junction between the two roads straight down towards Mersey Square. It was a slightly odd journey in that it passed over the Mersey twice, once over Bridge Street towards Heaton Lane, and then back over the Mersey Bridge to the square itself. He elected to walk by the tram lines.

It was always an interesting journey, seemingly taking in some of Stockport's busiest streets. Cyclists, horses, and carts filled the roads while bonneted women in smart blouses and skirts, and flat capped men filled the pavements. The less well-off mixed with Stockport's aspiring middle classes on its bustling highways. Occasional street traders were often seen challenging the well-presented shops, most of whom had their awnings drawn down to protect customers and goods from the sun and the rain. There was always something to see. The air was much the same as in Bolton. A vague smell of smoke permeated throughout in damp conditions; it would take a stronger breeze to clear it. Not so today, thought Austin, it was a day not unlike when he first took a seat on the upper floor of a horsecar.

In a little over twenty minutes he was standing in Mersey Square. From there it was a walk up Daw Bank, underneath one of the town's best known landmarks, its railway viaduct, and then on towards the junction with Bann Street. He liked Bann Street. It was short, and directly adjacent to the raised section of Holllywood Park. Had a house been available on this street when he was looking for one, he would definitely have rented it. Austin enjoyed a walk through the park; it was the favourite part of his journey to and from work. On a warm summer evening he would sometimes catch Emma and the children still enjoying its amenities, but there was no sign of them today.

Hollywood Park's central boulevard, with its well-tended gardens and steps to its other levels, was always inviting after a day in the mill. As he walked through it, he could see older children playing with a ball on the lower level field; in a few years perhaps they could be his own. The remnants of Hollywood House on the corner of Grenville Street and Bloom Street, to his left, could still be seen. It had been demolished two years earlier after a fire rendered it uninhabitable. That was before their time here. Number 49 was at the river end of Farr Street so he tended to walk down Grenville Street and on to Ealing Road, passing Yule Street before reaching his home road. It had taken forty minutes this evening. The walk had certainly helped but he still felt the need to talk about it with Emma. She would understand; she always did. He would wait until after supper, after the children had been tucked in to bed.

'Something happened today, Emma,' said Austin.

Emma looked up. She had already started to sew a blouse that Annie had torn earlier in the day.

'I could tell something was wrong. You were unusually quiet over supper,' replied Emma.

'Do you remember Johnny Cuthbertson?' said Austin.

Emma winced. Yes of course she remembered him, and what had happened. It was not a memory she treasured. They only vaguely knew Johnny, but after the accident everyone seemed to know him.

'He lost an arm and an eye on that machine. Only thirteen years old. Do you remember?'

'I could never forget that. What happened today, Austin?' replied Emma, anxious to avoid a detailed recollection of the Farnworth incident.

'I didn't see it, but heard it. I was taking a new man around the factory when it happened. It was at the opposite end of the room to where we were. The lad wasn't fast enough. I've always said they should stop those mules every so often to clean up. But they won't. You've seen them. One wrong move and the machines will have you. We heard a scream and that was it. When we got there the overseer was tending him, but there was blood everywhere and you could see what was left of his arm dangling uselessly from his shoulder. It was more than a break. I bet he lost it,' replied Austin.

Emma could see that her husband was becoming somewhat emotional. Concern and anger quite obviously welling up inside him. A distraction was called for.

'There's nothing you can do about it, Austin. I read the Factory Times as well. It's happening almost every day in nearly every mill in Lancashire,' replied Emma.

'I know. But it shouldn't. I don't want ours working in a mill, or in a mine,' said Austin.

Emma knew he meant well, but when the time came, she also knew that they might not have much choice. But that was for another day.

'You had a letter from home,' announced Emma.

It was a deliberate attempt to get off the subject. She should have mentioned it over their meal but had forgotten. On reflection it was just as well.

Austin acknowledged the information and got up to retrieve the letter from the usual place, a small letter rack placed on an old pine sideboard they used for storing useful household items. He opened it and started to read.

'Will you not read it to me, Austin?' enquired Emma. It was his usual practice.

Austin looked up, slightly surprised that he had omitted to.

'I will. It's from Annie. She's still working in the card room. John's got a job in a chemical yard, she doesn't say where, but he's also talking about wanting to join the militia like I did. Father is still not well; always coughing. She says that Bolton corporation is busy with electrifying the trams. They are building the gantries and overhead lines very quickly. The talk is that it will start before the year is finished,' replied Austin.

'Read it all, Austin. I don't want to miss anything.' repeated Emma.

Austin resumed reading, finishing what remained of the letter, which was mostly a little gossip about some close neighbours.

'I suppose I shall write back and tell them about the accident,' suggested Austin.

'They don't want to know that. They want to know about Annie and Edward, and how you are. I'll write to your sister and mine tomorrow. I'll soon be due, Austin,' replied Emma.

Austin nodded, acknowledging the wisdom of her reply.

'You are right of course. I'm sorry I've been gloomy. I won't say any more about it,' replied Austin.

'I don't mind, Austin. You are right but we can only do what we can do. Look after our own and hope that the owners will eventually see sense. If it keeps up there will be strikes. They won't like that,' said Emma.

'I know. But I'm not political. I don't want to be in a union, but I will also not be a knobstick. What would I do?' replied Austin.

'We'll cross that bridge if we ever come to it. Why don't you read something to cheer us both up? What about that Teddy Ashton fellow you like? Another one of those Tum Fowt sketches. It's been a while since you had them out. Let's have no more news today,' suggested Emma.

Austin stood up.

'I'll find one.'

Emma was right, as she often was. He did not want either of them to go to bed in a bleak mood.

* * *

Thomas was born at home on Farr Street on the first of August. There was some discussion about Emma moving in with her sister for a few weeks, but in the end, Sarah first, and then Annie came to stay. The birth was as normal as it could be, unlike the difficulties presented with Edward's arrival. Within weeks the newly enlarged family settled into the quotidian routines of daily life. It was a happy time.

With Annie now four, five in 1900, there was a need to find a suitable school for her. While the children were very young, Austin had avoided being too dogmatic about raising his offspring as Catholics, but he wished to remain true to his word. He would not coerce Emma to attend a Catholic service, but on the occasions he had asked her to accompany him to Mass, she had acquiesced. Emma also seemed willing to see the children baptised in the Catholic faith, with both Annie and Edward receiving the sacrament in St. Gregory the Great's in Farnworth and St. Benedict's in Hindley. They both agreed that the right place for Thomas would be in the St Philip and St. James Chapel on Chapel Street.

The church had become too small for the growing Catholic population of Edgeley, and funds were being raised for a new one. But for now, it was what they had. Its single domed bell and clock tower stood in front of a small and unimposing building. But looks deceived. Shortly after arriving in Stockport and joining the congregation, he learned of its ignominious place in the history of the town.

Less than fifty years earlier, Catholics had been less welcome than today. The chapel had been ransacked by anti-Catholics, mostly boys and young men, wielding pick-axes, hatchets, sledge-hammers and crowbars. They had perhaps taken umbrage at the priest's Catholic missionary zeal, although few were certain what had actually caused the riot. However, what was clear was the damage that had been done. Every adornment had been destroyed, crosses, crucifixes, images, pictures and candlesticks. Windows had been smashed, the altar pulled down, and the doors broken. Even the chairs, benches, and organ had been smashed, although attempts to set fire to the building all seemed to fail. The priest and some companions only managed to escape by firstly hiding in the bell tower, and then escaping over the chapel roof to the next house. It was a sorry tale, thought Austin.

Fifty years later, forty-seven to be exact, the damage had long since been repaired, but the need was now for a building much larger. Sheer numbers had forced acceptance of Catholics, not only in Stockport, but across Lancashire's mill towns. There were still skirmishes to be had, but a grudging respect had developed out of a recognition that the country needed these, mostly Irish, Catholics to help power its economy. And after all, they were all Christians.

As autumn drew close the newspapers had become increasingly interested in what was happening in South Africa. The Boers as they were called, had become belligerent in attacking British ambitions in certain states of The South African Republic, and the Orange Free State. Austin had a more personal interest in the affair.

He had bought a newspaper on the way home from the mill and was anxious to share the news with Emma. He burst through the door and immediately launched into a news bulletin.

'The Boers are at it again. It looks like war, Emma,' said Austin.

A little unnerved, Emma was unsure what to say.

'It's a long way from us, Austin. It's not our concern,' replied Emma.

'But it might be,' said Austin.

'What do you mean?' replied Emma.

'I was in the militia. They could still call me back. I'm still young enough to go,' said Austin.

'They won't, Austin. I'm sure they have enough of the regular army to handle a few farmers. We are the British Empire,' replied Emma.

'They are a nasty lot; well-armed as well,' said Austin.

'Why is it happening, Austin? What do they want?' asked Emma.

'Well, they don't want us there, Emma. They want all the gold and diamonds for themselves,' replied Austin, a little nonplussed at the question.

'So, it's theirs is it? Perhaps we should just let them keep it,' said Emma.

'I don't know about that. They just keep attacking our men and there's talk that they might try and take Mafeking, Kimberley or Ladysmith. We can't allow that, can we?' said Austin.

'As I said it's not our concern, Austin. I'm sure they will not call you back,' replied Emma.

'I'm not so sure. We'll just have to see, won't we?' said Austin.

'We will indeed. Now what else is there in that newspaper of yours?' replied Emma, diverting her husband had now become something of a habit.

* * *

Austin's concerns about a recall to service had not been realised. After some early failures, Lords Kitchener and Roberts had been put in charge. They changed strategy, recovered lost ground, and overwhelmed the Boers with numbers. The two free Boer states were no longer, annexed into the British Empire. The, at best, vague threat of a recall into the army had receded, but in Farnworth the equilibrium of the family was about to be disturbed by matters far closer to home.

It was obvious that the postcard was from Farnworth, after all it dropped through the letterbox with the photograph facing up; it was a picture of the railway station. They usually received letters rather than postcards, and there was rarely anything in the second post, so this particular communication commanded Emma's immediate attention.

She picked it up, looking at both sides. There was only the address on one side but underneath the picture there were only two short sentences:

'Austin, father very unwell. Come back home, urgently. Annie.'

She had recognised Annie's handwriting, albeit it was far less tidy than in her usual letters.

Thoughts raced through her mind. She checked the postmark. It was today. Annie must have posted it only hours ago.

Emma had to quickly decide how to deal with it. Her daughter was at school, but Edward and Thomas would need to be minded. She would have to ask a neighbour to look after them while she went to see Austin at the mill.

After some childminding arrangements had been made with a sympathetic neighbour, Emma rushed out of the house. She knew Austin's route to work and would follow the same. Her worry was whether his employer would let him leave. Perhaps her presence would help amplify the urgency of the situation. After all, in her mind the postcard could only mean one thing given his age; her father-in-law was dying.

The air was damp and cold on the upper floor of the Portwood bound horsecar; a typical late November afternoon. It was unfortunate that the lower floor was full, but she had wrapped up well, anticipating the weather. The short journey gave her enough time to think about how to tell the news.

Emma had never been in to any of Austin's workplaces, so when she reached the front on the mill on Marsland Street, she had to ask for the location of the engine house. After getting past the initial surprise at being asked such a question, Emma was given directions together with some unsolicited advice.

'It's not really a place for women you know.'

She smiled, politely, and got on her way.

The door to the engine house was open, allowing her to peer inside.

'You can't come in here. It's dangerous,' shouted a voice, apparently behind a piece of machinery.

'I've come for Austin Melia. It's urgent. I'm his wife,' replied Emma, in the loudest voice she could muster.

'He's not here. He's in the boiler room. You can't go in there either,' instructed a man who had now emerged from whatever he was doing.

'I really need to speak to him. It's about his father. Would you mind fetching him?' requested Emma.

'He'll be back in less than a tick,' replied the man, clearly unwilling to leave his station.

Emma had little choice but to wait until Austin appeared behind her, on cue, two minutes later.

'Emma. What are you doing here?' asked Austin, both surprised and shocked at seeing her. Before Emma had a chance to respond he had another question.

'Is it the children? Are they alright? Where are they?'

'No. They're well. It's your father. I think you need to go back to Farnworth today. Read the postcard. It came after you left this morning,' said Emma.

Austin took the postcard and read it, the colour on his face starting to drain as he did so.

'If only we had one of those telephones,' mused Austin, before adding, 'I think I'll need to go tonight.'

'Will they give you time off?' asked Emma.

'I don't know. Perhaps. But it will be unpaid if they do,' replied Austin.

'We'll manage. Just go and ask,' said Emma.

Austin looked at the postcard once more and then took action.

'Wait here, Emma. I'll see.'

Emma watched him disappear through a door on the other side of room. It gave her a few minutes to study her husband's workplace from the vantage point of the entry door. A huge wheel turned wrapped in an enormous rope. Various other ropes, pulleys, valves and pipes all seemed to work in synchronised effort to power the needs of the mill. It was interesting, but at the same time slightly threatening, and no less baffling to her. A tinge of admiration and pride in her husband's skills ran through her mind, tempered somewhat by the thought of whether he would see the same complexities in child rearing.

Austin reappeared.

'They will let me go early. I'll go straight to Farnworth from Stockport Station.'

'Won't you need some clothing, Austin?' enquired Emma.

'There are still a couple of items in Farnworth. You go now. Thank you, Emma,' replied Austin.

At that he took her out of view of the engine room, hugged and kissed her.

'I'll have to get Annie shortly. I don't really know what to say, Austin. You have my love and that of the children. If it is what we both think it is, I just hope it's peaceful. I'll be off now,' said Emma.

Austin nodded, then watched her depart until out of sight.

* * *

He's upstairs, Austin. Ma is tending him. Go straight up, Austin,' said his sister Catherine.

The family had gathered, thought Austin, as he climbed the staircase. After entering the bedroom, he could see that his mother and siblings were sat either on, or around the bed. Only Catherine and Cecily were absent. He had not seen his youngest sister, but now was not the time to enquire of her whereabouts. The atmosphere was sombre in the spartanly furnished bedroom; most of the chairs in the house had been brought upstairs. Two of his sisters were sitting on one side of the bed, while three of his other siblings were seated or standing opposite. Elizabeth and Margaret seemed close to tears, while Annie, John, and Ellen were putting on brave faces. His mother was the first to speak.

'You came. Thank you, Austin. He's been asking for you.'

'How is he?' asked Austin.

'His time is coming. We had the doctor round. He said to prepare ourselves,' replied Mary.

'Is there nothing he can do?' enquired Austin.

'He's...' Mary hesitated. 'He's dying, Austin,' replied Mary.

'No medicine?' asked Austin.

'I've got some morphine. He's had some. He's sleeping now. I don't think he can hear us,' replied Mary.

'Is there anything I can do?' asked Austin.

'Pray for him,' replied Mary.

The doctor said we should get a priest,' interjected Margaret.

Austin looked a little askance at his mother.

'Surely not. It can't be so close. Surely not,' repeated Austin.

He looked at his father more closely. His breathing seemed heavy, deep and slow, with unnaturally long pauses between breaths. The skin on his father's face looked pallid and drawn. It was true. His father was dying in front of him. Pangs of guilt and remorse crashed through his mind. It had not always been easy being with his father, especially when he had been drinking, but there had been good times as well. And he had been true to his word. Austin had spent a short time in the mine but it had been his father who had helped him get a job as a stoker at Foggs. Austin forced himself to suppress the emotional detritus of the past and focus on the needs of the present. He needed to take charge.

'I'll go to St. Gregory's and fetch a priest.'

'Alright,' replied Mary.

As Austin took a few steps towards the door, his father suddenly, and unexpectedly, stirred. Opening his eyes for no more than three or four seconds he blurted out a few barely audible words.

'No Dahdee, No more. No.'

It was a complete shock. Words from someone barely alive, and words which made no sense to the puzzled family group. Margaret was the one to ask.

'What does he mean?'

'I don't know,' replied Austin.

But he did think he knew. They sounded like the sounds an Irish child might make. He did not want to speculate but it was clear to him that his fifty-seven years old father had unearthed something, perhaps from the murky recesses of his childhood. It was not something he wanted to contemplate, and certainly not with his family in these circumstances. They needed to be distracted.

'I'll be off then. Liz, why don't you say a prayer for him?'

An hour later and Austin was back with a young priest who was visiting the parish on some sort of training. A young man, younger even than Austin.

'This is Father Jones,' said Austin.

'I'll get right to it,' said Fr. Jones in a distinctive Welsh accent.

'Some tea, Father?' asked Mary.

'Yes please, Mrs Melia. Your family can stay in the room if they wish,' replied Fr. Jones.

The priest examined Edward, quickly coming to the conclusion that it would not be wise to try and wake him. He then proceeded to explain what was about to happen.

'The Last Rites are a group of sacraments, Confession, Extreme Unction and Viaticum. You might know that as Communion...'

He continued in Latin, reverting to English from time to time to explain what he was doing, and why. It was finished in less than half an hour. As he concluded, Elizabeth burst in tears. Austin walked over and put his arms around her.

'We are a strong family, Liz. We need to be there for each other.'

Elizabeth continued to sob but seemed to derive some comfort in her elder brother's arms.

The priest went downstairs followed by Ellen, Annie and Margaret, leaving only John, Austin and Elizabeth in the room. All three turned to look at their father, who was clearly drifting away from them. Edward's breathing slowed even further, triggering a raw emotion of panic in Austin. He felt the end near.

'John, fetch Ma quickly.'

John looked at Austin, then his father, then rushed down the rickety, uncarpeted staircase. A minute later all four reappeared.

'The priest is still downstairs, Austin. What is it?' asked Mary, quite obviously concerned.

'I think we are losing him very soon, Ma. I just know it,' replied Austin.

His mother's hands started to tremble. She could see what was happening. Five minutes after Austin's instruction to John, Edward took one final deep breath, before his gaunt frame failed to summon up the strength for another.

The room was silent for a good two or three minutes before Austin felt compelled to say something.

'I think he's gone, Ma.'

Mary started to shed some tears, as did most of the other women present. Only Catherine remained resolute in emotional control. Austin decided to hug each one, first his mother, and then his sisters. John stood back, obviously upset but unwilling to show too much emotion.

'I'll bring Fr. Jones back up. I don't know if there is anything else he should do. And John, can you fetch the doctor?' said Austin.

His mother nodded in acquiescence, as did John. He wanted to be useful.

It had all happened so quickly, thought Austin. He had barely been in Farnworth a matter of hours, and yet had seen his father die in front of him. There was now the matter of a funeral to arrange. He would have to do it. As fortune would have it Fr. Jones was still present, so he could have a brief word with him. He would also have to get word to Emma.

There was so much to do.

* * *

For Austin, the dreary and often wet November days had become synonymous with his father's death. It was almost the second anniversary, and the memories of his loss were still fresh, and a little raw. He was always a little ambivalent about Guy Fawkes Night, probably due to some of the things his father used to say about what happened when he was young miner in St. Helens. Fifty years ago, it was not wise to be too obvious about your Catholic faith, especially on November 5th. When the Pope installed a new hierarchy of English bishops in 1850, anti-Catholic sentiment experienced a resurgence. Effigies of Guy Fawkes were replaced by effigies of these new bishops and the Pope. Austin's father had told him that there had been small groups of men roaming Liverpool, the city of his birth, looking for Catholics to intimidate, perhaps even attack and injure. He had said that he had been lucky to get home one particular Guy Fawkes night in one piece. As a consequence of these early experiences, his father would not let any member of his family out on November 5th, right up until the time they arrived in Farnworth. Fortunately, times had now changed. The day had become more of a spectacle, fireworks and bonfires, rather than an excuse for a religious protest. And Austin had started to see it as that, albeit with some reservations about its roots.

With these thoughts in his mind, he left the mill and started to walk up Marsland Street towards Great Portwood Street, his customary route. The November air was thicker with smoke than usual; it was to be expected given the day. There was also no movement of air, which had the effect of accentuating the density of the damp foggy canopy which now hung over the entire town. On reaching the corner he was immediately confronted with a commotion, and a flickering orange glow which seemed to originate behind the premises on the opposite side of the road. A bell being rung in a relentless manner signalled what Austin thought might be a fire engine. He turned in the direction of town to see two horses running towards him, pulling a cart holding a water tank, and eight or ten smartly dressed and helmeted firefighters. They passed one of Stockport's new electric trams at great speed, attracting the attention of everyone.

'It's a fire,' shouted a nearby woman.

Austin had already worked that out. But where? The fire glow seemed to be coming from the direction of the River Goyt. He asked another onlooker.

'Where is it?'

'Look over there. It could be Vernon's,' replied a bespectacled man, who Austin assumed was a millworker.

And then it became more obvious. As he turned back towards the Brinnington direction, he started to notice people disappear into the streets, Hayfield Street, Swann Street, Lancaster Street and Queen Street. They all led to Mersey Street, a road dominated by the Vernon Mills. It had to be there. Austin waited until the fire brigade had passed and turned up Lancaster Street before crossing over to follow. He doubted whether he could help, but there was always a chance he might be useful.

Heat seared through the dampness. The mills were aflame in rage, and the efforts of the now four fire tenders were puny in comparison. The Mersey Square fire station had only been opened a few months earlier, and so far as Austin was aware had only five apparatus. Therefore, four fifths of its contingent were present. Austin retreated from Mersey Street to the comparative safety of Queen Street. But others were more reckless in their enthusiasm to get the best view. There were perhaps forty fire fighters confronting the disaster, and possibly hundreds of others watching the conflagration.

He listened to the speculation offered by his fellow witnesses.

'How did it start?' enquired one.

'They say it was around four on the third floor. There,' replied another, pointing to the most obviously devasted part of the building.

'Men have died already. I know one, Billy Ashton,' interjected a third.

'He won't be the last.'

'There was no fire escape. They should have put one in after that extension,' said another.

'The bosses said the stone steps were all that were needed. I know that because Billy himself told me.'

Austin peered in the direction of the voice, recognising that he was the one who spoke earlier.

A woman called out across the street to a passing firefighter.

'Have you seen my Tommy? Thomas Ashton?' A look of deep concern and fear on her face.

The firefighter turned.

'I've not dear. I'll keep a look out for him,' he replied, before resuming his assigned duties.

Further up the street Austin could just about see a firefighter who had climbed to the end of an extendable ladder, and had perched himself, somewhat precariously, on the end of it. He seemed to be trying to assist another man out of an open window, perhaps only ten yards away from the rapidly encroaching flames. There were people pointing at him and shouting words of encouragement and admiration. It was hard not to be slightly overwhelmed by the bravery on display.

But there was nothing he could do. The firefighters were present and the police had arrived to manage the ever-growing crowd of bystanders. He decided to leave. Forty minutes of destruction was just about all he could take.

But it would certainly be a story for Emma. He just hoped it would be the last mill fire he would see.

* * *

Edward had been misbehaving at school again. He was completely unlike his sister, Annie, who the teachers seemed to regard as an angel. Thomas had a little bit of both of them in him. On some days he would follow Edward, while on others it would be Annie who would lead. It was an interest and a joy to watch them develop, but also more than a challenge. In Emma's mind, Annie was still too young to take Edward to school, and she was not too sure whether she would ever be able to handle his rascal like antics.

When St. Philip and St. James had been demolished to make way for what would be the new church of Our Lady and the

Apostles, Austin made a decision to start attending Mass at St. Josephs. It had the added advantage of an established church school, especially so, as it was just at the time when all three of their children would be in need of an education. And it was not a long way to walk, less than a mile, or twenty minutes or so from Farr Street. Austin got into the habit of walking with them when he could, leaving the pair in the school grounds on the days that he needed to be in the mill very early. On other days it would be Emma, controlling the eagerness of Thomas, who was always anxious to join his elder siblings in their lessons.

His time would come, mused Emma, as she tried to herd her flock away from the park.

'Edward, come over here,' said Emma.

Edward chose to ignore his mother; instead electing to encourage his brother to join him in chasing a stray terrier which had roamed towards them.

'Edward! Thomas! Come here!'

Edward continued to ignore his mother and maintained pursuit of his prey. Thomas at first froze, then turned round to look firstly at his mother, and then his brother. Emma held her hand out.

'Here.'

Thomas, somewhat reluctantly, started to take some steps towards Emma. Having won over Thomas, Emma turned her attention back to Edward.

Edward. Leave the dog alone. He'll bite you. Come now. We have to get to school. If the master sees you late, you'll get the cane. Do you want that?' shouted Emma.

At last, Edward's attention had been gained. It would not be the first time he had been caned. He decided to abandon the chase and grudgingly took some steps in the direction of Emma.

'Quickly. Stop dawdling! Think of the cane,' said Emma, perceiving some sense of victory in her quest to get them moving again.

Thomas, on reaching Emma, grabbed her outstretched hand. Meanwhile, Annie was already five or six steps ahead. She had no wish to be punished either, especially if her brother was to be the likely cause of it. When Edward finally caught up with the rest of the family, Emma leapt into action. She momentarily let go of Thomas and snatched at Edward's hand.

'Get off. I don't want to hold your hand,' whined Edward.

'You'll do as you're told,' replied Emma.

'No. I won't,' said Edward, attempting to wrest himself free of his mother's now firm grip.

'Behave yourself! I'll tell your father,' replied Emma.

Emma could see that Edward was close to a tantrum, so she rolled out one of her less used weapons, Austin. It was not that Austin would physically punish the children. Indeed, it was a very rare occasion when he did, but she did know that all three of her children enjoyed the approval of their father. They all liked him to think well of them, even Edward.

'He'll say that you're wrong,' said a still defiant Edward.

Hum, backchat as well, thought Emma. Edward was becoming a real handful.

'Don't you dare talk to me like that. There'll be no supper for you tonight,' replied Emma.

Edward pulled a stern face, but finally realised that his mother had the upper hand. He did not really care about the master's cane, but did not want to risk the wrath of his father, and he liked even less the idea of no supper that night. School it must be.

Emma maintained her grip on Edward. With her mischievous son under control the other two would meekly follow. There was little chance of her letting go until all three of them were firmly ensconced within the walls of the school buildings. She would have to have a word with Austin about Edward's behaviour. His increasingly rebellious nature was becoming a problem, not just for him but for Thomas as well. She certainly did not want Edward to influence Thomas any more than he did already. But what were they to do?

* * *

Austin needed to think.

He had moved his family to Stockport nearly five years earlier. They were settled. The children were faring well at St. Joseph's School, although Edward's behaviour had become a constant thorn in Emma's side. He saw less of that but what he had noticed was his son's proclivity towards lying. He would frequently blame Thomas for his own tomfoolery, even when it was obvious who the culprit was. Annie remained an angel, and while Thomas had his moments, his behaviour was nothing like Edward's.

But that was not what was on Austin's mind. He had heard about an opportunity in a mill in Littleborough and was more than interested in it. The question for him was how to approach the subject with Emma. He had, after all, promised her that they would not move too often after Hindley. She knew that Stockport might not be the last move, but Austin was unsure how she would react. Excitement or dread? He needed to think it through before talking to her about it.

He had finished an early shift at the mill and had been at home for less than an hour. Emma had started to prepare a meal and all three children had gone off to play in Hollywood Park, enjoying the warm July sunshine.

'Austin, can you fetch me some bread?' said Emma.

'Of course,' replied Austin.

This was an ideal opportunity to take some time to think. Within minutes he was standing adjacent to the front door. He had a decision to make. Where should he walk? He could walk down Farr Street, Lark Hill then on to Brinksway; perhaps walk by the Mersey. He could take a walk in the park, though the children might be a distraction, or perhaps take a stroll up towards Edgeley Park. The Hatters had moved there the previous year, although it had done little for their performance in the football tables. Perhaps next season they would do better; it could hardly be much worse. Austin considered that he might see them practising, but again this would be a distraction. Brinksway it would be.

Upon reaching Brinksway he made a decision to cross over and walk by the river. Up ahead, and across the river, stood the three red brick mills belonging to the Stockport Ring Spinning Company. To his left, a gentle roar of water spilled over a Mersey weir built to help measure the flow as it passed through the town. And further away, a steam train was shunting coal trucks into the Heaton Mersey Sidings. Austin decided to walk in the direction of the Gorsey Bank Mill, about a mile up the river.

The Mersey was subdued today, unlike its angry self in the wet days of winter. Clumps of Giant Hogweed growing by the side of the often-steep bank attracted flying insects by the dozen, and male Dragonfly patrolled in an effort to protect their breeding sites. Wild berry bushes grew in random formation, and butterflies could be seen settling on various species of shrubs and wildflower. For a second, he felt that he could almost be in the countryside, a little like their Sunday walks on the edge of Hindley.

Splash!

The water had suddenly been disturbed by someone falling in. Austin had not seen him; he must have been hidden from view by a bankside bush or shrub. He ran towards the flailing shape of a man in the water. The man looked elderly, and he was in trouble. Another nearby walker had grabbed a long stick, with the clear intention of using it to reach out to him. Two others had also gathered, and a fourth shouted words to the effect that he would run to fetch a police constable. Austin took no time to think about the situation. If he failed to act now, there would be tragedy.

He slid down the steep river bank and jumped straight in.

They were both lucky. The river flow was slow, and the elderly man was still close to the side. Austin grabbed his arm. As he did so, the elderly man made a feeble attempt to clutch Austin with his other arm, but then lost his grip; a vacant stare of defeat appearing in his eyes. It was better that way. As Austin turned towards the bank, he saw that the two bystanders had also descended, bringing a long stick with them. They stretched out a stick from the edge of the river, one man holding the other for balance. Using his free arm, and treading water, Austin was eventually able to reach, and hold, the end of a protruding stick.

'Grab it,' instructed Austin. The stricken, elderly man, still had a free hand but he seemed unable to comply. It looked to Austin like he was losing consciousness. It was therefore down to Austin to maintain his grip on the stick with one hand, and the elderly man with the other.

The two fellows on the bank pulled back on the stick, gripping it as they would a rope. When Austin was within reach, one man grabbed Austin and the other the elderly man. It was only then Austin loosened his grip on both stick and man. By the time the company had climbed the bank, dragging the hapless victim with them, they realised that a crowd had appeared to watch the spectacle, now apparently controlled by a police constable.

'Give them some space,' he demanded.

A crowd of perhaps twenty or twenty-five had gathered, and were mostly stood in the rescuers path.

'Are you well?' asked the police constable, who introduced himself as Knighton.

'I am, sir,' replied Austin.

'This fellow looks like he needs some help,' said PC Knighton.

The police constable set to work in front of Austin, the rescuers, and the crowd, and after a few minutes had brought the man around by means of artificial respiration. It was time for some questions.

'What's your name?' asked PC Knighton.

'Thomas Mangh, sir,' replied the elderly man who now had a name.

'Can you stand?' asked PC Knighton.

Thomas moved a little but it was soon obvious that he was in no state to walk anywhere.

'I'll have to fetch a horse ambulance. Are you able to stay with him?' asked PC Knighton of the rescuers.

'We are, sir,' came the reply. Austin nodded. He would have preferred to be on his way to some dry clothing, but he did as he had been asked.

'And what is your name, sir?' said PC Knighton to Austin.

'Austin Melia,' came the reply.

'That was a brave action you took, sir. It won't go unnoticed. I must be off now,' said PC Knighton.

It was a good forty-five minutes before the horse ambulance appeared. In that time Thomas Mangh had started to come around a little, and had started to speak. His efforts in answering were not always intelligible, but the story appeared to be that he had been attempting to gather blackberries and had slipped and fallen in. When PC Knighton reappeared, some further details were obtained. The man was aged seventy-five and had lived at the workhouse over in Shaw Heath for some time. It sounded to Austin like a rather sad story, but not an uncommon one. In the circumstances it made Austin feel especially lucky; he had a home and a family to go to.

But now what was he to do? He would have to go home in a set of wet clothes and without any bread. He had also been away for well over two hours; Emma would be worrying about him.

Perhaps today was not the day to bring up the subject of moving again.

* * *

It was another week before Austin chose to tackle the subject of moving to another town. In that time, he had become the talk of the street, and the Beehive. His bravery had become etched into memory through the services of the Manchester Evening News, who on 14 July 1903 had determined that the story should appear under the heading of 'Gallant Rescue at Stockport'. Austin had no idea who had conveyed the news to the paper, but he did for a day or two enjoy the admiration of family, work colleagues and neighbours. When the glow of his gallantry started to fade, Austin thought he might take advantage of Emma's tempered esteem. Tempered in that despite the fact that she thought it was an act of bravery, it was also an act of foolishness. Although Austin could swim, the Mersey could be quite unforgiving at times. Not only could Thomas Mangh have drowned, but Austin could have lost his life as well. And where would that have left Emma and the children? Probably at the mercy of the goodwill of Sarah and her husband in Bolton. Emma had a way of ensuring that Austin's feet remained firmly on the ground.

Austin felt he had to say something before the event was completely forgotten. A promenade with the family in Alexandra Park on the following Sunday provided an ideal opportunity. The park itself lay adjacent to Sykes Bleaching Works, but an ancestor of the family had the foresight to plant hundreds of trees in the vicinity. These helped to shield from view the bleachworks and its reservoirs, and focus attention on the park's immaculately maintained thoroughfares, lawns, play, and planted areas. As with their nearest recreational area, Hollywood Park, Alexandra Park was a welcome escape from the densely built red brick residential streets and towering cotton mills of Stockport.

The children were playing tag with others some distance away, and Emma seemed to have finished talking about her sister's latest piece of news from Bolton. Austin finally decided to take the opportunity to speak about some favourable circumstances that had arisen in his working life.

'Emma, you know I've been telling you about how new machines are being developed using electricity,' said Austin.

'I do. I've used the electric tram quite a few times now, Austin. And I've seen the electric lights that are appearing everywhere. They say everyone will have electricity in their homes one day,' replied Emma.

'Well, we'll see about that, but what I really wanted to talk about is something I've seen in 'Engineering'. I've read about a company that is installing a steam turbine in its mill. It will be the first cotton mill in Lancashire to do so, Emma,' started Austin.

'Is that so?' replied Emma, only mildly interested at best.

Austin had finished his prelude. He knew that Emma could see electric powered devices appearing almost everywhere, but the more arcane aspects of steam power would be a harder sell.

'I'm really interested in it, Emma. I've made some enquires and there is an opportunity. The machine will likely be installed in the spring or summer of next year, and they are looking for engineers to help with the installation,' said Austin.

The penny dropped for Emma.

'You want us to move there, wherever it is? Where is it, Austin?' asked Emma, hoping that it might be a little nearer home.

'Littleborough. Near Rochdale,' replied Austin.

'I know where it is. It's on the canal isn't it?' replied Emma.

'It is. The Rochdale,' replied Austin.

'What's the name of the company?' enquired Emma.

'Fothergill and Harvey. I'm told that they are good employers. And it will mean a bit more pay, and I'll get the experience. It will be good for us all,' said Austin.

'The children are settled. You know that,' replied Emma.

'But it might be good for Edward. A new school, new masters. I'm not sure the teachers at St. Josephs are that fond of him.' said Austin.

Emma had reservations about whether a move at this stage would be good for their children, but could see the excitement in her husband's eyes. And more money coming in would always be useful.

'When would they want us to go?' asked Emma.

'After Christmas,' replied Austin.

'So, you've kept that quiet, Austin,' said Emma.

'I didn't want to say anything until I was sure. I still need to see them and get something in writing. There wasn't much to be gained by saying anything until this stage. I expect to see Mr Harvey by the end of next month, and perhaps get a letter in September. There will be plenty of time to sort things out, months,' replied Austin.

'We'll need somewhere to live,' said Emma.

'I'll sort something out. It's an adventure, Emma.' replied Austin.

'I do hope so, Austin,' said Emma, appearing more than slightly sceptical.

'I did promise that we would not move very often, but it has been nearly five years. That's fair isn't it? And it will be good for the whole family. Just don't tell anyone just yet. I'll also have to keep it from the Beehive until everything is certain. It will be our secret,' replied Austin.

Emma nodded in acquiescence.

'There is a lot to think about. Edward!'

Emma had spotted her recalcitrant son up to mischief again.

'Edward, stop chasing the ducks,' shouted Emma, anxious to ensure that dead or injured animals would not be added to the list of misdeeds Edward had now accumulated. She momentarily turned round to face Austin and sighed.

'Perhaps it is time for a change.'

Chapter 5

LITTLEBOROUGH

'What's that?' shouted Edward.

'It's the future, son,' replied Austin.

Edward was pointing to an enormous machine which had just trundled down Littleborough's main road, Church Street, from the direction of the Gas Works and Hare Hill Mill. Austin, Edward and Thomas had just emerged from Hare Hill Road, and were standing on the corner outside Robert Hall's advertisement-festooned grocer's shop; all in aid of an errand for Emma. Austin had already learned that the locals called that point 'Top 'o' Littleborough', a strange reference to a point which to him seemed very close to the centre of town – they would have to learn as they went along. Annie had chosen to stay at home with her mother.

'But what is it?' repeated Edward.

Thomas cowered a little behind his father, underneath metal signs attached to the stone gable end promoting Colman's Starch, Fry's Chocolate, and Van Houten's Cocoa. The machine looked like a steam engine only it was being driven on the road. With two small wheels being used for steering at the front, underneath a puffing chimney, and two larger wheels towards the rear holding up its load, the vehicle seemed to be hurtling towards them at five or six miles an hour. It was an alarming scene for a five-year old. Edward had two extra years, and his generally more confident character, cocky even, suggested no such similar fears. He would have happily climbed upon the contraption given half the chance.

'It's a Foden steam lurry,' replied Austin.

'A lurry,' enquired Edward.

'Yes. They call them steam lurries. It's a cart for carrying things but instead of horses it's powered by a steam engine,' clarified Austin.

The engine thundered past, its rear wheels pressing down on the road's worn cobblestones, and its rhythmic puffing frightening a nearby horse. The owner of a cart it was pulling raised his fist at the passing engine driver as he sought to bring his beast under control.

'They will be everywhere before long. Look at that one. It's carrying beer for Parsons & Co. I can see the time when there won't be any brewer's drays being pulled by horses,' suggested Austin, appearing confident in his prediction.

The children looked up at him. God had spoken, and he knew all about steam engines.

With the groceries bought and paid for, Austin summoned his inquisitive children from the sweet counter. He had kept a close eye on Edward while in the shop; his son had already discovered the delights of this particular area, and Austin was afraid that he might just decide to help himself to the tempting glass jars on display.

'Not today, Edward. Let's get you back home to your mother.'

'Home.' Home was now some staff quarters in a building adjacent to his new employer's home, 'Town House'. Austin had not needed to find any accommodation on their move to Littleborough. His new employer, Mr Harvey, had offered the accommodation as a stopgap, although when the family arrived Emma decided she liked it, and had encouraged Austin to ask whether they could stay for longer. Mr Harvey had agreed to the request and had set a very reasonable rent, perhaps even allowing Austin to save a little more than he had been able to in Stockport.

In the weeks since they arrived in Littleborough the family had already become used to the walk from Town House to the town centre. It was not a long walk; a few hundred yards up Hare Hill and Sale Street, and you were already on the access road to home. The local council had only two or three years earlier bought Hare Hill House and its grounds, and had laid it out as a park; now a key landmark on Town House Road. Not that the town was short of open space. Their new home was unlike the heavily built-up, industrial, and much larger town of Stockport. With a ten, perhaps fifteen, minute walk from the town centre, and anyone could easily find themselves in relatively open countryside. After the park came the technical school on the left and the cricket club on the right. Past these and Town House was in sight. In time it would no doubt be obscured by the trees its new owners had planted in its grounds.

The two children began to run when they saw the house, Thomas chasing after Edward as fast as he could. From Austin's perspective there was little to fear here, no handcarts, horses, steam wagons or any of these new automobiles. He could let them run towards home without cause for concern.

When Austin arrived in Littleborough, he had been surprised to find that the Harvey family had only just acquired Town House the year before. There were three groups of granite stone buildings in the grounds, the main house itself, an old mill, and a property behind the mill known as Lower Town House. Town House was old and had been in the possession of the Newall family for hundreds of years, before being sold to the Harveys by a Mr Molesworth, a descendant of the Newalls. It commanded magnificent views of Blackstone Edge and the moors which surrounded the centre of Littleborough. An old mill stream ran through the grounds, and some sporadic beech trees were growing on the hill behind the buildings. The multi-storey building known as 'The Old Mill' was not actually being used as a mill, but looked like it had been used for the storage of wool. Overall, Austin and Emma considered it an almost idyllic spot; they were more than happy to be there.

Both Edward and Thomas were already in the front room of their cottage when he opened the door. Emma greeted him with some news before asking about her groceries. She teased him a little.

'We've had a visitor, Austin. Haven't we. Annie?'

Annie nodded, exaggerating the movement.

'And who might that be?' asked Austin.

'Mr Harvey. He says he wants you to meet his brother on Sunday,' replied Emma.

This was unusual, thought Austin. He regarded his employer as Mr Harvey, Ernst Harvey, and had never met his brother.

'Was that it, Emma? Did he say anything else?' asked Austin.

'No. He had a word with Annie but was only here for a few minutes. He said he would not stay for long. What do you suppose he might want?' said Emma.

'I don't know. Probably work.' replied Austin.

Mr Gordon Harvey always seemed to be away doing things. At least he had been during the time they had been living in Littleborough, so it was certainly an interesting development. Austin resolved to ask Mr Ernst Harvey, or 'Ernst' as he had already been encouraged to call him when not in company.

* * *

Austin did not have to wait long to see Ernst Harvey. In fact, the following day his employer sought him out. He was clutching a set of plans and was anxious to have a discussion with Austin and another more senior engineer.

'Austin, come and join me in the meeting room,' said Ernst, clearly expecting Austin to follow him to a room used for meetings of all sorts, including board meetings.

Upon arrival Ernst unrolled the plans, securing each corner with heavy objects lying about the room. Ernst then proceeded to scratch his chin and think a little before speaking. As he did so, Austin looked over his shoulder and started to study the drawings. It was the first time he had seen them, so he was keen to study them in detail. The designer's name was in the corner: Mr. George B. Storie, Station Buildings, Rochdale. Consultant Engineer.

'I have just received these today. So, we can all study them together,' said Ernst.

'Yes, sir,' replied the two other men.

Austin soon came to know that it was Ernst who was the technical expert in the Harvey family. He had a good affinity for engineering, and a good knowledge of engineering matters.

Fothergill & Harvey, the family company, were lucky to have someone of his ability in the business.

Ernst broke the silence and started to speak.

'This will be the first steam turbine in a cotton mill in Lancashire.'

It was obvious that he was proud of the fact.

'...and it will be installed in this mill at Sladen Wood. It will be rope transmission, rated at 225 brake horsepower and will drive 750 looms in the weaving shed. The 30 by 8 feet Lancashire boiler will deliver 500 degrees Fahrenheit steam at 105 lb per square inch. A Galloway Superheater will be placed in the downtake at the back end of the boiler. Eventually, the pressure will reach 200 Ilb per square inch, but let's get to 100 first...' continued Ernst.

Austin's heart began to beat a little faster as Ernst explained the technical detail behind the design and the installation plan. This was why he had come to Littleborough. It was exciting. He was already learning about turbines and was as anxious as his employer to get his hands on the new machinery.

An hour and a half later and the meeting appeared to be concluding.

'The turbine will be supplied and erected by Greenwood and Batley Ltd of the Albion Foundry in Leeds, and the condensing plant and mill gearing will be made and supplied by William Sharples and Co of Ramsbottom. You will both need to go and meet them on regular occasions over the next few months. That will be it for today. I'm going to take these home with me tonight, but will give them to you to study over the next few days. I hope you are both as excited as I am,' said Ernst, drawing the meeting to a close.

Austin let his colleagues leave first but asked to have a word with Ernst before he returned to his usual duties.

'Ernst, you want to see me on Sunday?' questioned Austin.

'My brother, Gordon, does. I've told him about you and he wants to see you,' replied Ernst.

'Was there anything in particular?' asked Austin.

'No. But expect to talk about politics, Austin. My brother has lots of, er, views. Expect to answer some questions,' replied Ernst.

'Anything I should read up on?' asked Austin.

'Expect the unexpected. He's like that,' replied Ernst.

Austin must have shown some concern and doubt.

'Don't worry, Austin. He's a good man. Just tell him what you believe. Be honest with him,' added Ernst, before leaving the room. He turned back to face Austin a few steps into the corridor.

'I'll see you on Sunday.'

* * *

Soon after acquiring Town House, and with the help of his sister-in-law, Gordon Harvey had enlarged the formerly diminutive gardens, planting a herbaceous border, laying flags, and installing a sunken garden with a fountain. He was pleased with their efforts, and had started to encourage locals to enjoy its amenities on Sunday afternoons. Austin took Emma and the children into the garden with the expectation that he would see Gordon Harvey at some point in the afternoon. Ernst could be seen in the gardens, as well as some faces that he recognised from the mills. He spotted Austin ten minutes after the family had arrived.

'Hello again, Mrs Melia. Hello, Annie. And these must be your sons,' said Ernst.

'They are. This is Edward and Thomas,' replied Emma, while pointing to her two sons.

'They certainly look active and healthy,' said Ernst, as Edward pulled away to play with some other children, Thomas following.

'Would you excuse me? If I could just borrow your husband for a short time,' said Ernst.

'Of course. I'll be here,' said Emma, addressing Austin.

Austin followed Ernst to meet his brother and was soon introduced.

'So, Austin, how are you finding the mill?' enquired Gordon Harvey.

'Very interesting, sir,' replied Austin.

'Call me Gordon,' commanded Gordon Harvey.

'Yes, sir. Gordon, as you wish,' said Austin.

'Let's go in the house for a few minutes. Ernst, perhaps you could look after Mrs Melia. She probably still doesn't know many people here,' suggested Gordon.

'Of course,' replied Ernst.

Austin followed Gordon into the house and then into the main hallway. Gordon paused by an old stone cupboard which bore the date 1638, an echo from a previous era. Nearby stood an attractive stone fireplace, also endowed with a date and some initials, '1783' and the letters 'L S N'. Austin could already sense the history of the building.

'We have plans to extend the house, a couple of new wings, and I'm going to create a library,' said Gordon.

'Yes, sir,' replied Austin, still attuning towards addressing his other employer on Christian name terms.

'You must be wondering why I wanted to see you, Austin. Well, I did want to meet you, but I also wanted your opinion on Fothergill & Harvey, and how we treat our employees. You are after all new to the business. Who better to ask?' said Gordon.

'Yes, Gordon. I have been very impressed with the dining-rooms at both the Greenvale Mill and Sladen Wood. They are better than any I have been in. As good as the coffee taverns in Stockport, and the food and heating facilities are admirable. And the prices are reasonable. I have already used the reading room and library at the club in the village, but have not tried billiards yet. There were few of these things at the mills I worked for in Stockport and Hindley,' replied Austin.

'Very good. You know we have never had a dispute with the workpeople in years. Once people start working with us, they rarely leave. Some spend their whole working life with us. Perhaps you will,' said Gordon.

'Of course,' replied Austin. It was too early for him to speculate on the long term. After all he was still only thirty-four.

'But my question is, can we do more?' asked Gordon.

'Perhaps with schooling, sir,' replied Austin, forgetting again. He knew from Ernst that Gordon Harvey had an interest in education.

'Well, you probably know about my interest in this area. I believe in local school boards. I'm a nonconformist and I intend to see all children should receive the education the 1870 Act intended,' said Gordon.

Austin shuffled a little. The family were Catholics and he saw little problem in his children receiving a church education. He wished he hadn't mentioned education but it was the first thing to spring to mind.

'I understand, sir,' replied Austin.

'And what does a working man like yourself think about free trade, Austin?'

'I've read what Mr Balfour and Mr Chamberlain have to say about it. I've also read your letters to the Rochdale Observer. All I have to say is that I think we are better off with it. The unions agree with me as well. I've no truck with these protectionists,' replied Austin.

He was pleased with his reply and knew his employer would be as well. It was also the truth. He had been careful in forming an opinion based on reading about it. Indeed, he had even had a discussion about the subject with Ernst Harvey.

'Excellent. We'll make a Liberal out of you yet, Austin. I'm going to stand again for Rochdale at the next election, and next time I intend to beat Colonel Royds. You know I lost by only 19 votes in 1900?' said Gordon.

'I did, sir,' replied Austin.

'It's Gordon, Austin. We lost because the electors were unwilling to saddle our party with the duty of rectifying the muddles of the Tories and those Liberal Unionists, especially over the Boers issue. We are still trying to understand how we can make the Transvaal work, started Gordon, before realising that he had drifted into an area that was perhaps of little interest to Austin.

He then reverted to his earlier theme.

'You know there is always a place for people like you in the Liberal Party. We need men who can talk to the workpeople about reform. Reform and fair taxes. The proper place for wealth is not the Exchequer but in the pockets of the people. The company's good fortune in the war will be invested for the benefits of its workers. I think you know this by now, Austin. A friend of mine used to say that I like to give people the pure milk of the Liberal word. This is true but we all have a duty to do good. Well... Perhaps you can think about what I have said. We should return to the gardens. Your wife must be wondering where you are,' said Gordon.

'Of course,' replied Austin, as he turned towards the doorway. Gordon Harvey had already taken a few steps, clearly expecting Austin to follow.

It was a strange conversation. Not quite what he was expecting. Austin knew that his employer made a point of meeting all Fothergill and Harvey employees, and was even on first name terms with many. That was understood. What Austin was not too clear on was what exactly Gordon Harvey was expecting. Surely not to become involved with the Liberal Party? He was not a natural Liberal, nor even a Tory for that matter. In fact, he was not really that political at all. Austin just wanted to work and provide for his family. He did not really want to join any political party, not really wanting to be seen as an activist or a party member. He might be a member of the Steam Engine Makers Society, but its tradition of conservatism had appealed to him when he joined. At least his employer had not asked for his views on the Irish question. If he had then perhaps Austin might not have been seen as such a 'natural Liberal' at all. Irish home rule was one of those subjects where he had been heavily influenced by his father, and Austin was not too sure where Mr. Harvey stood on the question. It was a subject better avoided.

Austin and Gordon Harvey soon found Emma, who was still talking to Ernst Harvey.

'Thank you, Mrs Melia. I promised I would not keep him for long. And now if you'll excuse me, Ernst and I will need to see some of our other guests today,' said Gordon.

'It was a pleasure to meet you, sir,' replied Emma.

The two Harveys separated and starting talking to other visitors to the garden.

'What did he want, Austin?' asked Emma.

'I don't really know. He wanted to meet me. We talked about politics for a few minutes. It was strange. I think he would like me to join the Liberals you know,' said Austin.

Emma smirked.

'That would not be like you, Austin,' replied Emma.

'I know. That's what I'm afraid of. I shall avoid the subject if I can. He's a nice man though, and a good employer. We are lucky to be here,' said Austin.

'We are,' agreed Emma, pausing for a second or two to reflect and make an appeal.

'Perhaps we could stay for a long time, Austin?'

'We'll see. Who knows what the future might bring,' replied Austin, lapsing into reflection.

'I think I've had my fill here, Austin. Let's go for a short walk near the reservoir,' said Emma, referring to a body of water close to Lower Town House.

'Alright. We can talk about what he had to say there. I'll fetch the children,' replied Austin.

* * *

By the following spring, family life had settled into its new routines in Littleborough. Stockport had already started to fade into memory, with family members making new friends, and occasionally inviting either Sarah, or a member of the Farnworth Melias over for a weekend stay. It was not too far, an hour on the train if you were lucky; two if you were not.

Austin's walk to 'Summit', the area within which the mills stood, was much different to Stockport. He would sometimes take the same route as Gordon Harvey, up over a steep path by a hill ridge and some moorland farms. He had often seen his employer ahead of him during fine weather. Ridge walks were reserved for fine days where the view could be appreciated. Higher up in the hills and it was possible to see the Rochdale Canal, more often than not hosting canal traffic negotiating its way up and down the valley. Almost running parallel to the canal, the L&Y Railway was also in view. It too was busy, frequently carrying laden steam trains racing past lethargic narrowboats, sailing flats and packet boats. It was easy to see the problem for the canal companies here, and right next to his employer's mills. Canal boats, and their literal 'one horse power', could not compete with the engineering challenge of a fast steam train. Each journey to work Austin could see that the days of the canal as serious competition to the railway were numbered. Steam power dominated everything.

On other less clement days his route to work would be via the carriage drive past Gorsey Hill Wood and Gale house, and then a brisk walk up Todmorden Road to his usual location at Sladen Wood Mill. Although there were mills in the valley, the air was generally cleaner than Stockport and Farnworth; he enjoyed the walk and the exercise it provided.

Austin was fully engaged on installing the new mill engine during most of the first year of his time in Littleborough. However, once the work was completed, he began to be called elsewhere in the valley. Fothergill and Harvey's first mill, Sladen Wood, had been started in 1859 and its second, Rock Nook Mill was built in 1886. The company had been successful in the years since and had acquired others nearby, including Greenvale Mill and Ealees Bleaching, Dyeing and Finishing Co. Thus, Austin's engineering skills were now frequently deployed across all of the company estate whenever help was needed. He did not mind this. After all it was all good experience, and one day he expected to be able to draw from it.

At home Emma had organised their cottage as she wanted it. The building they now lived in was an extension to the ancient Town House Mill, and was facing away from the main house. She had only ever lived in a brick terrace, and was fascinated with the hammer-dressed, slightly tilted, watershot stone used in its construction; its mullion windows and quoins. It was lovely, and she resolved to resist Austin the next time he wanted to move; she knew that eventually he would, whether through choice or circumstance.

* * *

'Annie. Find me the *Sunlight Almanac*. I think it's in the cupboard,' said Emma.

'I'm still hurting, Ma,' whined Thomas. Emma had begun to rub behind his ears as her son had been complaining of earache.

Annie returned with a small red booklet titled *Sunlight Almanac for The Home 99*. It was a few years old and they probably needed a later one, but it would do for now.

'Alright Annie, open the part that says 'On the Care of Sick Children' and tell me what it says about earache.'

Annie turned the pages of the booklet, pausing occasionally at the distracting, and therefore more interesting, advertisements for Sunlight Soap and other Lever Brothers products.

'Ma, it hurts. It's not helping,' said Thomas, who was by now attempting to wriggle away from Emma.

'Quickly, Annie,' said Emma.

'I've found it,' replied Annie, now pleased with herself.

'Read it to me,' instructed Emma.

Annie started to read, slowly at first but then quickly gathering speed.

'It says you can try any of these. Heat equal parts of Lever's Glycerine and laudanum in a spoon over a candle, and pour it into the ear. If no laudanum is at hand, use instead tobacco tied in a bit of muslin heated in oil or glycerine and put in ear–'

'We have no laudanum. What else does it say?' said Emma, interrupting her daughter.

'Tie half a teaspoonful of black pepper in a bit of muslin, soak in whiskey and insert gently into the ear–'

'We've no whiskey either. What next?' said Emma. Annie continued to read.

'Rub mustard oil or chloroform liniment behind ear.'

'Goodness, we are not doing well at all,' said Emma, who was still gently massaging Thomas's ears. Emma nodded to Annie.

'Roast an onion, take out heart, and put it hot into the ear,'

Emma shook her head from side to side.

'Hold the ear over a jug of boiling water,' continued Annie.

'I think we can do that, can't we Thomas? I'll warm some water.'

As Emma warmed a pan of water, Edward appeared. He had been playing on his own outside.

'You won't see the steam tram tomorrow, Tom.' It was a deliberate taunt to his younger brother.

'Be quiet, Edward. I'll see you don't if you continue to misbehave,' said Emma.

'I'll go on my own,' replied a defiant Edward.

'Your father will see about that. Just wait until he gets back. Be nice to your bother, or else...' Emma left the threat in the air.

Edward backed down. On this occasion it was simply not worth it.

* * *

The second week of 1905 had been seen as an important week for the children. It was the week that Rochdale Corporation had finally set for the last steam tram to run on the Littleborough line. Its other routes having been converted to electric the year before, Littleborough would be the last.

A sizeable crowd had already developed by the time Emma and her children had reached a suitable vantage point. Austin was still at work but the children had finished their studies for the day. There had been growing excitement in school, not just about the steam tram, but the prospect of electric trams finally appearing in the town. Edward, Thomas, and Annie had seen them before, in Stockport, but to many of their schoolfriends a connection to Rochdale's existing electric tram network would be a new innovation.

'Look! It's coming,' said Emma, pointing in the direction of the noise.

The odd-looking contraption snorted, puffed and clanged as it slowly made its way towards them. Starting at Drake Street in the centre of Rochdale, it had made its way via Entwisle Road to the Halifax Road, and then on towards Littleborough on its narrow-gauge track. The machine had certainly seen better days. It had an articulated design, with a front section, the steam engine, devoted to supplying power. It was connected to and pulled a separate rear section, a double decker passenger carriage. Emblazoned across the side, in between the upper and lower sections, were the words 'The Last Steam Tram to Leave Rochdale'.

About a minute later the steam tram driver was in full view. Dressed in a cap and a boiler suit, much like a steam train driver, he firmly held the steering handle as he approached the now cheering spectators. A conductor was leaning out of the windowless open spaces on the upper floor and was attempting a wave. The machine slowed to a stop as it reached the densest part of the gathered crowd, and both driver and conductor jumped off to talk to people.

'Can we get on? My friends are.' pleaded Thomas.

Emma agreed, but soon realised that they would have to wait. It was a bit of a surprise in that most of the town must have used the tram at some point, and yet the novelty of it being the last steam tram must have provided some extra appeal. And on this day, the driver and conductor were also celebrities. Everyone wanted to talk to them, including Edward, who had already marched off.

'Can I drive it, mister?' said Edward, a little petulantly, to the stocky tram driver. He had interrupted a conversation he was having with a local barber.

'Get off with you,' replied the driver, already irritated with Edward.

'I'm going to have a go,' said Edward, ignoring the driver's response.

Edward climbed up into the open cab and started to fiddle with the handles. The driver noticed and started to shout.

'Down lad. Leave that alone. You'll injure yourself and others.'

Edward ignored him and continued to pull at the handles. A few yards away, Emma had spotted what was going on and was heading towards him, leaving Annie to 'look after' Thomas on a paved area next to a shop. The engine and carriage lurched. Edward had been successful in releasing the brake, and the slight camber of the road had encouraged a little movement. Without power it would not get far but the movement was enough to attract the attention of the crowd and the engine driver. He sprang into action and jumped into the cab, firstly securing the brake and then securing Edward by the ear. Edward screamed.

'Get off.'

The driver ignored him and grabbed his other ear, apparently satisfied that he had engendered what he regarded as the right response.

'I'm sorry. I'm sorry,' said Emma, finally reaching the steam engine cab.

'He's a menace,' said the driver.

'I know. I'll take him. His father shall know of this,' replied Emma.

'He's lucky he didn't get a thick ear,' said the driver, still unsatisfied.

'Edward. There will be no supper for you tonight,' said Emma. It was a last resort but she needed something to mollify the driver.

The driver, apparently satisfied, finally released Edward's ears, allowing him to climb down and sheepishly head towards his mother. It was not quite what he had in mind. Emma seized his arm, dragging him towards the paved area where Annie and Thomas were standing. Quite a few of the crowd had been watching the incident and were casting disapproving glances in Emma's direction. She was furious with her son.

'Right. We are going home,' said Emma to the three of them.

'Why can't we stay?' whined Edward, apparently impervious to his mother's mood.

Emma clipped him around the head. It was not something she was inclined to do very often but her patience had run out. Edward needed to get the message.

'Home.'

Annie, Thomas, and Edward fell silent, and meekly followed their mother away from the meddlesome eyes of those in the crowd, many of whom were still watching.

'Your father will hear of this, Edward. I'll not be surprised if you get the strap.'

Edward's head hung low. He had done it now.

* * *

Edward's behaviour seemed to settle a little in the weeks following the incident with the steam tram. Austin had made sure of that, keeping his son on a tight leash until there were signs of less exuberant behaviour. Any sign of mischief and he was immediately brought into line. Fortunately, it was enough for Austin to just show Edward the strap; he did not have to use it. Frequent display and the exercise of it on an inanimate object seemed to do the trick. On occasion, Austin had received the strap during his own childhood, and he did not want to use it on his own children unless he absolutely had to.

In recent months he had often considered that it might come to that, but dearly hoped that it would not.

As the summer wore on Ernst Harvey's absences from the mills had increased. He was often on business in Manchester, and was frequently away for several days. It mattered little to Austin, but it was outside his employer's usual pattern and therefore worthy of comment. The reason for his absences became apparent in the middle of August when there was an announcement across all of the Fothergill & Harvey mills. Alexander Harvey, the father of Gordon and Ernst Harvey, had died.

Alexander Harvey had started the business in 1858 with his business partner, Thomas Fothergill. Until recent years he had been the driving force behind its growth and expansion, and at the time of his death was believed to be the oldest member of the Manchester Royal Exchange. He was held in high esteem, not just in the cotton industry but also by the employees of the company. Like his sons he had been a pioneer in social, political, and land reform, and had been a 'Guardian of the Poor' for Manchester. Perhaps his most notable achievement had been as a member of the committee that had helped establish 'half-holiday Saturday' for workpeople, a benefit still greatly appreciated across the cotton industry.

Austin had never met Mr Harvey Senior, but was expected to attend the funeral along with other selected represen... from each of the mills. It was at this funeral that Aus... number of employers from a multitude of other co... the Manchester area. The introductions during... afterwards meant little to him. After all, it was... business meeting. But in time one partic... with the chief tenter of a mill in nearby M... shape his later career.

* * *

In the months following Alexander Harvey's death, Gordon Harvey became increasingly diligent in the affairs of the company. Austin started to see him on a regular basis, usually informally, when walking around Sladen Wood Mill. On one occasion he had mentioned to Austin that he intended to relinquish his Liberal Party candidature and to devote himself to business, and helping improve conditions for his workers. But that was not to be.

1906 was an election year, and the local party had finally persuaded Gordon Harvey to remain a candidate. The local election was to be fought on a platform of 'Free Trade' and criticism of the Conservative Party's expenditure on arms. It was not a clean fight. The Socialist candidate, a Mr. Hobson, circulated scurrilous allegations about the Harvey's treatment of employees which resulted in a libel suit. Meetings were noisy and tensions ran high throughout the campaign. The odds seemed stacked against the Gordon Harvey candidature, given the mischievous accusations and a speech by George Bernard Shaw in support of Mr Hobson. The Liberal offensive campaign had to take drastic action.

On the day of the poll, 13 January 1906, Austin was asked to join two coachloads of mill hands and other employees from the Greenvale and Sladen Wood mills. He could hardly refuse. They were to tour Rochdale and Littleborough for several hours, generating support and enthusiasm for the Harvey campaign as they did. To get the message about the Harveys across, one elderly weaver, seated at the front of the vehicle, carried a placard: '52 years with the Firm'.

Whatever the reason, it worked. Gordon Harvey won in dozens majority of 1,436, a Liberal victory replicated pleased with tituencies across the country. Austin was it would mea loyer's result, but realised soon after that would be Ernst Harvey, not Gordon

Harvey, who would unquestionably be the key influence in his career. Thereafter, his brother's influence would be more through what he achieved as a politician rather than as an employer.

* * *

Austin looked up. He had been reading a copy of a March 1907 edition of the Rochdale Observer and had decided to share a piece of news with Emma.

'We've never really talked about these suffragettes have we, Emma?'

'We haven't. Why do you ask?' replied Emma.

'Well, three Rochdale suffragettes have just been jailed for demonstrating in London. I'm not sure they should be doing that. I'm surprised they have the time,' said Austin.

'Are they married?' replied Emma.

'It doesn't say. It does say 62 of them were imprisoned. 62!' Austin seemed visibly shocked.

'I'm not surprised. I would too,' said Emma.

'What do you mean?' asked Austin.

'We should have the vote. All the women I talk to think so as well. Why shouldn't we?' said Emma.

'Haven't you got enough to do looking after me and the children?' questioned Austin.

'What's that got to do with it?' replied Emma.

'It's a full-time job isn't it? Don't you think your place is here? You've not had to work. Am I not a good provider?' asked Austin.

'I don't know why we never talked about this before. If you mean do I think that my place is in the home. Well, it is and it isn't,' said Emma.

Austin frowned. Emma was full of surprises and contradictions.

'I don't understand,' replied Austin.

'That's easy. Doesn't looking after the children mean taking an interest in their education? Doesn't looking after the children mean understanding why food prices rise? Should food be taxed? Doesn't looking after the children mean making sure they have a roof over their heads? What affects you, affects me. If the government takes a decision that affects your work, it affects me. Shouldn't I have a say in that? When the issue in an election is peace or war and a man votes for war, does he himself have to fight? No! He doesn't. The men who fight are seldom qualified to vote, and the men who vote are never compelled to fight. And who pays if we go to war? Just the men? No! We all have to. It would seem we are not capable of voting, but we are capable of paying the consequences of what men vote for. It's all wrong, Austin. Wrong! And you can't tell me otherwise,' said Emma, confident in her arguments.

Austin looked at her, stunned by the cogency of her arguments. He started to flail around, looking for some robust counterpoints. He would try a different mode of attack.

'You would never go on one of these marches, would you, Emma? It might not be good for my position at the mill, especially if you were arrested, and perhaps even sent to prison. What would we do?' said Austin.

Emma saw through it straight away.

'I would, Austin. It is something I do believe in. I wouldn't want my Annie living in the shadow of a man all her life. Besides, I happen to know that many of these women chose to go to prison. They could have paid a fine, but wanted to stand-up for women everywhere. As for the mill, it's well known that Mr Harvey is in favour of reform. I think he will be a supporter of the suffragettes, don't you?' replied Emma.

'I don't know. I've never talked to Ernst about it,' said Austin.

'Well, perhaps it's time you did,' replied Emma.

'Look. We both know that women have different interests to men...I–' started Austin.

'We do,' replied Emma, interjecting. 'But we also have a lot that are the same, and we have a right to have a say in those things.'

'Have I not made some good decisions on behalf of the family? Do I not discuss with you who I will vote for?' said Austin.

'You have and you do. But that is exactly my point. When we discuss things together, a better decision is always made. So why should the vote be any different? You know what they say: 'two heads are better than one'. It's the same with the vote. If both men AND women can vote, then better decisions will be made by government. It's right and it's fair. And you can't tell me otherwise,' replied Emma.

'Promise me you won't get us into any trouble with these views you have,' said Austin.

'I can't promise you anything like that, Austin. It would not be what I want, but I and a number of the other women around here intend to support the cause. You know I get on well with the cook, Mrs Lansbury, over at Town House, don't you?' replied Emma.

'I do. What of it?' asked Austin.

'Well, she and I are going to see Mrs Pankhurst speak in Rochdale in the summer,' replied Emma.

'You never told me. I don't think that's a good idea, Emma. There might be trouble,' suggested Austin.

'She's opening a women's club, currently planned for August 31st. Are you going to try and stop me going?' asked Emma.

Austin could see confrontation ahead and wished to avoid it.

'Of course not. Just...don't get into trouble,' Austin replied.

Satisfied she had the upper ground, Emma decided to change the subject.

'Let's have some tea. I think we've had enough politics for one day. We should have had this discussion a long time ago, Austin,' said Emma.

'Perhaps we should have,' replied Austin.

He was relieved and more than a little surprised at Emma's position. Perhaps he should not have been, but one thing was for certain. He would have to be very careful what he said about the suffragettes in the future. After all, she might just have a point.

* * *

The 'steam tram incident' involving Edward two years before had not been forgotten, either by Emma or by Edward. However, he was now aged ten and had arguably developed a little more common sense. At least that was what Emma hoped. In the year following the episode she had avoided letting any of her children anywhere near any public events, but she considered it unfair to deprive them of attendance at these communal experiences forever.

Littleborough ran lots of parades and processions throughout the year, including an annual Whit Walk, somewhat unusually held on a Friday, The Cooperative Society's Children's Gala, Parish Church Procession and The Annual Cycle Parade. For the children the calendar was marked with these days; they were something to look forward to, sometimes to even participate in.

Both Edward and Thomas had been showing an increasing interest in water, and Austin had invested some time in teaching them the basics of swimming in the Town House Reservoir, yards away from their cottage. With so much water around them it was considered by both parents a sensible thing to do, and it was a disappointment to Emma that Annie resisted. Unlike her brothers she liked to keep away from water. Now with an increased confidence of being in water, Edward and Thomas had started to apply pressure on both parents to permit them to go up to Hollingworth Lake so that they could try out the boats, or join an excursion on a canal barge. Both parents resisted, still a little afraid that Edward would either get them, or himself, into some sort of trouble.

But one way or the other they had to give way on attending the annual parades.

Cycling had enjoyed a boom in popularity during the closing years of Queen Victoria's reign, perhaps more so in the time that Edward VII had been king. Emma approved in that she saw cycling as a pastime that both men and women could enjoy. Cycling clubs had mushroomed, and where the men still resisted female membership, women's only clubs had appeared. Emma had long since decided that it was something that Annie might eventually participate in. One day she made a serious attempt to divert the boy's attention from their interest in barging and boating, determining that they could all watch Littleborough's Cycle Parade.

Emma liked to ensure that the children were not only well-behaved, but well-dressed when appearing in public. Processions and parades were almost the ultimate local spectacles. It would not do to have her brood looking like ragamuffins. The boys often resisted, they didn't see the point, but Annie did not mind at all dressing up for an occasion. And a Littleborough cycle parade was an occasion.

Annie, dressed in a smart wide brimmed hat and a short sleeved and long muslin dress, stood on Hare Hill Road next to her brothers and mother. They were waiting for the first of the parade carts. Her blue pastel coloured sash wrapped around her waist stood out in sharp contrast to the cream, and only slightly embroidered, dress. Both Thomas and Edward were wearing dark brown, short lapel jackets, long trousers and caps. All three of the children were wearing clogs, but Emma had ensured that each one of them had been cleaned to perfection before leaving the house. Emma was proud of her work, and so long as the three of them were well behaved, satisfied with her children. At least Edward was not going to embarrass her this year.

A horse and cart driven by two older children appeared in view. It was still at least a hundred yards away and partly camouflaged by shop canopies. Union Jacks were hanging from the buildings, and people higher up the road were peering round, with some stepping out for a better glimpse.

'Ma, it's coming,' said Edward, as he stepped out.

'Edward. Step back. It won't be long,' replied Emma.

Edward looked at her, but then shuffled back to his standing position next to Thomas. He would follow his mother's instruction for now, but that did not mean he could not have a bit of fun as well. Satisfied, Emma took her attention away from Edward and waved at a woman on the other side of the road.

'Annie, look. It's Mrs Stainthorpe. Wave Annie.'

Annie dutifully obeyed, and along with Emma directed her attention back at the approaching lead cart. They could now see more detail. Hosting a placard advertising some evening entertainment, a dance, it was chaperoned by a smiling old man and a helmeted police constable. The crowd started to clap and cheer as it passed, and Emma encouraged her children to follow suit. A marching brass band followed the horse and cart, and then the cyclists appeared, all in fancy dress and apparently supporting their favoured charity. The parade represented the convergence of a cycling club, a sort of sporting event, and a fund-raising initiative. It was a strange but heart-warming spectacle.

Edward seemed quite interested in the assorted display of cycling machines, men, boys, and some women, at least for a time. But then a thought crossed his mind. He leaned over to whisper in Thomas's ear, not that his mother could have heard anything over the din of brass playing, and the excitable cheering crowds. Thomas laughed as he listened to his bother. Yes, of course he would.

The parade continued to wind its way past the onlookers. Some of the cycles looked like they had seen better days, but they had nonetheless been polished up for the event. It was a good thirty minutes before the last cyclist could be seen, a Penny Farthing. Beyond that was another horse and cart being driven by a single man, and also carrying a placard with the words 'Thank You' emblazoned across its rear.

Yards away from their small family group, Thomas suddenly jumped into the road, waving his cap in one hand and a red ribbon he had pulled from his pocket in the other. The startled horse snorted, raised its head and jumped to the left, catching its owner by surprise. Within the space of a second or two it had pulled the cart onto a single wheel, lifting the other off the ground as it spun round to face the opposite direction. It had all happened too quickly. The hapless driver struggled to regain control, as the clearly frightened horse showed every sign of wanting to bolt. The crowds on both sides soon realised this and quickly drew well back.

Seconds after Thomas had jumped into the road, Emma had hold of him by the scruff of his neck. Clearly in fear for his life she literally dragged him to the side of the road, concurrently shouting at both Edward and Annie to 'Get back!'. Thomas's initial tomfoolery, followed by Emma's reaction and a gasp in the crowd, had all but ensured that the horse would go no further. It had somehow managed to turn both itself, and cart, back towards the direction it had just emerged from.

And then, thirty seconds after Thomas's first move, it bolted back up the road, the driver doing his best to bring the panicked animal under control. The last vision most of the crowd had of it were the words 'Thank You' rapidly receding into the distance. Emma was mortified. For the second time in as many years one of her sons had seriously misbehaved. She almost expected it of Edward, but Thomas? Well, that was just not like him.

'I saw all that,' boomed a voice from behind.

Emma turned. It was a police constable. Her heart missed a beat as she summoned up the courage to face him.

'I'm so sorry. His father will hear of it. I promise,' said Emma, dearly hoping it would be enough.

'I'm afraid this is a more serious matter than that. What are your names?' said the police constable.

'I'm Mrs Melia. This is Annie, and these are my sons, Thomas and Edward,' replied Emma.

Edward smiled and then pointed at Thomas.

'It was him, not me.'

'I know who it was. Mrs Melia, where do you live?' said the police constable.

'Town House Cottage,' replied Emma.

'The Harvey's place?' said the police constable.

'Yes,' replied Emma.

I'll need to see you and your husband about this later today,' said the police constable.

'Yes, of course. Austin will be back by six o'clock,' replied Emma.

'You should take them home, madam. Just make sure you are in when I come. I'll need to see both of your sons this evening,' said the police officer.

Emma was quietly fuming, both shocked and embarrassed by Thomas's behaviour.

'Yes, of course we will be there, Constable.'

She seized Edward with one hand and Thomas with the other and starting marching back up Hare Hill Road towards the turn at Sale Street, Annie following. In the distance the horse and cart seemed to be finally under control as its driver attempted to calm it down before making a turn. The police constable stayed in position, patiently waiting for the cart's return.

* * *

Austin arrived home a little later than usual with a piece of news, blurting it out before Emma had a chance to talk about the cycle parade incident.

'Do you remember Thomas Fletcher?'

Emma nodded.

'He's died. He was the one that helped employ me three years ago. You remember? He had been manager at Sladen Wood Mill for 42 years and was a Methodist. He helped advise me on schooling for ours, him being a member of the Littleborough School Board. It's a shame. I did take to him straight away. A fair man. Very fair,' said Austin, drifting into reflection.

'I'm sorry about that, Austin. But there is something I must tell you. Something happened at the parade today. Thomas got into trouble. And there is a policeman coming shorty to talk to us about it,' replied Emma.

Austin switched his attention to the problem at hand.

'What did he do? Where are they now?'

Emma summarised the incident, advising Austin that they were upstairs, confined to their bedrooms.

'I'm surprised at Thomas. Are you sure it was him and not Edward?' asked Austin.

'I am. I saw it. It was definitely him,' replied Emma.

'Right. Let's get them down,' said Austin, before shouting up for them.

Both Thomas and Edward appeared, Thomas hanging his head, but Edward expressing an insolent stare.

'Why, Thomas?' asked Austin.

'I don't know,' replied Thomas, clearly ready to burst into tears.

'And what have you to say about it, Edward?'

'Nothing, sir. It was Thomas.' replied Edward.

Redirecting his attention back to Thomas, Austin asked again.

'Why Thomas? And what are you going to say to the police constable? Would you like to go to jail?'

This was too much for Thomas. He started to wail.

'Edward... told... told... told me to do it,' replied Thomas, now struggling to get the words out.

'I never,' denied Edward.

'What did he say, Thomas?' asked Austin.

'He... he... he... said it would be funny,' replied Thomas, between sniffles and tears.

'And do you think it was funny?' asked Austin.

.N... n... n... n... no,' replied Thomas.

'Don't you dare lie to me, Edward. Did you tell Thomas to frighten the horse?' asked Austin.

'No, sir, I never would do such a thing,' replied Edward.

Before Austin had a chance to challenge Edward, there was a knock on the door. Austin stood up to answer it. As expected, it was the police constable.

'Come in, Constable,' said Austin.

The two men sat down on opposite sides of a pinewood kitchen table the family used for almost everything.

'My name is Police Constable Slaithwaite. I'm here about your son's misbehaviour at the Littleborough Cycle Parade today. This was a serious incident, Mr Melia.'

'Yes, my wife has told me about it and I've talked to the pair of them about it. They will be punished, Constable. Of that you can be sure,' said Austin.

Edward and Thomas remained seated on a rug placed in front of the fireplace, next to Emma who was listening.

'I'm really sorry, Constable. I've had words with them already. It won't happen again,' interjected Emma.

'That maybe so, Mr and Mrs Melia. But I do want to talk to the younger one. Thomas is it?' asked PC Slaithwaite.

'It is,' replied Austin.

'Come to the table, Thomas,' said PC Slaithwaite.

Emma pushed from behind at Thomas's shoulder, encouraging him to comply. Seated, PC Slaithwaite started to tell him off, Austin and Emma both squirming, red faced on their respective chairs.

'Now, lad. That was a very bad thing to do. Someone could have been killed. Has no one ever told you how silly it is to deliberately frighten a horse? Do you understand me?' said PC Slaithwaite in a stern voice.

'Yes, sir. No, sir. I'm sorry, sir,' replied Thomas, who was by now starting to shake in fear.

'Do you know what happens when people break the law?' asked PC Slaithwaite.

Thomas just stared, nodding left to right.

'Prison. Would you like to go to prison?' asked PC Slaithwaite.

'No.' replied Thomas. It was too much for him. He started to cry, looking first at PC Slaithwaite, and then his mother, for comfort. Emma wanted to reach out but felt it was better to let the police constable get his message across. It might also help with Edward.

'Well, this time you were lucky. No one was injured, not even the horse. But if it happens again you know what the consequences might be now, don't you?'

It was intended to be rhetorical. Thomas just nodded that he understood.

'I think that will do for now Mr and Mrs Melia. I won't take any further action on this occasion. That will be all,' said PC Slaithwaite.

'Thank you, Constable. Thank the policeman, Thomas,' said Austin.

Thomas wept an almost inaudible expression of gratitude.

'I'll be off then. I just hope I don't have to come here again,' said PC Slaithwaite.

'You won't, Constable. I'll make sure of that,' replied Austin.

PC Slaithwaite, picked up the notebook he had been using and headed towards the door. After he had left, Austin summoned both Edward and Thomas to stand in front of him.

'Thomas. To bed. No supper tonight. Now go upstairs now. Edward, I don't believe you. Go and get me the strap,' instructed Austin.

Thomas disappeared, and Edward retrieved a leather strap from a drawer Austin kept for safekeeping.

'Austin. I'm not sure,' said Emma.

Austin ignored her interjection.

'Edward, bend over. If you don't tell me the truth you get the strap tonight. Did you tell Thomas to frighten the horse?' asked Austin.

Edward had bent over and now had to resolve his conundrum. If he lied, he would get the strap; if he told the truth he might not, but would still be punished. What should he do?

'Thomas did it,' replied Edward.

Whack! Austin applied the strap to Thomas's backside, as Emma winced.

'Answer my question. Tell the truth,' demanded Austin.

Edward's backside was already smarting. He was not too keen on receiving another. He had a quick change of heart.

'I did, sir.'

'Why did you lie to me and your mother?' said Austin.

'I didn't want to get into trouble, sir,' replied Edward.

'Well, you did, didn't you? Stand up. You are not to leave the house for the rest of the summer. You will help your mother with extra chores until I say so. No supper tonight. Now, get out of my sight,' said Austin.

Edward ran upstairs to join his brother. Annie, who had been hiding behind her mother throughout the whole dressing-down, remained frozen in place.

'You are not in any trouble, Annie. She's been as good as gold today, Austin,' said Emma.

'That's good to hear, Annie. Now come and give me a hug,' said Austin.

Annie walked over and put her arms around Austin.

'Now leave us. I need to talk to your mother in private,' said Austin.

'Go outside,' said Emma.

Annie went outside to play on her own.

'What are we to do with him?' said Austin.

'I've tried, Austin. I don't know,' replied Emma. Although unspoken it was obvious who they were talking about.

'He's got another three years in school. Perhaps when he's working, he will improve,' said Austin.

'Perhaps. But I'm going to find it difficult holding my head up around here now. It's a small town and everyone knows about him. That's twice it's happened. What if Mr Harvey hears about it? He might not want Edward near Town House for fear of mischief,' replied Emma.

'He's still a child, Emma. I doubt the Harveys will bother. I'll ask the priest for advice,' suggested Austin.

They agreed that it was something of a last resort but it might be worth a try. Perhaps he would have some ideas about how Edward's behaviour might be brought back into line.

* * *

The rest of 1907 passed without incident, with Edward maintaining an enforced 'low profile'. Emma had kept him busy throughout the summer and autumn with jobs and errands, leaving little time for mischief. After a month of receiving some equally strict instructions, Thomas was let off the hook, and by the middle of the summer life for him had returned to normal. Emma would occasionally remind him of the stupidity of his actions, but for the most part had forgiven him. Thomas of course was eager to do that little bit extra to expedite his return to favour, an approach which no doubt helped. Edward resisted from time to time, but every time he did Austin would extend his strict routine of extra chores. He clearly resented the fact that he had to take on some of Annie and Thomas's work, but had to accept that he had little choice.

A widespread flu epidemic across Rochdale in January 1908 signalled a change of approach. While neither parent succumbed to it, all three children seemed to catch the unwelcome virus, with Edward particularly affected for some weeks. He recovered, but the illness did help inspire a softening towards him by both Emma and Austin. Little else of note took place during the spring and summer of 1908.

All three children had attended the Catholic primary school associated with St. Mary the Annunciation on Featherstall Road during their time in Littleborough. Unlike the experience in the larger towns, pupil numbers at the school were below capacity, so the children received more attention and a better education than they might have done in Stockport.

Annie turned thirteen in the spring of 1908, and left school with well-developed skills in reading, writing and maths. She was now of an age where she was expected to earn a full-time wage, and to contribute more to the family purse. Neither Austin, nor Emma, were particularly keen on their sons and daughter working in the mills, but the lack of local opportunities elsewhere had forced their hands. Austin in particular had seen too many children injured to be comfortable with the idea. Nonetheless, pragmatism was required. There were far poorer cotton mill employers than Fothergill & Harvey. At least they had the welfare of their workers in mind, even if they were prepared to employ children, 'little doffers', as they were called. And of course, Austin could continue to keep an eye on her. Annie's earlier experience, as a half timer working in the carding room held her in good stead. She was taken on a full-time basis during the summer and by the end of the year had been accepted as a full-time company employee.

Fluctuations in the cotton trade during 1908 and 1909 triggered job losses, short time working, and cuts in wages. The effects of mill owners' actions to help protect their profit and loss accounts also fanned the flames of discontent, resulting in various disputes of one form or another. Fothergill's good relationship with its workers acted to mitigate any serious issues within its mills, but at the zenith of the industrial conflict, during autumn 1908, few mills in the county were unaffected, either directly, or indirectly through supply issues. The cotton dispute was finally settled in the first week of November. As with a similar situation in 1903 Austin himself remained largely unaffected by it, although Annie did find herself working on a short time basis for a few weeks. Mills generally re-started on 9 November to the general relief of both owners and workpeople.

* * *

Annie was perhaps the most reluctant member of the family when Austin and Emma told the three of them that they were to leave Littleborough. She had been happy in their cottage, and had made a number of friends in both school and at Fothergill & Harvey. She did not want to go. Thomas and Edward were nonchalant about the move. Thomas was still at school, and Edward had only recently started as a 'half timer' the year before. Austin and Emma did not want their children working in the mills until they were at least eleven. Edward was still at least a year away from leaving school, so the question of finding full time occupation had not arisen. While she liked the cottage and Littleborough, Emma had become more sanguine about moving. Although to a degree inured to criticism, she did feel that some of the women she mixed with had a deprecatory view of the way she handled her sons, especially Edward. Whether justified or not, and she felt the latter, a move to another part of the county might provide a fresh start. After all, Edward's behaviour did seem to have improved as he grew older.

The opportunity came, unexpectedly, during the summer of 1909. Austin had been approached by the manager of a mill in Middleton. Fothergill's reputation as a good employer had attracted the interest of other 'modern' thinking mill managers across the county, and it was on a visit to Sladen Wood that Austin came to the attention of Benjamin Simpson, a director of the Townley Mill in Middleton. Benjamin Simpson was not just a director of the company. He was also the manager of the mill and had a good idea of what he needed. He was looking for someone at the right age and with the right experience, and Austin seemed to fit the profile.

For Austin the job appeared at just about the right time. He had learned a lot at Fothergill & Harvey and certainly appreciated their treatment of him. But he wanted to do more. Indeed, he felt capable of taking on much more responsibility but the opportunities in Littleborough appeared to be limited. The company's success in retaining employees had a detrimental effect on career advancement, which irked Austin somewhat. He wanted to test himself, to exercise his skills and abilities even more than he had been. Middleton seemed to offer that. A role as the senior engineer at the mill, and a possible path to a board position. Difficult though it was to leave Ernst and his colleagues at Fothergill & Harvey, he knew when the role was offered that he would have no choice but to take it.

Bags and belongings packed, farewells made, the Melias set off on the short journey from Littleborough to their new home in Middleton, full of anticipation and expectation. It would be a fresh start for them all and a new chapter in their journey through Lancashire.

Chapter 6

MIDDLETON

'Next time we move can you find somewhere in Bolton, Austin. I would dearly like to be closer to my sister. Wouldn't you like to see your family more often?' said Emma.

'It's a bit too soon to be talking about that, Emma. We've only just got here. What do you think of the house?' replied Austin, deliberately changing the subject.

As with Harveys, the company had provided Austin and Emma with some rental accommodation, almost in the shadow of the recently constructed Cromer Mill, which itself was only ten minutes further away from Townley Mill, his new work location. It was not unlike their last cottage, having a fancy name and being set back from the road, a considerable way from the typical Lancashire red brick terraced rows they had both grown up in. Dale House was an old property, built at least a hundred years earlier, possibly older, and it showed. Some of the stone slates on its roof were missing, its front door rickety and the outside walls already bowing. Externally, it looked like it had recently been rendered, and whitewashed, to give it a fresh and more inviting appearance. Before they moved in, Austin had been told that it had been built in as a logwood mill in the eighteenth century, and used for extracting dyes from timber - that would have made sense given the proximity of the River Irk located only a few yards away. However, a few years before Austin and Emma arrived, the building had been converted into living accommodation, and was therefore 'perfectly usable as a house', at least according to his new employer; notwithstanding the fact that the southern half of the building looked more like it ought to be demolished. Whether or not it was deemed to be habitable would no doubt be down to Emma. In the meantime, it seemed to Austin that his employers probably thought that the convenience and reassurance of having their engineer living within walking distance from the mill was a far more important factor than the comfort of his family.

'I don't know, Austin,' replied Emma, clearly a little dubious.

'It would allow us to save more,' Austin suggested, hinting at the possibility that one day they might own their own house.

'And we could certainly keep Edward in school a little longer,' he added.

This had been a family talking point in the weeks before they left Littleborough. Austin had agreed that Edward could start work as a 'half timer' once he reached the age of eleven. However, when he did reach his twelfth birthday, both Austin and Emma agreed that it was not worth the risk of letting him work full time. In Austin's view, he might 'do either himself or another an injury'. Austin in particular did not want to take the risk, at least not until his son's behaviour improved to his satisfaction. Edward would have to stay on at school until he reached the age of thirteen, which would be in May 1910.

Emma seemed a little more persuaded by the savings argument, and despite some deficiencies in their new home, was eventually won over by her husband's willingness to 'fix' a few things that in her mind 'needed fixing'. She fully intended to hold him to that promise in the months ahead.

* * *

Austin's journey to work in Middleton had far less bucolic appeal than his journey to Sladen Wood. There were mills in Littleborough but they were certainly not on the scale of Middleton. Their new home was on the edge of the built-up area of the town, almost rural but not quite. While Dale House might not have been directly surrounded by edifices built by the cotton kings, they were nonetheless not too far away. Behind them stood the towering textile shrines of the Don, Rex and Soudan mills, and in front of them stood the famous Cromer, its capacious single storey capable of housing 66,000 ring spindles. It had only been open for four years, a more recent testament to Lancashire's still dominant textile industry. Where there were no mills there were reservoirs, without which there would be no steam to help power the engines vital for the processing of cloth.

Austin shrugged as Emma's complaints passed through his mind. It was not as pretty a location as Town House but it was the best he could do. And it was convenient. A few strides over the footbridge adjacent to the house and he was on Hilton Fold Lane. A few more strides and he could be on Middleton's tram network on Oldham Road; the Hilton Fold Depot itself was located only minutes away; though catching a tram to work was unnecessary. A few yards down Hilton Fold Lane, a turn at Green Street, and another at Spring Vale, and he would be standing outside the dye works. Another hundred yards and he would be facing Townley Mill. It was an easy walk, more like Farnworth than Littleborough. Emma might not like it so much but he was in his element, one step closer to Manchester, the beating heart of Lancashire's textile industry. Opportunity seemed all around him.

* * *

Edward was furious when Austin told him that he would be staying on for another school year. His father had once promised him that he could work full time when he was old enough, just like many of his friends of a similar age that he had in Littleborough. He just couldn't see the point of more schooling. He had learned all that he felt he needed.

'One more school year, Edward. It's for your own good. I'll get you a job in the mill next summer,' said Austin.

'You promised!' replied Edward.

Emma sat silently in the corner. This was a conversation Austin alone needed to have with their son.

'With moving to Middleton we can afford to keep you on at school. The more you learn the better the job you will get. And let's be truthful. Your writing skills need improving,' said Austin.

Edward grimaced.

'I hate school. We should have stayed in Littleborough then.'

'Are you questioning me, lad?' challenged Austin.

Edward pulled a face but remained silent. He now knew better than to answer back.

'Well then?' added Austin.

'No. No, sir,' replied Edward.

'Good. I'm pleased you see the sense of it. Now get on with your chores,' instructed Austin.

Edward sloped off to collect some coal for the fire. One way or another he would get his own back. He just had to work out how.

* * *

Fr. Wigman was not one of Edward's favourite people, but then again Edward was not especially fond of any of the teachers at St. Peter's. The recently extended school stood near the old, and modestly sized, parish church on the corner of Albert Street and Taylor Street, not far from the centre of Middleton. The parish had been saving for years to replace the church, and it was now due for demolition 'next year', at least according to Canon Wigman. He had announced it a few weeks earlier towards the end of Sunday Mass.

St. Peter's Irish roots were evident everywhere around the school. Almost all the Roman Catholic teaching staff had Irish roots in one form or another, and there were other reminders all around, pictures of the 'old country' on the wall, religious icons, St. Patrick, and other mementos of a lost world. All designed to augment the link between the Irish community back home and the one here in Middleton. It was no surprise to find that the first church and school had been built by Irish navvies.

Edward did not really care about any of that. He just wanted to get out and live life. But before he could do that, he had to negotiate his way through his last year of education, and somehow avoid the wrath of Mr Murphy. Mr Murphy was probably the oldest teacher in St. Peter's School, and not exactly patient and evenly tempered. And to cap it all he was losing his hearing.

Edward sat on the boys' bench sited at the end opposite to the teacher's desk. There were four rows of boys' benches and four for girls, each separated by a space for walking in between. Two or three boys had to double-up on the front bench, so at times had their back to the teacher. There were maps of Great Britain and the world on the wall, a clock, a bookcase filled with both books and educational materials standing next to the teacher's desk, pictures of Ireland, class produced offerings on almost all of the surfaces, and a statue of St. Patrick placed on a pedestal in the corner. Behind the teacher's desk stood the classroom's windows. They were a large, long rectangular shape with panelled panes, and clearly designed to deliver as much natural light as could be obtained. This was Edward's world for most of his school day.

Edward tore off a piece of paper and started to chew it. Within a minute or two it had disintegrated into an inchoate piece of ammunition. He removed it from his mouth, then squashed, rolled and re-formed the material into a tight ball, squeezing as much surplus liquid as he possibly could from the increasingly noxious object. Paddy, Edward's partner in crime and who always sat next to him, started to smirk: he knew what was coming.

Mr Murphy turned towards the blackboard and started to write in chalk, something to do with Italy. Edward seized the moment. He lifted his weapon of choice, a wooden ruler, and quickly loaded his ammunition. All he needed to do now was to choose his target. Paddy whispered something in his ear, provoking a smile from Edward and a change of direction for the ruler. It would be Clodagh today. No doubt a hard target on the front girls' bench but then again more satisfying if successful. It was certainly worth a try.

Whoosh!

'Ouch!'

Edward scored a direct hit on the back of her head. His aim had already garnered the admiration of the other boys on the back bench, its precision being absolute.

The teacher spun around as soon as Clodagh had shrieked.

'Who did that?' shouted Mr Murphy.

'Answer me, boy!' He did not seem to be addressing anyone in particular.

With lightning speed Edward had already put his ruler down, unobserved by his teacher. He sat as stony-faced and innocent looking as he could, just like every other boy in the class.

Clodagh started to cry.

'It's... It's hurting.'

'Be quiet, girl,' replied Mr Murphy, becoming increasingly frustrated and agitated.

Clodagh's crying slowed to a whimper.

'Stand up!' Mr Murphy was clearly addressing all the boys.

'Clodagh. Where did it hit you?'

'On the back of my head, sir,' replied Clodagh.

Mr Murphy looked at Clodagh, and then the boys, all of whom were now standing.

'Bench one, sit down.'

The seven boys on the front bench sat down. In Solomonic judgement Mr Murphy had determined that the front bench could not have hit Clodagh on the back of the head. He narrowed his interest.

'Right. It will be the cane for all of you boys now standing.'

'It wasn't me, sir,' cried out Conor O'Reilly. He was standing in the middle of the second row.

'Then who was it?' questioned Mr Murphy.

'Not me, sir. I don't know,' replied Connor.

'Boy. Come here,' demanded Mr Murphy.

Connor obliged.

'Hands or backside?' enquired Mr. Murphy.

Connor stood silently in front of the teacher, unwilling to provide an answer.

'Bend over the chair,' instructed Mr Murphy.

'Whack! Whack! Whack!

Three whacks. It would be worth it, thought Edward, as Connor returned to an upright position rubbing his backside and nursing his pride.

'Right. I'll ask again. Who did it?'

Still standing, none of the boys opened their mouths.

'It was you wasn't it, Melia?' challenged Mr Murphy, directing his gaze at Edward.

'No, sir, it wasn't. Ask Paddy,' replied Edward. Mr Murphy had caught Edward dip Ciara O'Neil's pony tail in writing ink the previous week, and would often have him at the top of his list when making accusations.

Mr Murphy looked at Paddy who remained expressionless.

Edward knew that none of the boys on the back row would tell on him. And if any of them did, they would surely pay later.

'Bench two come here. Line up in front of me and bend over the chair, one by one.'

Edward could see that all of the back three rows were going to get it. The other boys would not like it, but what could they do?

When it came to Edward's turn, he duly obliged. But it was a smirk he had on his face rather than pain when he walked back to the desk. He regarded it as a win. As well as undertaking some fine target practice, he had managed to completely disrupt Mr Murphy's class. And what did he care. He knew already that he had learned enough 'reading, 'riting and 'rithmatic' to last a lifetime. As for Geography, Italy and the Vatican City, what use was it? Target practice would be far more useful, especially if he intended to follow his father's footsteps and join the army. He was saving that one for the future.

* * *

As far as home was concerned, both Austin and Emma had begun to think that Edward had at last started to mature. Complaints about his behaviour had diminished since their arrival in Middleton, so why would they think anything else? However, Edward had just become a little better at not getting caught, and that included being seen to be a little less defiant towards his parents. It was a game for him, and one day he would get his own way, with or without the approval of his father and mother. In the meantime, there were only a few months of school left. Having endured his time in school this far, he could put up with a little more, just. And besides, he needed his father's help in getting some work in a mill.

Austin wanted to cement his new status as the senior engineer in Townley Mill, and had started to give lectures on steam engineering to his peers in the local industry. Friday 9 October

1909 was something of a milestone for him. Fridays were always fish pie day, not as popular within the family as potato pie day, usually Thursdays, but still not too bad. Indeed, Austin quite enjoyed Emma's interpretation of the Catholic tradition of avoiding meat on Fridays, a little less stoic than his own upbringing which involved very plain fish, and even plainer cooking. He arrived home in quite an excited state.

'Emma, look. I've got some news.'

He waved a paper he was holding at Emma who was dressed in a cooking apron.

'It's the Cotton Factory Times. They reported on my lecture last week. Shall I read it to you?'

It was a rhetorical question as far as Emma was concerned.

'That's fine, Austin. But I need to check the pie. Read it while I look,' replied Emma.

Austin opened the page and started reading.

'It's under the Middleton section. It says: Mr A. Melia of Middleton, gave a lecture on 'Steam Elementary'. He dealt with saturated steam and its properties, and showed how to calculate the evaporation of water and the amount of coal required in order to raise any required quantity of steam according to the various pressures. The heating of mills was very ably dealt with, and the enormous cost of heating new mills especially in comparison with old ones. He contended a great mistake was made in raising steam to a pressure of 180llbs, and forcing it through a reducing valve to 90llbs. The better system, he contended, was to raise it to 90llbs and put it through. The cost of raising steam to a very high pressure was considerably more. A capital discussion followed. Mr Charles Lancashire presided.'

He was visibly pleased with his recitation of the article and looked towards Emma for further approval.

'That's very good, Austin. Now I really must get on with supper,' replied Emma.

Slightly deflated, Austin added more.

'But don't you see, Emma. This could mean people will take notice of me. It might mean a better job.'

'Austin! We've not been here for even a year,' replied Emma, distracted from her task and more than slightly alarmed at the thought of moving again.

'I don't mean now. In the future. Besides I've got some other news. I've been talking to someone about making soap,' said Austin.

'That sounds like a barmy idea, Austin. What do you know about soap? Just call Edward and Thomas will you. They're on the Green kicking a ball.' replied Emma.

Austin turned towards the door, shouted for his sons to come in, and then returned to the conversation.

'That Bolton fellow, Lever, he does it. He's got a big factory in Port Sunlight,' said Austin.

'But that's my point, Austin. How could you compete with Lever's goods?' questioned Emma.

'We would work it out. It's not worth doing if there is no profit in it. I'm going to talk to him some more. Who knows where it might go? And I've also got some ideas about making ice cream carts,' said Austin.

'Austin, really. Don't you think we've had enough business talk for one day? Let's sit down with our fish pie. Annie, put the knives and forks out. It will be on the table in a few minutes,' replied Emma, now more focused on getting the meal on the table.

'Alright, Emma. How was school today, Edward and Thomas?'

'Very good, sir,' replied Edward.

'Very good, sir,' replied Thomas, mimicking his brother, much to Edward's annoyance.

'Your father got a mention in the Cotton Factory Times today,' said Austin to his children, all three of whom were now sitting at the table.

'Would you like me to read it to you?' asked Austin.

Emma shrugged her shoulders. It looked like another reading was on its way, whether they wanted it or not.

* * *

Emma's days were much like many of the other Lancashire women. The days of the week were defined by specific tasks or traditions, rituals even. Across the county Mondays were almost always wash days. The set-boiler fire sited in the rear kitchen would be lit quite early in the day, so that several gallons of water could be heated to a temperature suitable for washing soiled clothing; it was usually boiling. A peggy-stick would be used as a stirrer, and later, a four-legged dolly-peg would be used to turn the clothes, once they had been removed to a peggy-tub. Some rigorous work on a rubbing board would be followed by running everything through one of the latest mangles – Emma had insisted that Austin bought one of the newest models when they moved to Middleton. If the weather was good, they were all hung out to dry outside. If not, the kitchen would be dressed with damp cloth hanging from every available rack. Mondays were not the easiest of days for any of the family.

It followed that as Monday was a wash day, then Tuesdays were devoted to ironing. With both Mondays and Tuesdays fully committed to housebound domestic duties, any grocery shopping had to take place on other days. Emma tended to shop on either Wednesdays, Thursdays or Fridays, sometimes over two of those days, depending on the time she had available. If it was a Friday, she would often pass women cleaning their front steps. They called it 'donkey stone day', named after the block of reconstituted sandstone used to rub freshly water swilled steps and pavements in front of each terraced house. Emma had been spared this task given the type of house they lived in, and would usually use Fridays to bake for the week ahead. They were the 'baking days' for her. Saturdays were often for market visits, a mix of food shopping and sometimes even a bit of leisure and entertainment, depending on whether Austin wanted to accompany her and Annie. If he did, they usually agreed to meet in town after he finished work at lunchtime.

Emma had no specific loyalties towards any particular shop. It was always about price and value for money. Loyalty was an expensive indulgence, and she saw it as a shopkeeper's duty to be loyal to her by keeping prices 'keen' rather than the other way around. But she did have a soft spot for the Co-op. Just as in Farnworth, Middleton's Central Stores building on Long Street was perhaps the town's finest building. Underneath the clock bearing the name 'Smiths Derby', the store sold almost everything needed, from provisions and drapery to ironmongery. If Emma could buy at a competitive price at the Co-op, then that is where her money would go. Perhaps it was a loyalty, of a kind, but it was loyalty based on common-sense money management.

As 1909 shed its days, the family settled into a life of domestic routine. Austin continued to explore his ideas in manufacturing soap and ice cream carts, while Thomas attended school with some enthusiasm, and Edward counted down the days. Annie's bond with her mother grew stronger, as Emma began to tutor her for a possible future marriage. She was after all nearly fifteen and starting to show a bit more interest in the opposite sex. For Edward, 1910 would be the year he finally broke free of the yoke of schooling, a step closer to the freedom he so wanted.

* * *

The death occurred on Friday, but it was not until Sunday morning that the newspapers were full of reports on the passing of King Edward. Emma had her own views on the matter, fuelled by the rumour and gossip circulating throughout the country. It was Sunday, so Austin agreed that he would take Edward, Thomas and Annie to Mass, so that Emma could meet her sister, Sarah. Sarah did not visit very often, so both Austin and Emma agreed that it would be expedient for Emma to miss Mass that day. Austin would make excuses for her absence to Fr. Wigman, in the unlikely event that he noticed and asked.

News travelled fast when the King died, but until people saw it in black and white, in the newspapers, it was just a rumour. Any doubts Emma might have had were dispelled by the walk down Oldham Road. The 'A' boards announced his death one after another: 'King Edward Dead'. It was blunt but effective; everyone would buy a newspaper that day.

Middleton's railway station stood on the corner of Oldham Road and Townley Street. It had only two lines and two platforms, and was very much a branch line, a first or last stop for travellers. Sarah had needed to plan her journey with precision, as it was a Sunday and services were limited. Emma walked into the station at half past ten, five minutes before Sarah's train was due. It gave her a few minutes to buy a 'News of the World' which had 'The King is Dead – God Save the King' emblazoned across the top. All the news articles were about the King and Alexandra, his wife, and her grief. They had a new king now, George V. It was all so sudden, unexpected, and not ten years since the death of Queen Victoria. She thought about Austin. He might have seen the newspaper advertising boards but he would not have read a newspaper. There would be a lot to talk about today.

Sarah's steam train announced its arrival with a hiss from its air pump, as the engine driver used its steam to alter the air pressure in the braking system. Emma smiled to herself as she recalled Austin's overly detailed explanation of how steam train engines operated.

It did not take long for Emma to see Sarah.

'Sarah!' Emma waved while quickening her pace.

With only three people disembarking, Sarah caught Emma's eye straight away. Seconds later, and after an embrace, Emma began to talk.

'A good journey?'

'Yes. Very quiet. Did you hear the news?' asked Sarah.

'I've bought a newspaper. It's everywhere,' replied Emma, knowing exactly what news Sarah was referring to.

'Where's Austin?' asked Sarah.

'Mass. With the children,' replied Emma.

'Of course. I had forgotten,' replied Sarah.

'Let's walk home,' said Emma, already leading the way.

'Are the children well?' questioned Sarah.

'They are. Annie's looking forward to seeing you,' replied Emma.

'And Edward?' queried Sarah.

'He seems to have settled down. He finishes school soon. Austin has sorted a job out for him in the mill,' replied Emma.

'I thought you didn't want them in the mills, Emma. Unsafe you said,' said Sarah.

'We don't, but there isn't much else around here. Austin will make sure he is with someone who will look after him, as he did with Annie,' replied Emma.

'So, the King is dead. What do you think, Emma?' asked Sarah.

'Well. You know about the gossip about him, don't you?' said Emma.

'Gossip?' queried Sarah, unsure about which particular gossip her sister was referring to.

'His latest mistress. I thought everyone knew. It's been going on for years,' said Emma.

'I've heard some, but perhaps not everything. I don't take as much interest in that kind of thing these days, Emma,' replied

Sarah, unwilling to admit that she might not know quite as much as her sister.

'He's always been up to something with someone. There was Lilly Langtree. You know the actress?' said Emma.

'Yes. Mother used to talk about her. It was the talk of the street. She got pregnant; the scandal of it,' replied Sarah. She was older than Emma and probably knew a lot more about it than her sister.

'Then there was that Daisy Brooke. That went on for years. And then that Keppel woman. 25 years younger than him. That's been going on for years as well. Well... It did. I wonder how Princess Alexandra will deal with her,' said Emma.

'I wonder,' replied Sarah. She had heard about Alice Keppel before but had not really talked about it.

'Don't tell Austin we have been talking about it. He wouldn't approve. He's never really been one for scandal or gossip. At least that's what he says. But if I ask him about anything like that, he's not shy about giving an opinion. He just doesn't like to be accused of gossiping,' said Emma.

'Of course not. I would never,' replied Sarah.

The two women giggled at the thought.

'Nearly there,' said Emma.

The pair had just turned left up Hilton Fold Lane. Middleton's Hilton Fold Lane tram depot stood on their right. A smooth rolled traction engine had been hooked up to a tram carriage and it was just about to pull it out of the shed.

'It's only got one deck,' remarked Sarah.

Emma avoided an 'Austin type' technical explanation and simply agreed.

'Yes. A lot of them are like that in Middleton. You get on at the front as well. What time will you be leaving tonight?' replied Emma, changing the subject.

'I've got a return ticket for eight,' replied Sarah.

'I'll make sure we get you to the station on time. Austin and the children will be back shortly. They'll all be hungry. Austin says Catholics don't eat breakfast before Mass. He's quite strict about it,' said Emma.

'Was it wise to marry a Catholic, Emma?' asked Sarah.

'You should know better than to ask me that, Sarah. He's a good man. Loyal. Fair. Honest. Loving and committed to me and the children. I couldn't ask for more. I can put up with some of his Catholic foibles, and I did agree to bringing the children up as Catholics when we married,' replied Emma.

'I'm. I'm sorry. I didn't mean anything by it,' said Sarah.

'You are forgiven. You are after all my sister. Look. We are nearly there,' replied Emma.

They had just passed the old brick works and crossed a small footbridge over the River Irk at the top of Hilton Fold Lane. A whitewashed Dale House could be seen at the other side of a patch of slightly overgrown grass encircled by shrubbery and trees.

'Your house looks so grand,' said Sarah.

'It's not all ours. There are two other families living in parts of it as well. But it's not so bad,' replied Emma.

'I'm hungry as well, Emma,' said Sarah.

'We had better get in the kitchen then, Sarah,' said Emma.

* * *

'Where's Thomas?' asked Austin.

Edward was sitting on a chair in the kitchen, arms folded. He was expecting some news from his father.

'He's playing Ring Taw on the Green,' replied Edward.

'Are you not playing with him?' questioned Austin.

'I've left school now. I won't play with marbles any more. Besides he's just practising. He wants to win more at school,' replied Edward.

'I've got you some work at Townley Mill. You'll be a little piecer on a mule just like I was. Tommy Evans is the spinner; he'll take you on. He's a good man. You just need to do the job and behave. He'll pay you a fair wage, unlike some of the others I know,' said Austin.

'I want to be a tackler,' replied Edward.

'Don't be silly. It's not a job for someone with your education,' said Austin.

'And a piecer is?' replied Edward, sardonically.

'Don't answer me back, boy. You'll do as your told. Serve your time and you might be a tenter. But until then you'll bring a wage home as a piecer,' said Austin.

'It's just that I want to work with machines. You know I like them, Dad,' replied Edward, realising that sarcasm would get him nowhere. An explanation was needed.

Austin looked at him.

'You never liked school. If you want to work with engines or machinery you'll have to go to a technical school. I'll help you if you want but you'll have to change your attitude to learning. Think about it. It won't be easy,' said Austin.

'Yes, Dad,' replied Edward.

'Now go find Thomas. I want a word with him,' said Austin.

Edward stood up and walked towards the door. There was little else to say on the subject.

* * *

Edward clutched the wage he had been given by the spinner. It was Monday evening, the start of his second week. On every day the previous week he had waited for his father to finish so that they could walk home together. But not on this occasion. He wanted to find a quiet spot, count out the money he had just been given, and come to a decision on what to spend it on. This is what he wanted. Freedom to work and money to spend. Life was about to get better.

Despite finishing later than Edward, Austin had arrived at home earlier than his son, much to the consternation of Emma.

'Where's Edward?' questioned Emma.

'He finished before me. I had expected to find him at home,' replied Austin.

'Well, he's not. Where can he be?' asked Emma, slightly concerned.

'He'll be fine. He got his first wage today. He'll be along soon,' said Austin.

Emma shrugged her shoulder and resumed working on the family's evening meal.

An hour later Edward appeared at the door looking pleased with himself.

'Where've you been, Edward?' questioned Austin.

'Oh. Nowhere. I've just been having a walk by the river. What are we having for supper tonight?' replied Edward.

Austin ignored the question and issued an instruction.

'Empty your pockets and give your wage to your mother.'

Edward looked at him, initially unwilling to part with anything.

'Give her your wage, Edward,' instructed Austin.

He took the money he had out of his pocket and placed it on the kitchen table. Austin walked over, picked it up and counted it out.

'Is this it, Edward?'

'It's all I have,' replied Edward.

'That's not what I agreed with Tommy Evans. I know he's not a cheat so where's the rest?' questioned Austin.

Edward lifted his shoulders and eyebrows in an attempt to communicate a lack of knowledge.

'Well?' said Austin.

Edward was cornered. He knew there was no point lying but he had to say something.

'It's gone.'

'Where has it gone, Edward? Don't you dare tell me you lost it,' said Austin.

'I've spent it,' replied Edward.

'You've no right to. On what?' questioned Austin.

'I can't say,' replied Edward, unwilling to provide any details.

'You can say. On what?' repeated Austin.

'I've got a right to spend my money, haven't I? I earned it.' replied Edward.

'Annie. Where is your wage?' asked Austin, turning towards his daughter who had been trying to be as inconspicuous as she could.

'I gave it to ma,' replied Annie.

'And why did you give it to your mother, Annie?' asked Austin, in a more emollient tone.

Annie hesitated, unsure of what to say. She did not want to fall out with either her father, or Edward.

'Food and board, Dad,' replied Annie.

Austin turned back to face Edward.

'Food and board. Annie is making her contribution. Don't you think you should do the same?' said Austin.

'I,' started Edward.

'That wasn't a question, Edward. One last time. What did you spend it on?' said Austin.

'Wills cigarettes, sir. I'm old enough to buy a smoke, aren't I?' replied Edward.

'It's not a question of age. It's a question of you making a contribution. You need to learn that, Edward. Next week you give all of your wage to your mother and you won't get any spending money. Is that clear?' said Austin.

'But...' replied Edward.

'Is that clear?' said Austin, not letting Edward finish.

'Yes,' replied Edward, now presenting a defiant expression.

'Good. And you will wait for me every night as well, until I say otherwise,' said Austin.

'Yes, sir,' replied Edward, recognising defeat.

Satisfied, Austin started to talk with Emma about plans for the following weekend. Annie turned away from Edward whose defiant expression had now melted into gloom and despondency. Noticing Edward's dejection, Austin decided to offer a ray of hope, an offer that he thought his son might actually seize.

'Edward.'

Edward looked up, expecting further admonishment.

'You will be allowed to keep some money for the technical school. That is if you are serious about wanting to learn about machines and engines,' said Austin.

Edward's mood lifted a little.

'Yes, Dad. I do want to learn about these things,' replied Edward.

'Well, let this be an end of it then. You will give you wage to your mother and she will give you the money for the trams and any fees,' said Austin.

'Yes, Dad,' replied Edward.

Austin was satisfied. It was not exactly what he had planned but it had worked out very well indeed.

* * *

Another year passed.

Edward seemed to have settled in and was apparently actually enjoying learning about engines at the technical school. It was also a bit of an adventure for him, away from the routine of life in Middleton. A No 7 tram on the Rhodes to Oldham route would take him into the centre. Once in Oldham it would be a walk to a lecture at the old Mechanics Institute on Manchester Street, or attendance at the new college that the Platts had established on Ashcroft Street. Oldham felt like a lively place to him and he enjoyed going there.

Spring 1911 brought with it the usual festivities and commemorations, the annual Whit Walk in Birch, and the May Day show with its decorated horses. But there would be an extra event this year: the new king was to be crowned on

June 22nd and, much like the rest of the country, Middleton would be celebrating it, with a bonfire on Parson's Field off Hollin Lane. It was to be enormous, with the clear intention of it being seen for miles around. Everyone in the town planned to be there.

Coronation day was a Thursday, but most of the town's employers had shown some flexibility in allowing workers time off to help construct the fire. Some had even provided materials. Austin had agreed with Emma that they should all meet back at home and walk to the bonfire together, following some of Middleton's lesser- known footpaths. That way they might avoid the crowds. It was not only a family occasion, nor even one just for the town. It was a celebration for the whole country.

The unlit bonfire was visible even from the cricket ground which stood on the corner of Rochdale Road and Hollin Lane.

'It's. It's enormous! It's like a chimney,' exclaimed Annie.

A column of wood stood in the middle of the field in the shape of an elongated pentagonal cone. Erected a safe two hundred yards from Hebers Cottage, it was more than a pile. Indeed, it was more like a carefully crafted timber monument to the skills of the people who constructed it. To the side of one panel of the surprisingly even shaped wooden pentagon lay some long ladders, perhaps thirty feet or so. Above the top rung of the resting ladders there was at least another fifteen or twenty feet of the pile. A man stood to the side of a flagpole with a Union Jack fluttering in the wind. It looked like he might have just raised it.

'Maybe fifty feet,' said Austin.

'How is he going to get down?' queried Annie.

On cue, the man started to descend.

'He's like a monkey,' said Edward, admiring the man's physical dexterity.

'It's a wonder it doesn't fall down,' observed Emma.

'No. It looks like they've used nails and rope to fix everything in place. It's safer than it looks,' replied Austin.

'I wonder when they will light it?' said Thomas.

'About eight 'o' clock. At least that's what I was told,' replied Austin.

'Well, it's nearly eight now,' said Thomas.

Almost as soon as the flag man had reached ground level, three others and two police constables started to usher the crowd well away from what soon would be a pillar of fire.

'Stand twice as far away as the tower is high,' instructed each of the bonfire marshals.

It took a good five minutes for the crowd to reach an acceptable distance, but as soon as they did, two firemen appeared with blazing torches. Within a matter of a minute or two the base of the pyre was alight. Minutes after that the entire edifice was ablaze, all the way from the top to the bottom of its core. Angry fingers of flame radiated out, as if trying to escape from their wooden confinement.

'They must have oiled the centre of it for that to happen,' said Austin, clearly admiring the ability of the beacon's architects to create such a magnificent spectacle.

By this time the crowd must have been in the thousands. Speculation that the whole of Middleton was attending was probably not far wrong. A few street vendors had now appeared, selling food and beer. The bonfire had become a party.

Forty-five minutes or so of gazing into the flames was just about enough for Edward. It might well be impressive, but there was only so much to see. He mentioned to Emma that he intended to get some food, but then slinked away to find a beer seller. It took a while to exit from the main body of the crowd into a clearing, but he eventually managed it. A police constable stood by a beer stall talking to another policeman. Edward ignored him and joined a small queue. The constable cast a suspicious eye at him when it was Edward's turn, but must have decided that he was of age. Satisfied, Edward picked up his opened bottle, took a swig, then started walking around the back of the crowd.

He noticed a friend from the mill, and waved at him before taking another swig. As he did, he caught the eye of a girl, who happened to boast what he thought was a magnificent cascade of jet-black hair. It was her hair that really interested him. It was longer than any he could remember at school, or in the mill; in any case most girls at the mill were braided or made-up in some way. It was beautiful. Edward immediately felt that he had to take a closer look.

The girl looked away and started taking to an older woman as soon as she realised that Edward had spotted her. Probably her mother, thought Edward. He moved a little closer, not too close, but close enough to get a better look. Now all he had to do was to attract her attention. What should he do?

He need not have worried. She turned to face him.

'Edward Melia.'

Edward blushed, as the girl and her companion stared at him. He really had no idea what to say.

'Are you still a naughty boy?'

She was already teasing him. He studied her features for a few seconds. She had certainly changed from how he remembered her, but he had no doubt who she was. No longer in neat pigtails, Bridget had matured into an attractive young woman. Her alabastrine skin stood out in sharp contrast to her black hair, and her sharp green eyes completed a picture of youthful attractiveness. The colour of her eyes had been an object of fun at school, but not anymore. Edward gazed at her, momentarily spellbound by her appearance. How could he have not seen this at school?

But what should he say to her, especially with her mother present? It was an awkward situation. And yet he had to say something.

'Are you enjoying the fire?'

That was clumsy. Edward suddenly wished he had thought of something more interesting or sophisticated to say.

'Don't you recognise me?' asked the girl.

'Of course, I do. You're Bridget O'Hanrahan,' replied Edward.

'Are you on your own? Is Thomas with you?' asked Bridget.

'No. Everyone is here... somewhere. I've lost them for now,' replied Edward.

'Why don't you come and stand with us until you see them?' suggested Bridget.

Edward nodded and took a few steps closer.

'This is Edward, Mother. We were in the same class at school.'

'I remember you. You were often talked about,' replied Mrs Hanrahan, showing a slight hint of disapproval.

Edward squirmed a little. This was getting even more difficult. He needed to change the subject.

'I'm working at Townley Mill now. A piecer. But I want to work with engines. I'm going to the technical college in Oldham.'

'Are you now. Will you be working with steam engines like your father?' replied Mrs Hanrahan.

'I don't know yet. Perhaps,' said Edward.

'I'm working in the carding room at Cromer Mill,' interjected Bridget.

'Annie, my sister, is a back tenter in the card room at Townley Mill,' said Edward.

Bridget's face hinted at a smile, and her eyes intimated mischief as she volunteered her next comment.

'You're quite a handsome boy now, Edward.'

Edward was flummoxed. What was he supposed to say? It was both a compliment and an insult. He now regarded himself as a man, after all now he was earning a wage. He flushed again.

Mrs Hanrahan saved Edward from responding.

'Bridget! Really! You should not be so forward. You can see Edward is embarrassed.'

Unfortunately, it made him feel worse, more embarrassed even.

Bridget seemed unperturbed by her mother's comment. She even turned and grinned at Edward once her face was out of the view of her mother. Was it satisfaction, or mischief? Edward could not be sure. It was probably best not to say anything at all.

'I can see Thomas, Edward. Look. Over there,' said Bridget, gesticulating towards Edward's brother and Annie. It appeared that they had come to look for him. Edward waved and shouted in their direction.

'Over here!'

'I had better be going. Perhaps we will see each other again, Bridget,' said Edward turning to face her.

'Perhaps we will,' replied Bridget, ignoring the obvious doubt on her mother's face.

Edward walked off to meet his brother and sister. Once out of earshot Mrs Hanrahan turned to Bridget.

'I don't want you seeing that boy, Bridget. He's always been trouble.'

Of course not, Mother. I would never do such a thing,' replied Bridget.

Satisfied, Mrs Hanrahan turned back to face the increasingly impressive fire, as Bridget cast an unseen sly glance at Edward's receding form. He was indeed handsome.

* * *

In Austin's mind the lecture had gone well.

Since arriving in Middleton, and being elevated to the rank of a chief engineer, he had given something like two dozen lectures on various aspects of steam engineering. They had been invariably well received, and had achieved the planned effect of him becoming a well-known and respected engineer, not just in Middleton but in Stockport, Oldham, Rochdale, and other towns on the east side of Manchester.

Not for the first time had he been approached by a mill manager to take up the position of senior engineer in a mill. Henry Jones had attended several of Austin's lectures, and had no doubt been impressed with its content and delivery. He had even asked some questions at one such lecture, and had been answered in Austin's accustomed style, with professionalism, knowledge, and courtesy. What Austin had not realised at the time was that Mr Jones had been undertaking a bit of research. He needed a competent engineer to take charge of not just one works, but two.

Barlows had been in business for over fifty years. The company owned a bleachworks in Castleton, Rochdale, and Spring Valley Dye Works and Moston Mill in Newton Heath. Moston Mill had been built the previous year as a Calico print works, and was in need of a full-time senior engineer. Austin was deemed to be the man to run the engineering function, but Henry Jones acknowledged that he would have be persuasive. After all, Austin was already a senior engineer in Middleton, and he had been in that role for less than three years. To entice Austin into the role would require more than a bigger pay packet, but Henry Jones did have a few other advantages over his current employer. Moston Mill was a larger and more modern mill, and there was the bleachworks. Austin could be offered the responsibility of both the dyeworks and the mill. With a bigger salary, a newer and larger mill, and a second location, how could Austin refuse? These were the thoughts in Henry Jones's mind when he made the offer to Austin after attending a lecture in Middleton that Autumn night.

Austin had a lot to think about as he walked out of the Jubilee Free Library on Long Lane. The lecture, which he described as 'Steam (Elementary)', had been given almost exactly a year earlier, but to a different audience, and in a different town. He would have been thinking about that, and the questions posed, had he not had the offer, but he now had to come to a decision. He had less than a week to make a choice, to stay on at Townley Mill, or to take what was certainly a very attractive position in Moston. Emma's views were always helpful, but first he needed to think it through himself.

The 'plop' of a street lamp being lit provided a momentary distraction. A few dozen yards to his left, a lamp sited in front of St. Leonard's church suddenly started to cast a soft, warm amber glow on the paved area below. A flat capped lamp-lighter started to withdraw his lighting stick, the tool used to lift up the hinged panel under the lamp and switch on the gas supply. The acetylene flame at its tip still burned; its carbide of calcium fuel still suitable for more work. The process was a living science lesson, the combustible effects of a few drips of water on calcium carbide being put to good use.

Austin did not usually walk by Middleton's cemetery, but a route by the Church Army Mission Hall offered a short cut home. The footpaths he had to take were certainly unlit but were relatively short, and in no time at all he was walking by Cromer Mill. The lights from the windows of its expansive single storey ring spinning operation glowed as the night shift still laboured. Another ten minutes and he would be home.

The children had already eaten by the time he arrived, as was often the practice on the evenings he lectured. Annie was in her bedroom, Edward was out, and Thomas was reading, as Austin recounted the day's events. But he saved the most interesting piece of news until after the meal.

'I've been offered a new job, Emma.'

'I would rather we didn't move, Austin. I feel I've only just settled in,' replied Emma, already alert to the prospect of another round of disruption.

'It's a chief engineer role with responsibility for more than a single mill. I would be its first senior engineer; it's a new mill. More pay. It's in the Moston and Newton Heath area,' said Austin. He had started to use the term 'chief engineer' rather than tenter; it felt more modern and prestigious.

'Would we have to move?' asked Emma, unsure of exactly where it was.

'No. It's called Moston Mill and has been built close to Moston Station. I could catch a train from Middleton every day,' replied Austin.

'So, you would be home later and have to set off earlier?' suggested Emma.

'Perhaps a little. But it would be worth it. It's an interesting engine as well. A foreign one, made by Carel Brothers of Ghent in Belgium. There aren't many of those around. It would be good experience,' said Austin, already providing signals of his intentions.

'You're going to accept it, aren't you? I can tell you are. If we are not to move then it will be fine with me, but what about the children? Are they to stay at Townley?' said Emma, other questions already in her mind.

'Why should they not? I doubt Edward will remain a piecer for long, and Annie is settled in the carding room. As for Thomas. Well, I'll find something for Thomas when the time comes. He could always join me at Moston Mill,' replied Austin.

'Then so be it, Austin. You'll have my blessing if you want to accept it,' said Emma.

Relieved, Austin had only one more thing to say on the subject.

'One day we will have a house of our own, Emma. With the extra pay from this and selling my interest in the soap business our savings are almost there. It's a pity the ice cream machine didn't work out, but I think it was worth a try. It's probably just as well. I didn't really have enough time to make either business successful. You know I could take a mortgage out, or join a building club, but until I'm certain where we will settle...' Austin's comments tailed off into reflection as Emma began to ponder over where that might eventually be. One of these days she would put her foot down.

* * *

The sinking of the Titanic and its loss of life almost two weeks earlier had shocked the nations on both sides of the Atlantic. It was a tragedy, of that there was no doubt, but it did feel somewhat remote to the lives of the Melia family. Even the fact that the captain of the Carpathia, the Titanic's rescue ship, was Bolton born, was only of passing interest. More exciting to Emma was the recent visit to Middleton by Adela Pankhurst, who had come to speak at the local branch of the NUWSS. Less strident, and more moderate than her mother, Emma would always attend any locally organised events where the younger Pankhurst was to speak. For at least a week after one of these suffragette assemblies, Emma would be rather more animated about women's rights than during the rest of the time. Austin would often feel the effects of the movement's radical thinking, including Emma's latest views about him undertaking a little more of the housework. When such ideas were floated, Austin's sympathies with Emmeline Pankhurst's ideas tended to dissipate, though he never wanted to become combative with Emma. It was better to think of some distraction, or treat, than to argue. While likely seeing through any of his ruses, Emma tended to soften when Austin dreamt up some entertainment for her.

Austin believed that he had found an ideal amusement for Emma, and had obtained tickets for it already. It would be a night out just for the two of them now that the children were almost adults. And it would also be a surprise.

Emma had been asked to dress for a visit to the theatre but that was only partially true. The April weather was unusually warm and clement, so they decided to take a tram down Oldham Road for a couple of stops, and then walk the rest of the way to the theatre on Corporation Street. Emma's excitement grew as they neared the theatre's entrance. After all, a night out was quite a rare treat, although one now becoming more frequent with Austin's elevated status. But instead of joining the queue that had formed, he led Emma away.

'Austin, what are you doing? Where are we going?' asked Emma, clearly confused.

'You'll see,' replied Austin.

'Tell me. I need to know,' said Emma. She always had a bit of difficulty with not knowing.

'It's a surprise,' said Austin.

'But I've dressed for the theatre,' replied Emma.

'That's alright. You look lovely, as I said when we left,' said Austin.

'That's not what I mean. Where are we going?' repeated Emma.

Austin led Emma down Old Hall Street in the direction of Manchester Road. Amused, slightly frustrated, and perhaps even slightly irritated, Emma chose to stay silent. She didn't have long to wait. At the junction of Wood Street, Long Street and Old Hall Street, the destination suddenly became obvious. A large crowd had developed outside the newly constructed building on Manchester Road, all seemingly eager to go in and try out this new form of entertainment.

'They won't get in without a ticket. That's for sure. At least not tonight,' said Austin, confident in his ability to access that which others clearly could not.

'It's the new picture house,' exclaimed Emma, now delighted with Austin's choice of entertainment.

'Tickets only. Tickets only. This way if you have a ticket,' advised a burly man dressed in some sort of garish mauve uniform with strange yellow epaulets on his shoulder.

Austin took out their tickets and waved them at the man.

'This way, sir and madam.'

The crowd parted to let him through as the usher directed them towards a large open door. Emma felt special as the usher roped off the area they had just passed through. She felt like a royal. No wonder they called it The Palace.

Neither Austin, nor Emma, had ever seen a moving picture before. Austin had read about the technology but to actually see it. It was another wonder of the twentieth century. There seemed no boundaries to what the future offered.

A second usher inspected the tickets and pointed to where they should sit.

'Row F is over there, sir. Your seats are near the aisle.'

Emma and Austin talked about what they were going to see as they sat down. The theatre was already three quarters full.

'It won't be long now, Emma. Most people are already here.'

There was a buzz in the air. Everyone in the room seemed excited. Perhaps for many it was also the first time they would see what they were now starting to call a 'film'.

'I had heard it was opening, but I never expected to come here on its first night,' replied Emma.

'I got them through one of my engineering friends who is related to the manager here,' said Austin, smiling.

At eight most of the electric house lights were turned down. A voice boomed out from the darkness.

'Quiet please, ladies and gentlemen. The show is about to start.'

The excited chatter around the auditorium quelled, almost into silence, as the antique ruby curtains drew open. Seconds later, the first bars of a piano score floated across the room as an almost hidden pianist started to play. The screen in front of them flickered into life with a title card: Charles Dickens,

A Tale of Two Cities, Directed by Charles Kent. Two cast cards were followed by a scene setting description.

And then.

The audience gasped in amazement. For most it was likely the first time they had seen a moving picture.

Two giant characters appeared in costume, one male and one female. Exaggerated gesticulation caricatured emotion as the two figures spoke, unheard. The pianist's musical interpretation speeded and slowed, as he perceived action and empathised sentiment.

Both Austin and Emma sat still, and in silence, spellbound by what they were seeing. When the final title card announced 'The End', the curtain started to close and house lights were switched back on. The final bars from the pianist floated into the silence. Unsure of what to do, someone to the right of them started to clap, and then someone else. A few seconds later the entire theatre had burst into applause. But with no one there to receive it the appreciation did not last.

A voice from behind boomed again.

'Ladies and gentlemen, there will now be a longer intermission. Refreshments are available.'

There had been two pauses of five minutes already in the showing, 'for changing the reel,' suggested Austin, who always seemed to know these things.

Three other moving pictures were shown with a bizarre array of themes. *Dr Jekyll and Mr Hyde*, *For the Cause of the South*, and *The Scarlett Letter*. It was the last one that provoked some comment from Emma. Set in 1600s Puritan America, it told the story of a woman who had to wear a scarlet letter 'A', for adultery, for having a daughter with another man while her husband was away.

Emma refrained from comment until they were out of the cinema and out of earshot.

'I enjoyed the evening, Austin, but I didn't like that last one. No one should have to wear anything like that, whatever they have done. She shouldn't have seen that other man, but to shame her like that. It's wrong. Anyone can make a mistake.'

Austin was out of his depth on this one – it was probably better to agree with his wife.

'I, er... I don't really know what to say,' replied Austin.

'Well, say something,' demanded Emma.

'I'm sure you are right, Emma. She shouldn't have gone with that other man,' replied Austin.

'But what about the letter she had to wear? Don't you think it was wrong?' questioned Emma.

The truth was he did not really have any strong feelings on the subject. It was a story after all. It was not real.

'It's just a story, Emma. Though I'm sure you are right about that as well,' replied Austin.

Emma seemed dissatisfied. She clearly wanted to provoke a discussion, although Austin was unwilling to engage. What was there to talk about?

'Would you like to go again?'

He knew what the answer would be had she decided to voice it. But Emma just smiled. The evening had been a success.

* * *

1912 closed much as it had in 1911, and for that matter the year before that. But far away from humdrum domestic life in Lancashire, both in geography and in social status, the reciprocation of people, actions, and events, were generating effects that would impact every member of the family, and everyone's family. The seeds of chaos had long since been sowed, and it was now just a matter of time before the repercussions of discord rippled through.

Life was about to dramatically change.

Chapter 7

EDWARD

The tram lurched to a sudden stop. It woke Edward who had seated himself directly behind the driver. He had been leaning with his cheeks against a window, a practice usually discouraged by the conductor, but on this occasion had apparently let happen. Edward had not planned to doze for more than a few minutes, but the effects of a day's work and a few hours in Oldham had caught up with him. He had slept all the way to Rhodes.

'Last stop, Rhodes,' announced the conductor.

Edward sighed. He had not got enough money to pay for the stops back into the centre of Middleton, and would therefore have to walk. It would make him late home but it did not really matter. The early spring weather was good and the walk would be pleasant, refreshing even.

He disembarked the tram onto Manchester Old Road's pavement, and was immediately confronted with Schwabe's enormous chimney. It was a landmark across Middleton, but he had forgotten how tall it actually was. At over three hundred and twenty feet high it was reputed to be the highest brick chimney in Lancashire, if not the country. The structure dwarfed Rhodes village, and any person or object that passed by; even a tram looked like a toy when standing near to it.

'Edward Melia.'

A female voice from behind interrupted his intellectual tarriance. He spun round to see who it was.

'Hello.'

It was her again, Bridget, and without her mother. It must have been a year...

'Bridget,' said Edward.

'So, you do remember me this time,' replied Bridget.

'Of course, I do,' said Edward.

'What are you doing here?' asked Bridget.

'I missed my stop. I've been to technical college in Oldham. You remember. I told you about wanting to be a mechanic, didn't I?' replied Edward.

'It was something like that. I've been to buy some bread and milk for mother. We've run out. How's Thomas and Annie?' asked Bridget.

'Very well,' replied Edward, remembering that Bridget lived in Rhodes. He recalled that she always travelled to school from the direction directly opposite to his. It felt like so long ago.

'You've changed again,' said Bridget.

'So have you,' replied Edward with a cheeky grin.

It was hard to decide where the conversation might go from here, although it was perhaps already obvious to both that there was an appetite for it to continue. Edward began to stare at her, wondering what to say next. He was again struck by her green eyes, soft white skin and deep black hair. An unexpected paroxysm of desire swept through his being; he could not just say goodbye and leave.

'Have you ever been to a moving picture?'

Bridget returned his look, initially unsure how to respond. Was it a question or an invitation?

'No. Why do you ask?'

'Would you like to come and see one with me?' asked Edward.

It was a direct question she had to answer. Should she? What would her mother say? But then Edward was not the boy she knew at school, having now matured into a handsome and presentable young man. In the milliseconds before answering she studied him. He had taken to combing his hair in a long slicked back style that was becoming popular, probably using that Brilliantine scented oil that was now all the rage. His square facial features, dimpled, jutting chin, and stocky build presented a picture of health, strength, and reliability. What was not to like? Perhaps he had been a bit of a terror at school but he was almost a man now.

She delivered her answer.

'Of course. But mother might not like it.' Bridget knew full well her mother would object. She had always been suspicious of Edward.

'What about Saturday? We could go to a matinee,' suggested Edward, ignoring the maternal threat.

'That would be perfect. I'll tell mother I'm meeting a friend after work. We could go after three,' replied Bridget, already engaging in subterfuge with her mother.

Edward often went to college on Saturday afternoons but would give this week a miss.

'I'll meet you at the Market Place tram stop at three on Saturday then. We'll go to the Palace. My ma and dad said it was the place to go for moving pictures,' said Edward.

'Goodbye, Edward. I'll see you on Saturday,' replied Bridget, adding a soft smile.

There, he had done it. He had asked her out and been accepted. It had happened so quickly; he hardly had time to think about it, thought Edward, before turning back towards home and setting off at a brisk pace, heart pounding with anticipation.

Bridget continued with her errand, thrilled with the prospect of being taken out to a moving picture, and with Edward, but already guilty about misleading her mother. She would never agree to Bridget being unchaperoned, least of all with Edward. But she liked him. She had always had a soft spot for his mischief at school, even on the rare occasions when she had been the object of his pranks. But that was long in the past. He most certainly would have grown up by now.

* * *

Saturday cinema was a success. After all, Edward was on his best behaviour, a true gentleman. That first visit to the cinema was followed by a second, and then a third. Edward's sixteenth birthday passed in May, and so did Bridget's, who also had a birthday in the same month. The weather had warmed during the latter part of spring, and offered the prospect of walks in the countryside surrounding Middleton. Middleton was not a large town, and both were acutely aware that the more clandestine meetings they had, the higher the risk of being seen, and being recognised. A walk in the country seemed to be the answer. Edward suggested that, as it was near to her Rhodes home, Alkrington Hall Woods would be reassuringly secluded and a good place for walks.

Walks in the woods became a regular pastime for them both. Edward's whereabouts were far less of a concern to Austin and Emma, especially now that he had reached the age of sixteen. Still a minor, but no longer a child, and he was earning a wage. So long as he kept out of trouble with the authorities, and work, he would be left to his own devices. Meanwhile, Bridget would disguise her secret meetings with Edward by forming a habit of regular walks, with or without him. She would often come home with a small posy of wildflowers gathered in the fields, verges, and forests around Rhodes. Her mother approved, and actually encouraged the routine, believing it was good for her daughter's health.

There was one particular copse of bushes in the wood which had been designated as their meeting place. Most of the time Edward would just sit, or stand and wait, but if there were other people around, he might hide until they had gone. The woods were more popular in late spring and summer, but avoiding people was a lot easier when everything was in full leaf. Saturday afternoons were their preferred meeting days, but Sundays as well on occasion.

Edward waved. He recognised Bridget from a distance despite the gentle breeze. The action of the wind served to pendulate the bushes and tall shrubbery around the winding path, momentarily hiding her form. She returned the wave as there was no one else in sight. When they met, they kissed, showing nothing of the awkwardness of their first embrace only a few weeks earlier.

'I've missed you,' said Bridget.

'And I've missed you as well,' replied Edward.

He held out his hand and Bridget took it straight away, a universal signal of affection and intimacy.

'Where shall we go today?' asked Edward.

'Can we go closer to the Hall?' suggested Bridget.

'We need to be careful not to be seen when we get close to it. I think the Lees own it; you know the big millowners. My ma says one of the suffragettes is related to them, Marjory Lees I think her name is. Ma is always talking about suffragette stuff,' replied Edward.

'Did you hear about that Emily Davidson woman? Threw herself under the King's horse at Epsom Races?' said Bridget.

'My ma has talked about nothing else for the last few days. Dad has had enough of it. He said he couldn't understand why anyone would want to do such a thing,' replied Edward.

Bridget just shrugged. She had no idea either.

Edward led Bridget off their usual path into a denser and untrodden part of the forest.

'Let's find somewhere quiet to sit so that we can talk.'

Bridget seemed happy with the suggestion, but had to let go of his hand and follow, as the shrubbery became thicker.

'What about there?' said Edward, pointing at a barely visible small tract of grass, highlighted by a break in the forest canopy.

Bridget did not answer but acquiesced to his suggestion. Within a minute they were both sitting on dry wild meadow grass, already a good length given the time of year. Moderately high ferns almost surrounded the clearing, completely hiding their presence should they decide to lie.

'Let's move to the edge, under that tree,' suggested Edward.

They moved. It was only a few feet, but by changing location they would be invisible to anyone around and from above. Low hung branches, now in full leaf, supplemented their camouflage. The woods were criss-crossed by footpaths in all sorts of directions, but at least now Edward felt they were safe from inquisitive eyes.

Bridget had been carrying a kind of cardigan. She had not needed to wear it, but now found a use, laying it down and sitting on it, then lying back and resting her head on its edge. The sounds of early summer were all around. Swifts, wrens, blackbirds, various finches and tits were in song. Through the overhang, nebulous remnants of cumulus floated in the inviting blue firmament above. It felt like a summer should be: peaceful and relaxing.

Minutes passed in silence.

Edward then made his first move, leaning over and kissing her on her perfectly shaped nose.

Bridget giggled, enjoying the attention.

He then kissed her on the lips before drawing back as if to test the water. But Bridget was willing. She lifted her head and leaned it against her clenched left hand, now held off the ground by her elbow. Edward mirrored the action and faced her. They kissed again, and again.

Five minutes passed.

Bridget lay down again but Edward wanted more. He leaned over to kiss, but this time he also started to undo the buttons of her blouse. Slowly at first, but then a little quicker as his sixteen years old hormones started to take control. Bridget's cheeks began to flush as he did so, and her body began to tingle with excitement. She wanted to go further but there was also danger. She wanted Edward but should she let him do this?

Blouse unbuttoned and loose, Edward moved his hand underneath and started to caress her breasts.

'Edward. I don't know,' said Bridget, excited but confused with the conflict between rational thought and primeval instinct.

Edward hesitated.

'It will be alright. No one can see.'

But that was not what she was concerned about. Was it her virtue? Her religion? Her unseen mother whispering advice in her ear?

Edward resumed his gentle caress.

'Do you love me, Edward?'

'Of course, I do.'

Edward started to sweat as the urge to finish what he had started already seemed in jeopardy. His mind was willing her to remove more of her clothing, but Bridget wanted to regain control, both of herself and her situation.

'I'm not ready for this, Edward. Not today. Can't we just kiss?'

Edward drew away and lay on his back. He took a big breath and sighed out loud.

'I'm sorry, Edward. I, I, I just can't.'

The moment had passed for the both of them.

It was another five minutes before Edward said something.

'Let's walk up to the Hall.'

Without answering, Bridget raised herself off the ground, brushing off some grass and other bits that had caught in her clothing.

'Perhaps next time,' said Bridget.

'Perhaps,' replied Edward, rather dubiously.

* * *

Edward and Bridget's relationship flourished during the rest of the summer. As Bridget's confidence in Edward's intentions grew, she became increasingly relaxed about his ardour, his enthusiasm to physically consummate their bond. What had seemed so unwise and foolish at first, just seemed natural as they began to talk more about a future together. After their first time, Edward expected it almost every time they met, and Bridget acquiesced. Talk about marriage and somehow involving their parents seemed whimsical to Edward at first. He mostly agreed with what she said, but would typically find some excuse to delay moving their association to the next step. There was 'plenty of time for that', 'we are still only sixteen' or 'when I get a better job, we can start to plan for that' were typical responses. He even found reasons for not saying anything to either of their parents. Bridget would say something like, 'I will talk to mother about you. She will understand you are not the schoolboy you once were', but Edward would draw back in horror at the prospect, typically framing a response in terms of work and income. But the more he resisted, the more Bridget pressed. She had given her mind and body to him, and wanted a clear commitment, an engagement; she cared little for how long that might be.

Edward began to fear it. At sixteen he felt that he still had much to do, a life ahead of him, and he did not want to contemplate marriage, not now. By September their meetings and liaisons had become less frequent. He had started to avoid her rather than share his true feelings and intentions. Bridget accepted that their walks would be less frequent, as the trees shed their leaves and the weather became less amenable, but she still wanted to see him.

And then one early autumn afternoon Bridget dropped a bombshell after meeting Edward. They had planned another cinema matinee, but Bridget's news soon diverted them.

'We were seen, Edward. Now we'll have to get engaged.'

Edward's eyes widened as he processed the implications of her statement. He certainly thought differently to her.

'No. We should not see each other as much. People will soon forget about it if there is no gossip.'

'It's too late. Mary Manion is a complete gossip. She will have probably told her mother already, and her mother will talk to mine,' replied Bridget.

'How do you know she saw us?' asked Edward.

'She told me herself. I told her that mother already knew but I don't know if she believed me. We didn't really get on that well at school either,' said Bridget.

'We shouldn't go to the cinema. We need to talk about this,' replied Edward.

'I know. We need to plan how we should tell yours and mine about us getting married,' said Bridget.

'We are not going to get married. At least not yet,' replied Edward.

'But I might be with child,' said Bridget.

'No. You are not,' replied Edward, horrified at the prospect.

'I don't know Edward. I might be. I, I can't say,' said Bridget.

Edward let go of her hand, already wanting to distance himself from Bridget and the situation he seemed to have got himself into. He needed some time to think and plan, but for some sort of escape, not a marriage.

'We can't see each other, Bridget. There is too much risk.'

'What do you mean?' replied Bridget.

Bridget did not seem to have quite understood his earlier comment, so he had to try again.

'I don't want to get married until I'm a lot older.' There, he had finally been explicit in his intentions. There would be no early wedding.

'But we've... You know,' replied Bridget, obtusely.

Edward knew exactly what she meant but chose to ignore it.

'I know it's cold, but its's not raining so let's go for a walk down Manchester New Road. There is less chance we will be seen there. We can cut through the woods later,' suggested Edward.

Bridget had other ideas.

'I want to go home.'

'I'll walk you. But Manchester New Road is still a good idea,' replied Edward.

'I'll go on my own,' said Bridget, now quite obviously upset by the course of the discussion.

'No. I'll take you,' insisted Edward.

'No! Leave me alone!' shrieked Bridget, oblivious to the fact they were still walking on some of Middleton's busier streets.

Edward was taken aback by the unexpected outburst and replied in a more muted tone.

'Hush. People are starting to look.'

'I don't care,' replied Bridget, in a barely less audible volume.

Bridget stopped walking, catching Edward by surprise.

'Go home. I'll find my own way back.' She was being as clear to him as he had been to her. Even to Edward's barely developed sense of empathy, it was obvious that he would have to leave her be.

'I'll see you next week.'

Bridget ignored his comment and walked straight past him. Edward turned and watched her back disappear into the distance. She did not turn to either wave or look at him. He knew then that this would not be the last of it, and that his life might become a little awkward for a time. Talking his way out of it might not be an option. Something more radical might be called for. He would just have to see.

* * *

Several days passed. Bridget had not tried to contact Edward, and Edward had not attempted to contact Bridget. He started to relax. Perhaps it was for the best. It would give her time to think it through. The more Edward mulled over the discussion he had with her, the more convinced he became that all would be well. He was sure that she would soon begin to see the situation his way. They were both very young; far too young to think about getting married. It would be a long time before they could afford to rent a house, never mind have a baby. It was common-sense really.

Another fortnight passed.

Edward arrived home from Townley Mill as he did every day, sometimes with Thomas, and sometimes without him. His father now worked in Moston and had to get a train to Middleton Station before walking home, so he was always home after the three siblings who remained working at the Middleton mill. As Austin could sometimes be an hour or more later than the children, Emma would usually give them their evening meal almost as soon as they got home. It was not unusual for all three to have finished, and be attending to evening chores, reading, or studying by the time she and Austin sat down to eat. However, unknown to Edward, Bridget had put into motion a sequence of events that would ultimately break-up the family for a time.

'Edward, after your father and I have eaten we would like to have a talk with you about your mechanical studies and work,' said Emma.

She had implied that Austin was aware of the discussion they were about to have, but that was not entirely true. She did not want to alarm or worry him just yet.

'Yes, Ma. I need to do some reading tonight as well,' replied Edward.

Edward disappeared into an upstairs room to join Thomas, who was already reading one of his father's volumes, a book on Steam Turbines.

'Steam engines eh? You know there are other things happening. Automobiles are the future, internal combustion engines,' said Edward.

Thomas ignored him at first but then chose to answer.

'I've seen the steam wagons on the road. I'm learning about steam.'

Edward rummaged through a drawer and pulled out a notebook he used at college. He began to read through it.

An hour later Emma called upstairs.

'Edward, can you come down.'

Edward complied, joining Austin and Emma in a part of the house they now called the dining room.

'I had a visitor today, Edward. Mrs O'Hanrahan,' said Emma.

Edward's heart missed a beat. He started to flush and shake. Was Bridget going to have a baby? What had she said to her mother?

'She said that you and Bridget have been seeing each other for months now. You didn't tell us,' added Emma.

Edward remained silent. Whatever he said would likely be the wrong thing. But he needed to know what Bridget had said.

Emma continued.

'She said that Bridget is very upset with you. And that you had promised to marry her. Is this true?'

He had no choice but to say something.

'I have seen her. I never promised to marry her.'

Emma stared at him for a good minute.

'Have you...' Austin interrupted Emma's question. He had remained silent up until now.

'Have you had relations with her?'

Edward elected not to answer, prompting Austin to repeat it.

'Has there been any naval engagement? Did you use a life jacket?'

Emma looked at Austin, totally bemused by the coded language he was using. Unsurprisingly, notwithstanding his youth, Edward knew exactly what his father was asking. He answered.

'What if I have? I'm sixteen; I earn a wage. She was willing.'

Emma put her head in her hands. She had caught up with the interlocution.

'You'll have to marry her now. I told Mrs Hanrahan that everything she said could not possibly be true. And it is. She could be having a baby.'

'She can't be. We're not married,' replied Edward.

'You know better than that, lad,' said Austin, becoming quite obviously irritated.

'I won't get married. I'm not ready for it,' said Edward.

'You'll have to, Edward. It's only right,' replied Emma.

'I'm too young,' said Edward.

'You should have thought of that before you did what you did,' said Austin.

'Then it's settled. I'll start to make the arrangements,' said Emma.

'But we don't even know if she's carrying a baby,' replied Edward.

'You can't leave her like that. What will people say when they find out. And they will. We have a reputation to keep. Your father is a manager at the mill, and neither of us would be able to hold our heads up in church. You'll have to marry her and that's that,' said Emma, sensing Edward was reverting to his old self: intransigent and disagreeable.

'I won't do it!' replied Edward.

'You'll have to or you won't be able to stay under my roof,' thundered Austin.

'Well, if that's how it's going to be then that's it. I'll find my own place to live. Anyway, I've nearly finished college,' replied a brazen Edward.

Austin had remained relatively calm throughout the discussion but was clearly very unhappy at the outcome. Emma spotted it and attempted to assuage the tension that had developed.

'Go and sleep on it, Edward. We'll talk about it again tomorrow.'

'I will, Ma,' replied Edward.

He also could see that his generally placid father seemed far more agitated than usual. A lot had already been said, and it would serve no purpose to say more and risk a heated discussion becoming a violent argument. For possibly the first time in his life he could not fully read his father.

Whether his father meant what he was saying was unclear to him. But from Edward's point of view it was time that he went out on his own. He believed he could get some employment working with automobiles. The only question was where this should be. Though one thing he was sure of was that it would not be in Middleton, not with Bridget and her mother likely to be calling round again. He needed to do something, and to do it quickly. That is what he would be sleeping on, not on the need to get married.

* * *

Two days later Edward had the outline of a plan. He would be leaving Middleton for one of the bigger towns or cities in Yorkshire. The ones around Manchester were too close, too accessible. He needed to put some miles between him and Middleton, and let time heal the disagreement. Edward did not want to leave on bad terms, but he had to do what he had to do. His solution was a letter and an early morning start. No one would be allowed to know where he was going; he would write to them in a few weeks once he had found work and lodgings. Perversely, he began to look forward to it. It was exciting, an adventure even.

There was awkwardness in the air. Thomas and Annie remained unaware of what had happened, but they could see something was wrong. Emma remained distant to Edward. They talked, but in a very transactional way. Edward responded in like manner, 'Yes, Ma', or 'No, Ma', there was little else exchanged. Austin had been avoiding him while Edward was complicit in that avoidance. Neither wanted to return to the discussion, yet both knew that it was an inevitability. All three feared another visit from Mrs Hanrahan. The matter remained unresolved. What could they say to her?

Edward prepared the detail of his escape. He would be leaving on Saturday. No notice would be given to work. He would simply take the savings he had accumulated, a few items of clothing, and catch a train. And he had chosen a city, Leeds. It was far enough away but not too far should he have need to get back to Lancashire. Busy and vibrant, and with a football team that topped the league, it seemed like the perfect choice. With feelings of trepidation and yearning to stay tempered with excitement, he began to count down the hours to executing his scheme.

* * *

Saturday morning.

It was a working day like any other, but today Edward rose a half hour earlier than usual, taking care not to wake anyone in the household. Thomas was still soundly asleep as he dressed, and he could hear the muffled sounds of his father's snoring from the room next door to theirs. He crept down the stairs, avoiding the seventh from the bottom, the one that always creaked if you stood on it at the wrong point. There was a bit of bread and butter in the pantry; it was enough for now. Placing his bag on the floor, the one he packed the previous night, he retrieved an envelope addressed to 'Dad and Ma'. Placing it on the mantlepiece over the fireplace, he took one last look around the room, and then he was off.

Moving quickly to the footbridge over the Irk, and then on to Hilton Fold Lane, Edward knew already that he was out of sight. Trams were being shunted in, out, and around the tram shed when he passed it, preparing for another day of commerce. He could have caught the first one of the morning, but it was not really worth it. A brisk walk and he would be at Middleton Railway Station. Once a train had left the branch line he could get off and catch one to Yorkshire. If he was lucky, he might get one that went direct to Leeds; if not, he would just have to change somewhere.

Edward was lucky. By half past nine he was standing at the entrance to Leeds Central Railway Station wondering what his next move might be. He had enough money to survive for up to a month, food and lodgings. That must surely be enough time to find some work, he thought, as the grey clouds parted and a few rays of autumn sunshine shone on Wellington Street. Picking up a copy of the Yorkshire Evening Post he began to walk. Edward knew that there would be plenty of work in the mills, but he wanted to work with automobiles. After over two years of attending technical school, and studying mechanics and engines, he knew the theory and had even had a bit of practice. Despite his youth he knew that he had skills that few others had, and that all he needed was a bit of luck. Garages selling and maintaining automobiles were popping up everywhere, and in Edward's confident mind all he would have to do would be to walk in and ask. So that was his plan. He would go from garage to garage looking for a job, and if that did not work there was always the situations vacant in the newspapers. He felt exhilarated at the thought.

It was only a few minutes walking to City Square, and luck was on his side that day. He chose to follow a family up a street which he suspected led to Leeds Market, judging by the conversations he had overheard. Something changed his mind minutes into the trek; he turned left up Albion Street. At Guilford Street he looked left then right. His heart leapt. There was an 'A' board in the street a few yards away to his right announcing a 'Rover Dealer. This Way'. An arrow pointed towards another street. With a spring in his step Edward walked in the direction of the arrow.

King Charles Street was perhaps only a hundred yards long. Once past some building renovation work that was taking place on the corner with Guildford Street, there were only two other buildings of note, a warehouse sited at the corner of the next street, and the Rover garage. Next to a sign painted directly on the wall announcing 'Rover Dealer Cars' stood a half-glazed garage door, just wide enough for a modern car. Edward peered through the window. He could see a Rover 12 standing over an inspection pit. There was no one visible but he could hear someone knocking at something underneath the vehicle. An electric light provided illumination to the rear of the room. Another man seemed to be writing or reading, sitting on a chair positioned under an old wooden table.

Edward saw his opportunity.

He took a few more steps to what appeared to be a yard. There were several other cars of various makes parked outside, and various spare parts stacked in the corner. The building itself looked very old, three storeys and built of red brick. Were there was once a door there was now only an outline. The doorway had been filled with unmatching bricks from another era. He would have to return to the main garage door.

He knocked.

The man at the desk turned round, looked at Edward, then returned to finish whatever he was doing. Edward obviously did not look like a customer.

He knocked again.

'John, there's someone at the door.'

The man working underneath the Rover could not see Edward but had temporarily stopped hammering and heard the knock. The other man put down his paperwork, walked over, and opened part of the door; it was of a concertina type. Edward decided to be direct.

'I'm looking for some mechanic work on cars.'

'We don't have anything. You'll have to try somewhere else,' said the man Edward now knew as John.

'Yes, we do. Wait a minute,' boomed the voice from the pit.

The other man climbed up a ladder sited at the opposite end of the pit, and appeared from the other end of the vehicle. It looked to Edward like he was the boss.

'I'm David. Have you worked with cars before?'

'I've been to college to study engines and how to fix them,' replied Edward.

Unimpressed, David asked again.

'Yes, but have you repaired them?'

'I've dismantled engines and reassembled them. I've even done a Rover one. I know how they work and how to fix them,' replied Edward, attempting to exude as much confidence as he could muster.

'I'm going to as you a few questions. If you answer them right, I can give you a few weeks work,' said David.

He then turned to John, either his business partner or employee; Edward did not know.

'We've got that Sagar-Musgrave job coming up. You know the brewery. They want some work doing on their car, and a couple of jobs on that lorry. An extra pair of hands would help for a few weeks, or we might not get it all done on time.'

'It's your decision,' replied John. Edward now understood the pecking order.

David then proceeded to test Edward with a number of questions on car engines, before asking where he was from and why he was in Leeds. Edward avoided answering with too much detail, but seemed to have generally satisfied his prospective employer with what he said.

'Where are you staying?' asked David.

'I don't know yet. I'll find somewhere this afternoon,' answered Edward.

'You can stay upstairs. It's not fancy but it will do until you find your feet. In fact, you can put your bag in there and start this afternoon. Oh, and I'll pay five shillings a day with the room for free. You'll have to work Saturdays,' said David.

'Thank you, sir. I'm sure it will be fine,' replied Edward.

'It's David. What shall I call you?' enquired David.

'Edward, or Ted,' replied Edward.

'Ted then,' said David.

And that was it. Edward had been in Leeds a matter of hours and he had already got some work and temporary lodgings. As he climbed the worn staircase to the top floor, he felt that life was about to lift-off for him. There were pangs of guilt for leaving the way he had, but he genuinely thought that he had been left with little choice. It was his life and he was going to live it the way he wanted to.

* * *

Emma was usually the first downstairs on working days. She started to lay out the kitchen table for breakfast, lit the stove, and readied a pot for some tea. It was a good few minutes before she noticed the letter on the mantelpiece addressed to her and Austin. She recognised Edward's handwriting straight away, ripped open the envelope and began to read:

'Dad and Ma,

I'm sorry I can't say this to you in person but I think it will be for the best. By the time you read this I will be well away, catching a train to another town. I packed a bag and have enough money to last for a few weeks if I can't find any work straight away, but I surely will. I am going to be a car mechanic.

Bridget is a nice girl but I am not ready to get married to her. Perhaps in time I will be ready, but I just can't even think about it at the moment. I want to do things and see more of the world.

Once I get settled, I will write and let you know where I am. Please don't be too angry or worried about me. Everything will be fine.

With love.

Edward'

'Austin! Austin! Please come down,' Emma shouted up the stairs.

Austin was already half dressed. He pulled on a shirt and rushed downstairs. It was unusual for Emma to shout like that.

'What's the matter? What's wrong?'

'Edward's left home. He said he would,' said Emma, anxiously. It was not clear whether she was about to shed a tear or be angry with her son. Austin read the note he had left.

'I don't know what to say. What can we do? He's already gone,' said Austin.

'Go and find him,' replied Emma.

'He's almost a man, Emma. You know he's always wanted things his way. He could be anywhere by now. I've also got to work today. I can't just drop everything and go looking for someone who is sixteen. Some would say he's made his bed...' replied Austin.

'He's our son. You could ask at the railway station,' suggested Emma.

'And then what? He could have gone to Manchester, Yorkshire, London even. We'll just have to wait until he writes,' replied Austin.

The enormity of what had happened, and the sense in her husband's points suddenly hit Emma. She sat down at the table and put her head in her hands.

'What will we say to Annie and Thomas? And what if that woman appears again?'

'We'll tell them the truth, that he has gone to find work as a car mechanic. We could say he's gone to Wigan, Bolton,

Yorkshire, or somewhere. It doesn't really matter. As for Mrs Hanrahan, well as the proverb says, we should not cross that bridge until we come to it. We don't know if the girl is pregnant. If she isn't then this will probably pass. If she is, well...' replied Austin, without finishing.

'It's a horrible thing he's done, but I never wanted this, Austin,' replied Emma.

'Ma, is breakfast ready?' Thomas had shouted down, interrupting their discussion.

'Not quite. A little longer,' shouted Emma back up the stairs.

'I'll help you with breakfast. I'm sure everything will be alright, Emma,' said Austin.

Emma composed herself and resumed her food preparation tasks. She would deal with Annie and Thomas when they came down, but knew that for the rest of the day she would be worrying about Edward. He had been headstrong about the Hanrahan situation, but he was after all her son and she loved him. Nothing on planet earth would change that, whatever he did.

* * *

Within days Edward had settled in. The 'few weeks work' extended into a few months. He wrote home after three weeks telling Austin and Emma which city he was in, and what he was doing. He provided all the details except a boarding address, suggesting that his accommodation was temporary, and that he would give a more permanent address next time he wrote. Before November was ended, he relented and wrote with the garage address. He knew it was a risk. If Bridget was pregnant, he knew that trouble could already be making its way towards him. But he also knew that there was a limit to how long he could delay being honest with his parents, if he were to have any chance of repairing the damage he had caused.

Emma insisted that Austin make his way over to Leeds as soon as Edward had divulged his address. Austin knew that Emma would never give up on Edward, and decided to visit him on a Sunday. Trains were not as regular at the weekend, but he managed to find something, and was in Leeds at the door of the garage in early afternoon. Edward was not obliged to work on a Sunday, but David had said that if he wanted to, then he would be paid. For Edward, in these early weeks, it was a godsend. He wanted to earn money and save, 'just in case'.

Edward and Austin's eyes met as soon as Austin had appeared at the garage door. Momentarily surprised, he went over and opened it.

'Dad, I'm working,' said Edward.

'On a Sunday, the Sabbath?' replied Austin, though he could see that Edward was in overalls.

'I don't have to but, well, it's the wage I want,' replied Edward.

'So, you got a job working with cars then,' said Austin, in a slightly derisive tone. His career had been built on steam.

'Yes, Dad. So, you found me then,' said Edward.

'You did write and tell us where you were. I'm thankful for that but you should have said sooner,' said Austin.

'I didn't know where I would be,' replied Edward.

'Your mother's been worried sick about you,' said Austin.

'I'm sorry but I had no choice,' replied Edward.

'You always had a choice, Edward. You know that,' said Austin.

Edward did not know what to say next. His mind then started to race. What had happened with Bridget? Was she going to have his baby? He did not really want to ask about it, hoping the subject would simply go away.

Austin pre-empted any questions Edward might have but was reluctant to ask.

'Bridget is not pregnant, though she is very upset. And Mrs Hanrahan is very angry with you. She visited again, and we had to listen to what she had to say, Edward. It was not a good thing. Your mother was very upset. Angry at what you have done, upset at the way you left, and generally disappointed with the way you dealt with everything. Is this how you are going to be when you are older?' said Austin.

Edward turned away from looking at his father. He felt, and no doubt looked, sheepish. His father was right and he did feel guilty. But then again it had all worked out. Bridget was not going to have a baby, and perhaps the whole affair would soon be forgotten about.

'Would you like some tea, Dad. I can make you some upstairs,' suggested Edward, attempting to deflect the conversation in a more agreeable direction.

'I will, but I can't stay for too long. I need to get a train back to Middleton. Work in the morning,' replied Austin.

Austin followed Edward upstairs and discussed with him what should happen next. Both men agreed that Edward should stay in Leeds, 'for the time being', until the dust had fully settled back at home. In time, Edward would return, not necessarily to the family home, but much closer to Middleton. Edward also agreed to write more frequently, even sending a postcard or two, keeping Austin and Emma informed of his whereabouts, working arrangements, and plans. While awkward at first, the parting was as good as could be expected, with Edward even promising a visit in early 1914.

* * *

Edward's current run of luck held further. The temporary job at David's Rover workshop stretched into over five months, but by late spring the surge of work that garage had experienced had diminished. He was told that they could no longer give him a wage, but that one of their customers was looking for somebody to look after their cars, and act as an occasional chauffeur. It was Mr Sagar-Musgrave, owner of the first car he had worked on, and a local brewery owner. By coincidence, the butler, a Mr Lowes, had called into the garage and asked David if he knew of anybody. Edward's work and his recently found skills had paid off, David had recommended him. It solved the workshop's problem, laying off Edward, and the customer's problem. Everyone was happy about the new arrangement, especially Edward.

He needed a driving licence. As luck would have it, he had turned seventeen in May and could apply for one at Leeds Council Office a short walk away. With his experience, even given his current address in a Rover garage, it was never going to be a problem. All he had to do was ask. There was a short period between Edward finishing at the garage and him starting his new job. David allowed him to continue to use the upstairs room for a few weeks, and Edward decided that the break would be a good time to visit home in Middleton.

Edward was expected when he arrived back at Dale House. He had, sensibly, dropped a postcard the previous day indicating the time he would arrive, and how long he planned to stay. He had chosen a Sunday and timed his arrival for dinner. The family ate earlier on a Sunday than in the rest of the week, and it was always the best meal of the week.

Crossing the footbridge at the top of Hilton Fold Lane brought back guilty memories of how he left. A few more steps and he would be standing at the front door. His heart began to pound in anticipation. Although he had written to his mother, and she had written back, on multiple occasions, he could not be sure what sort of reception there would be. After all, he had not seen her for nearly nine months.

Annie saw him as soon as he started walking around the grass oval in front of the house. She ran up and threw her arms around him.

'I've really missed you. All of us have.'

Edward hugged her in return.

'I've missed you as well. There is much to tell,' replied Edward.

'Let's go straight in. Mother is expecting you. She's prepared something special today,' said Annie.

That was a relief to Edward. It would be a welcome, not an admonishment. At least not yet. They both walked inside the house.

'Edward!' Emma ran over and hugged him as tight as she could.

'Ma,' replied Edward. He felt the need to continue.

'Ma, I'm sorry for leaving the way I did.'

'You waited weeks before you wrote, Edward. I was worried to death; I didn't sleep...'

Emma paused to let it sink in before continuing.

'But now it's in the past. Just don't ever do it again,' replied Emma.

'No, Ma,' said Edward, surprised his mother was able to leave the subject so quickly.

'How was the journey?' asked Emma.

'It was good, Ma. Leeds is not so far away. As I wrote on the postcard, I've just finished a job but I've found another. I'll tell you about it when dad is home,' replied Edward.

'He's out for a stroll with Thomas. They've gone up to the Rochdale to watch some of the boats. I doubt he will be long now; he knows what time we will be eating,' said Emma.

Edward remembered his father's habit. He liked to walk on the canal towpath and watch the various types of narrowboat sail up and down. It was the same canal that ran through Littleborough. He seemed to feel connected to it in some way.

'If you don't mind, Ma, I'll sit down and read the paper. I've starting buying one quite often, just like father. I like to see what's going on. There's talk of war, you know,' replied Edward.

'I know. Your father keeps telling me about these things he keeps reading. It's very worrying. But at least Parliament passed the Irish Home Rule Act. He approved of that. Your grandfather always seemed to want to see Ireland become independent, and Austin's the same. I don't know why. He's as British as I am, Catholic or not,' said Emma.

'Edward.'

'You're back.'

Austin and Thomas had appeared, just as Emma was finishing.

'I may be British but I still want to see a free Ireland. There's been enough bloodshed. I might not be political but there are some things...' said Austin.

'You're always saying that you aren't political, and yet you always seem to have a view. Anyway, let's not talk about that. Edward is home. I want to know what he's been doing,' said Emma.

Emma laid out the table for an early evening meal, a roast beef special as she had taken to calling it. It was just as Edward remembered, fresh vegetables and roast beef with a tasty garnish of gravy followed by an apple pie. He had missed his mother's cooking.

'You have a new job, Edward?' enquired Austin, as Emma and Annie cleared the table.

'Yes. It's working for a family who live on the edge of Leeds, the Sagar-Musgraves. They own a brewery in the centre and need someone to look after their cars, and drive them around. I've asked for a driving licence. It's a big house and I'll have accommodation in the servants' quarters. The wage is quite good too. Better than I could get in a mill. It's worked out quite well, Dad,' replied Edward.

'You'll write with an address, Edward,' interjected Emma.

'Of course, Ma,' replied Edward, not that he had much of an option.

'See that you do,' said Emma.

Edward nodded. Having had a run of good luck he would not want anything to interrupt it. He was starting to think he might always be lucky.

Edward spent most of the week at home, and for a time everything seemed to normalise. Given the amount of free time he had, Edward had wanted to walk around Middleton, but thought better of it. There was still a risk he might encounter Bridget, or even worse her mother. He wanted to avoid that. Even though many months had passed, the situation might still be very raw. It would serve no one's purpose to raise it again. Additional time at home, he still called it that, would also mean more time with his mother. He had left in a rush and he felt she deserved more of his attention. Before leaving for Leeds he promised, both to himself and his mother, that he would never get into that kind of situation with a woman ever again. Resolute in his assurances, the following Saturday he caught a train from Middleton to resume his new life in Yorkshire.

* * *

Red Hall had been built near the village of Shadwell a few miles out of Leeds, just off the Wetherby road. It was a pragmatic decision to take the job. Living in the centre of Leeds had been quite exciting after the comparatively quiet villages of Middleton and Littleborough. So, to take a job in somewhere so rural would have been something of a shock. But there were compensations. He had control over two cars and would no doubt find excuses to drive them, legitimate or otherwise. Indeed, during the first few weeks of his employment he made a point of being indispensable when a task involving a journey was involved. It was also not difficult for Edward to find fault with the running of the vehicles, an excuse to drive into town to collect a needed part, or discuss a problem with his old employers at the Rover garage. But a lot of the time it was not necessary. Mr Robert Sagar Musgrave, the family business brewery manager, would require Edward to drive him to and from the Leeds brewery almost every day. Sometimes he would require Edward to wait around for driving duties during the day, but on most days his only duty would be to collect his employer at some pre-agreed time. It was a good life, nothing like the trials of working in a mill or even the long days of working in the Rover garage. He felt lucky again.

The Sagar Musgraves were still in mourning for the death of the matron of the family, Mrs Clara Sagar Musgrave, who had died only two months earlier. Arriving only a matter of weeks later, Edward soon detected the sombre mood in the household. It was not only with the family, but with the staff as well; she had been well liked. Being a military man, a colonel in the West Yorkshire Regiment, Abraham Sagar Musgrave took far less interest in the business. He was also frequently away, so was not someone Edward had dealings with very often. As for the servants, in addition to the butler, there was a cook, Lucy Walker, and a maid, Mildred Strudwick. So long as he kept on the right side of the butler, and 'Mr Robert', as the staff called their employer, life would remain very easy indeed.

An advantage of living in Red Hall was that he would see daily newspapers after the family had finished with them. Mr Lowes showed surprisingly little interest in the news, and would pass on any read newspapers to Edward at the end of each day. Edward had a different view. The newspapers were not only an interest for him, but were a connection to the outside world. It was also starting to become an essential part of his job. On their journey to the brewery each day, his employer would increasingly ask for Edward's views on whether Britain should 'get involved' in the fracas that had been enveloping Eastern Europe during the summer. He had to have an opinion or Mr Robert might think him stupid.

It was Monday 3 August 1914. For Edward the morning routines were the same as any other day, but the mood in the household had changed. Edward knew what the topic of conversation would be on the way into Leeds.

'You no doubt saw the news over the weekend, Edward. Germany has declared war on Russia. My brother telephoned me last night. His unit has been told to be ready to mobilise. He also said that Germany had declared war on France. That's not in the newspapers I've seen just yet, but it will be. We could be at war soon. What do you make of this latest development, Edward?' asked Mr Sagar Musgrave.

'I'll do my duty, sir. My father sent me a copy of the Manchester Guardian from last week. It's a few days old but they are adamant that Britain should not be dragged into a war. They say we should stay neutral. They said that our attitude should remain doubtful, and that it will be both a crime and an act of supreme and gratuitous folly, if we get involved in it. My father agrees with them. He says we should be less like animals,' replied Edward.

'So said the Times, Edward. But I fear we will have no choice in the matter before long. Germany is demanding immediate passage of its troops through Belgium, which wants to be neutral. If they do march through Belgium, and into France, then Britain will have to make a decision. Should it defend France and Belgium, or stay out of it? My brother thinks the decision has already been made. We will know within days, perhaps even hours,' said Mr Sagar Musgrave.

'Yes, sir. I don't know what to say. We shall just have to see,' replied Edward.

'How old are you, Edward? Seventeen?' asked Mr Sagar Musgrave.

'Yes, sir,' replied Edward.

'You are still too young then. And I'm just too old by a year. I'm sure we'll find some way of doing what we need to. Do your bit as my brother said yesterday, when we talked about the very same thing,' said Mr Sagar Musgrave.

'Yes, sir,' replied Edward.

'I've got some meetings around Leeds today, so you'll need to stay with me. Abraham says that we should prepare for the worst, so that's what we'll have to do. God help us,' said Mr Sagar Musgrave.

Forty-eight hours later, with Germany breaking its treaty agreement with France and Great Britain, the King had declared that the country was at war with Germany. Every newspaper on August fifth had some variant or other on the headline: 'Great Britain at War with Germany'. And everyone suddenly had an interest in, or opinion on the subject. One matter though was clear, Germany was the transgressor and Britain was on the side of the just.

* * *

At first the war seemed remote. It was something read about in the newspapers. Naval battles took place, ships sank, and in the more distant fields of Europe, men started to fight other men on the battlefield. But the war soon seemed to extend into a global conflagration. Countries far away became embroiled in the turmoil. The Empire began to send men to defend the Motherland; Canada, Australia, New Zealand, India and South Africa. At home the call went out for 'fighting men'; they were 'urgently needed'. Tens of thousands started to sign-up across the nation, all heeding the call of King and Country.

None of this passed by Edward. Swept up in the fervour of 'doing one's duty' he felt he had to join the many. He knew that both his employer and his family would object. Both parties seemed to think that he might face a compulsory draft at some point, but both would likely tell him to wait until the letter came. But Edward saw it differently. It's not that he wanted to go to war, but he did want to be seen as a hero, a rescuer, a saviour of the country. As autumn started his mind had been made up. He was going to join up whatever anyone else had to say about it.

'Tell him I've gone to join up,' said Edward to Mr Lowes, the butler.

Edward wanted to avoid telling his employer directly, although he hoped that they would understand. He knew that there might be a problem if there was a face-to-face conversation, and he also knew that if he signed up in Leeds, 'Mr Abraham' might be involved in some way. That might also be a problem. His solution was to go back to Manchester and enlist there. The plan would be to enlist first, and then go back home to Middleton and tell his parents. It was a risk of course, as they would also know that he was too young. But then he knew of so many others of his age who were answering the call.

The recruiting sergeant already had a pen and paper in hand. It was a production line task for him and he needed to be quick. He barely looked at Edward as the forms were completed.

'Age and date of birth,' the sergeant demanded.

'18 sir. The 29th May 1896,' replied Edward.

It was a bare faced lie. Edward had been born that same day in 1897, but the sergeant seemed to show little interest.

'Trade?' asked the sergeant.

'Spinner, cotton mill sir,' replied Edward. This was also a lie but from Edward's point of view he did not want to give any more information away.

'Next of kin and their address?' asked the sergeant,

'Dale House, Middleton, Manchester, sir. No, er, Red Hall, Shadwell, Leeds,' replied Edward.

The sergeant finally looked straight at him. Edward flushed at the mistake.

'Well. Which is it?' demanded the sergeant.

'Red Hall, sir. I'm sorry,' replied Edward. He did not want to give the Middleton address in case his parents were difficult about him enlisting.

Irritated, the sergeant crossed out the Middleton address, leaving Red Hall intact.

'You'll report in Deal on the eleventh. Understood?' asked the sergeant.

'Yes, sir,' replied Edward.

'Next.' The sergeant had already lost interest in Edward and was already starting to fill in the paperwork for the next recruit.

Edward left the makeshift office. He was in the army now.

* * *

He came clean about his enlistment as soon as Austin and Emma were together at home. They were remarkably sanguine about it. He had expected them both to object, but the world had significantly changed since his last visit. Although seventeen, they both knew that the army would take him in June 1915, with or without their consent. And that was only seven months away. They could either make the best of the time they had with him, or use it to argue about whether he should join voluntarily this year, or be compulsorily enlisted next. In the end it was pragmatism that was required, not another argument. Edward had joined and would probably find another way, even if they made trouble for him.

The whole family were up early on the day of his departure, each member of the family giving him a hug and wishing him well. Emma, particularly upset, tearfully asked him to write 'at least once a week'. 'I will, Ma' was the reply. 'All the best, son,' were the last words from Austin, as Edward opened the front door and left for the station.

No one really knew when they might see him next.

Chapter 8

WAR

It was not deliberate; it simply happened.

With Austin and Emma apparently on the move every few years, Austin's relationship with his siblings had started to drift. Emma was much better, as women often are. She used to visit her sister in Bolton on quite a regular basis, and likewise, her sister visited her almost as frequently. During their time in Hindley the whole family would visit Austin's mother, brothers, and sisters, much more often. But Littleborough, Stockport and Middleton seemed so much further away. It was not really. A change, perhaps two, on the railway network, and another half hour or so in time, and they could still get there and back on a Sunday. But the demands of daily life rolled on. Letters and postcards replaced visits, and even they became less constant.

But the onset of war changed everything. Austin's brother, John, had been a member of the Farnworth Company of the Loyal North Lancashire Territorials since 1894. As a Sergeant it was inevitable that he would be one of the first men to be mobilised, and so it was. John's equally long tenure at Edmund Potter's chemical works in Little Lever had to be put on hold. Furnacemen could be far more easily replaced than a fully trained and experienced member of Britain's volunteer army. Kitchener needed him and his fellows, and by the end of the year he had already been deployed to the Western Front to help repel Germany's initial offensive moves. Ada, John's wife, had been left on her own to feed and clothe her four remaining children, one of whom was barely six months old when John was deployed.

As soon as he was told the news about John, Austin felt the need to step in and help. It was what families were supposed to do, rally round in times of need. Austin was the elder of the two brothers. At the age of forty-five the army considered him to be too old to be of interest. Seven years too old for the regular army and three years too old for the special reserve force; serving would no longer be for him. Austin's role would be to keep the domestic wheels of industry turning and to support the war effort wherever, and whenever, he could. So that is what he would try and do, with family first in the order of support.

John and Ada had moved from Kent Street to Lorne Street just after Edward had been born. It was deemed to be a bit closer to Potters, which would of course mean a shorter walk to work. So, there was now another Edward in the family. It was not that they lacked imagination, but tradition still demanded that the Christian names of previous generations be passed down to the next. Interestingly, John and Ada had named their own first born, Austin, although Austin was not sure whether this was after their own grandfather, or him. Sadly, he died at the age of five, although by that time they had another son, Thomas. Their third, 'Young John', also died as an infant, and their first daughter, Elizabeth, was born in 1910. Margaret appeared in 1912 and Edward in 1914. It was Margaret they were worried about. She was a sickly child and Ada always seemed to be fussing about her health, particularly as she had already lost two before.

Mary, Austin's mother, also tried to step in to help, but she was now sixty-seven and starting to suffer failing health herself. Austin knew that he and Emma would have to be the ones to support his sister-in-law, emotionally, and financially if necessary. There were going to be some tough times ahead for the family, and probably every family, as the war wore on. Unlike many, he was sceptical of the 'war over by Christmas' trope promoted by certain newspapers and public figures.

* * *

While Austin and Emma had been increasing their visits to Ada and Mary, Edward was nearly three hundred miles away at the Royal Marines Recruit Depot in Deal, Kent. He was in his first weeks of basic training, and doing his best to get on with other sappers from Manchester.

'I saw you on the London train,' said Edward.

'Yes. We should have known, shouldn't we?' replied another young man of similar age to Edward.

'I'm Edward Melia, Ted for short,' said Edward.

'John. John Pilling,' replied John.

Along with others, they had both caught the train to London and made another connection from St. Pancras to Deal. It was on the Deal train that they realised that they were probably heading to the same place.

'Marines?' enquired Edward.

John nodded.

'I've told them I want to work with motor engines. I have some experience. What about you?' asked John.

This was even more interesting to Edward.

'I didn't know you could do that. I worked in a car garage in Leeds. I've got a driving licence as well,' replied Edward.

'Did you tell them that?' asked John.

'I said I was a cotton spinner on the forms. Perhaps I'll tell them I'm good with engines when I get there,' replied Edward.

'You should. We'll still have basic training to do, but I'll learn more about engines and will end up with a trade as a mechanic. It will be more useful when the war ends; it will probably be over by spring,' said John.

'Some were saying that it would be over by Christmas, but I don't think so. My father thinks it could be much more than a year. The Hun have a good army. Not as good as ours, mind. But good all the same,' replied Edward.

'Well, make sure you tell them soon, or you'll end up behind a gun and not the wheel of a motor car, or lorry,' said John.

'I will. Where are you from? I know you got on at Manchester,' enquired Edward.

'Bolton, Bradshaw. It's a village on the edge of the town,' replied John.

'Oh. My father is from Farnworth. I bet he knows that village. They're living in Middleton now, though I've been living in Leeds. I told my employer – he owns a brewery you know – that I thought it was my duty to sign up,' said Edward.

'My Uncle said it was a bad idea. He didn't want me to go. Both my mother and father died when I was young. I live with him now. The truth is I'm not quite eighteen yet. I will be in a few weeks, but I didn't want to miss the fun. You won't tell on me, will you?' said John.

'Course not. It's the same with me,' replied Edward, realising that there would probably be quite a few of his new comrades who were under age, and that he was already sharing secrets with his new found friend.

* * *

Edward's initial training regime was the same as for any other short term service recruit, and after six weeks he would have been released for deployment with only some basic training in infantry skills. However, a timely conversation with a sergeant shortly after his arrival at Deal changed the usual course of instruction. Men were in short supply, and men with mechanical skills were at a premium. He was notified that he was to stay at Deal, and undergo a full six months training together with some more targeted schooling in the sort of machines the navy and army were using in the war effort.

One day's training at Deal was much the same as the next. A 5.30am bugle reveille would be followed by some housekeeping duties, a mug of tea, and an hour and a half parade. Another parade followed breakfast and another after lunch. Training in the use of rifles, naval guns, and swimming, were also included during the first months of 1915. The optimism of 1914 soon faded, with the frustrations of the failures to gain ground at Neuve Chapelle and Gallipoli. It was clear by spring that this was not going to be a short war, and that sense had rippled down to the new recruits. Edward realised that his 'three years or duration of the war' commitment could be a lot longer. Germany and Austria-Hungary were already proving to be more formidable opponents than almost anyone in the country would have believed a year earlier.

Unfortunately, Edward's erstwhile run of good luck was about to run out, and in an unexpected situation.

'Private,' instructed the corporal.

'Sir,' replied Edward.

Together with half a dozen other aspirant motor mechanics, Edward had been assigned to a temporary training area away from the barracks. It centred on a large building that looked like it might have been used as a barn before the war. The single large room was packed full of various types of mechanised machinery, including a couple of Thorneycroft J types, a Pierce-Arrow armoured anti-aircraft lorry, a Rolls Royce armoured car, and a Talbot armoured car. Some of these were at the cutting edge of military technology, and Edward and his comrades were expected to know each one of these vehicles inside out by the time they finished their training.

'Bring that wheel over here,' said the corporal.

Two of the team were being given instruction on changing a wheel on one of the Thorneycroft lorries. It was a simple task but there was always a process that must be followed. Edward had long since learned that he had to do things 'by the book'.

'Yes, sir,' replied Edward.

He picked up a moderately heavy single solid wheel which had been leant against a nearby wall, and then began to walk back to the three waiting men, the corporal and two other private trainees. It was ostensibly a straightforward and harmless command, the sort of thing that would likely be repeated lots of times.

With his eyes focused on the corporal he just did not see it. Without carrying the wheel Edward might have steadied himself, but with the object in his hands he stood little chance. Every instruction or command always had to be executed at pace. Edward was not even walking. In fact, he was almost trotting when he slipped on a small slick of recently spilled oil pooled on the hard concrete surface.

He screamed in pain. His left knee had given way and hit the floor as its greasy surface came into contact with his shoe. The wheel followed his legs to the floor, landing with a least half its weight on his knee and the other half on the ground.

'Get to it. Help him!' shouted the corporal.

The two trainees rushed to remove the wheel and help Edward to his feet.

'I'm alright, sir,' said Edward.

The corporal looked at Edward who by now looked ashen and in obvious shock. He decided that he was not alright.

'Let's get you looked over. Smith, Alderton. Take him to hospital.'

'Yes, sir,' replied the two privates.

After that there would be several weeks of compulsory rest for Edward. He was lucky in that he had not broken anything, but the fall had triggered a latent health problem that until now he had not been aware of.

He had expected to be assigned to Chatham in June, but it was not until July 15th that he finally walked, or limped, through the doors of the Chatham Depot. It was obvious to his superiors that Edward had a problem. Although he was walking again, he struggled to bend his left knee. It was clear that he would be unfit for duty in the trenches, and quite possibly in any role supporting mechanised units.

After persevering for a few weeks in July and early August, Edward was sent for a formal diagnosis, and to ascertain whether there was any chance he might be assigned to full duties. The medical diagnosis was not good. Edward had been told that he had septic arthritis, possibly ignited by his fall a couple of months earlier. They were also not optimistic about his knee, calling it ankylosis of the knee joint. It appeared that there was little they could do about it. He had lost over half the movement in that knee and it would likely be a permanent problem. With the medical investigation over, his fate was already sealed. The Royal Marines had no need of anyone who was not in near perfect health. Edward was medically discharged on September 1st 1915. He had been trained, and had tinkered with some vehicles for a few months, but had not fired a shot at the enemy. Edward was going home.

* * *

The Balderstone mill of Eagle Spinning Mill Company Ltd was just another one of the many mills dotted around Lancashire. Austin had heard of it but it did not really mean much to him. Moston Mill's bleachworks had even had dealings with them from time to time, but they were just another customer. All that changed on March 10th 1915, when the mill caught fire causing over twenty thousand pounds worth of damage. Austin had read about it in the Manchester Evening News and the Cotton Factory Times shortly after it had happened, but had almost forgotten about it a few weeks later.

Henry Jones, manager of the Moston mills, knew Arthur Bentley, manager of the Eagle Spinning Mill, quite well. Arthur was in more than a pickle. With so many men committed to war work of one form or another, he needed help to get his mill back up and running. Henry Jones thought he could help, but first needed to talk to Austin. He would help if he could, but he needed Austin's agreement that Moston Mill's operations would remain largely unaffected. The proposal was that Austin would step in for a period of six months or so to help get the Eagle Mill put back into wartime level operation. There would be a financial incentive both for Moston, and for Austin, on a successful implementation of the arrangement.

Austin agreed straight away, fully aware that his brother John was hundreds of miles away fighting in the trenches of the Western Front, and that Edward was in training in Deal. He wanted to play his part however he could, and if that meant helping out while the senior engineer of another mill was at war, then so be it. The journey was a little further than Moston, involving a change at Middleton Junction and a tram from Rochdale Station, but it was not so bad. And it was only for a matter of months.

Eagle Mill had some similarities to Moston Mill in that it was a ring mill, usually running over forty thousand ring spindles and sixty thousand mule spindles. The fire had destroyed a good number of those spindles and had damaged part of the mill engine. Once the structural damage had been repaired, and with the help of a retired engineer, Austin set to work on repairing the mill engine and installing replacement mules. By the time Edward had returned to Middleton the work was quite advanced, and there was an expectation that early in 1916 the mill would be back to full operation, or at least to the production levels appropriate to the wartime situation.

There were two personal benefits to Austin as a result of him undertaking this additional work. Although he already had a robust reputation amongst the engineers and managers of the cotton industry in the East side of Manchester, news of his achievement had already spread amongst members of the Royal Exchange. In time, this would help his career. However, of more immediate benefit was the financial incentive provided, a bonus for completing the work. Austin had been saving hard for some years, but this particular financial reward meant that the family would no longer need to rent. They were finally able to join the increasing ranks of property owners and buy their own house.

* * *

August 1917.

John had finally been issued with a gas mask. They called it a small box respirator. It was a life saver, although he hoped he never had to use it. Almost triangular in shape around the head, and with two large bug eye lenses for seeing through, it was not too heavy. An exhale valve and rubber hose from the mouth connected to a cannister which hung around his neck. Inside the oval shaped cannister, cotton and wire gauze filters acted to stop any poisonous chemicals passing through.

John's unit had been warned that the Germans might attempt a poison gas attack at any time, and they had all been told to carry their masks as a precautionary measure. Not a single man liked to wear them, but they all knew that they were necessary. Stories of what happened in Ypres two years earlier abounded. Hundreds of men had been caught by surprise, unable to defend themselves from the latest deadly weapon to be deployed on the battlefield.

'Gas! Gas! Gas!' The cry went out.

It was happening. John's comrades looked at each other in fear. Only slightly reassured by their new equipment, the concern was one of whether it would work to keep them alive.

They instantly started checking each other's apparatus, seals, hoses, and clips.

'What is it?' shouted someone unseen, from a trench about thirty yards away.

John did not recognise the voice but he understood the question. It was of course gas, but what sort of gas? The Germans had started with chlorine, but had more recently been using phosgene, and now mustard gas. Mustard gas was the most feared. Even a slight exposure to the skin would cause blisters and unimaginable pain.

'It's chlorine!'

Someone else shouted back. It was a relief of a sort, although the Germans could not be trusted. They now mixed chlorine and phosgene to increase the former's potency.

John lifted a mirror attached to a pole above the trench. He twisted it left and right to get a good look. It was heading their way. A greenish yellow cloud, no more than about twenty feet in the air was slowly rolling towards them, vaguely sizzling as it did. There was no obvious escape from it. He knew he was in the worst position he could be. The gas was heavy, and would concentrate the closer to the ground it was. John knew it would be even stronger in the trenches, but what could he do? If he climbed out, he might be shot, and if he attempted to retreat, he would be disciplined. And he was a sergeant. His invariably younger and less experienced subordinates would be looking towards him for comfort and reassurance.

'It will be alright lads. We've got the best kit there is. It will soon pass. Just hold your nerve,' he shouted across the trench.

'Yes, Sergeant,' replied two of his men; the others just stared in fear.

John knew that it could be hours of torment, hours of fear.

An unexpected breeze suddenly appeared. The rolling veil of poison, now barely yards away, began to shift to John's left, revealing what appeared to be a German infantry assault. Adumbrated shadows of masked men carrying weapons pointing at John became sharp outlines, targets.

'Fire at will!' came the command.

Dozens of Tommy heads appeared above their trenches and began firing rifles. The enemy had little chance. They were in close formation and difficult to miss, as each man fired a dozen rounds or more per minute.

'Rückzug! Rückzug!

It did not take very long for the advancing troops to realise that the game was up. They were being mown down by the dozen, and wearing masks did not help. The problems were no doubt the same for the German equipment, difficulty in breathing, lens fogging and misting, and the general heat and exhaustion caused by wearing them for hours on end. They might have had a chance had the light breeze not appeared, but this was not going to be their day.

What was left of the advance retreated back to its own summer baked mud shelter. Saved by a quirk of nature, the German advance had failed. John felt lucky on that occasion, but knew he could never be sure if it would hold another day.

* * *

20 November 1917.

The heat and sun had been almost unbearable during the summer. There was little protection from anything nature threw at him and his men at any time in the year. The elements were almost as deadly as the enemy. Sunstroke in the summer and frostbite in the winter. There was no escape from it. As the autumn weather brought rain, the landscape liquified. Occasional shelling removed whatever was left of the natural environment, reducing trees and shrubs to blackened rubble, and churning up the sodden earth time and time again. Corpulent rats, increasingly brazen, foraged for food in the shared earthworks. It was always a challenge to prevent them from finding and gnawing at the army's food supply, and it was no different for John's unit. There was competition to catch and kill them.

After weeks of little happening the men had started to become a little bored. It was near impossible to train in the trenches, so John had to keep them occupied by shoring up weakening defences, digging out gun emplacements, and other useful activities. It was hard work but they had to do something. There was only so much rat hunting that a man could do.

Less than a hundred miles from Calais was Cambrai, the capital of what the French call the Cambresis region. John had little interest in its culture or history. To him it was where the Germans were believed to have a local headquarters. He and his men were dug-in somewhere between Havrincourt and Villers, at the sharp end of the Western Front. What felt like an interminable wait was about to be ended with orders to attack.

After days of silence the British artillery abruptly opened fire. There was no warning to either side.

Tanks, dozens of them, were suddenly on the move. Without warning, several of those nearby suddenly ran straight over their own trenches, forcing men to rush away. Biplanes appeared overhead, all bearing in the direction of the German lines.

'Somethings afoot,' shouted John, barely audible above the noise.

'You can say that again. They look like Mark IVs.' said John to Tommy, his corporal.

'There must be a hundred or more,' replied Tommy.

As far as the eye could see, green coloured machines of war were advancing towards the German lines, each one distinguished by only a number and red and white recognition stripes at the front of either side. Lewis guns were blazing in response to enemy fire.

Then the order came through. They were to advance behind a mechanised steel wall of destruction.

'We're going over the top lads,' commanded John. He could see the terror in each man's eyes, but they all knew there was little choice.

'Move on my signal,' shouted John.

The twenty-six remaining men of his platoon readied themselves.

'Fix bayonets! Fix bayonets! Fix bayonets!' The order from his commanding officer echoed across the nearby trenches. Similar calls were being repeated up and down the line. The clicks and snaps of equipment being attached reverberated everywhere.

'Fweeeeeeeeeeet.'

Whistles were blown signalling everyone to move, whereupon the line immediately erupted into a cacophony of shouting. Hundreds of men, rifles pointed at the enemy, climbed over the trench line, and started nervously advancing through the smoke-filled chaos of shell holes and debris littered about no man's land. Some did not even make it past the line, falling to a lethal projectile even as they appeared over the top.

The shelling continued as they advanced towards the enemy gun positions. As they neared, John could hear orders being shouted in German. He had no idea what was being said, but could guess. They sounded panicked, much as his own people might in the face of an onslaught the other way.

'Behind that tank as best you can,' shouted John, pointing at the nearest one several hundred feet away. The tanks were taking the worst of the fire but there were still shots being fired in his direction.

Whistles were being blown and arms were waving to move ahead. Some of the brave, or foolhardy, were already too close. Men were falling ahead of him. How they had got there so quickly he had no idea, but there they were. Part of his job was to keep his platoon as safe as he could, and three years on the front lines had told him that being at the head of an advance was never a good idea. He was as brave as the next man but that did not mean he was foolhardy.

The Germans had been caught by surprise. They were unprepared for this change in tactics and were no match for the British mass tank advance. The belt of barbed wire they had erected were a feeble defence, and the tadpole tailed tanks soon crushed a route through for the infantry. By the end of the first day the battle had gained almost seven kilometres into the Hindenburg line. The following day more ground had been taken, but attempts to take even more were being fiercely resisted. The order came through to dig-in for winter and consolidate what they had.

* * *

30 November 1917.

John had ordered his platoon to start digging as soon as he was given the command. He knew that they might well be there for some months. It had happened before and would no doubt happen again. But the Germans had started reorganising, and had already developed new retaliatory tactics, their own response to the unwelcome British surprise.

Rifle shots and machine guns were being fired.

'Where are they? Anyone?' John could not see what was going on.

'Over there!' shouted Edwards.

More shots from a different direction.

'Shoot at will. But don't waste bullets. Shoot only when you've got something to shoot at!' shouted John.

He should not have needed to say it but some of the lads were a little trigger happy. And ammunition was not limitless. A couple of his platoon started shooting, then another half dozen more. He could not see what was going on.

'Aaaaagh!!'

A stray bullet had caught him in his left hand. Blood started to stream from the wound.

Tommy pulled some first aid bandages from the kit round his belt and wrapped them round John's hand. John was in pain but he still needed to think.

A heavily accented voice shouted from the nearby wood.

'You are surrounded. Put down your weapons!'

The firing continued on both sides.

'Tommy. See how many bullets the lads have,' John was struggling with the pain but he knew it was not life threatening. But he also knew he needed some proper medical attention.

There were less than twenty men nearby, spread over two foxholes. There had not been the time to dig a full trench so they were not in a strong position. John inspected his own Lee-Enfield, and counted the 303s he still had left. It had a ten round box magazine, and his best men could fire thirty rounds a minute. If they were genuinely surrounded there was no chance of getting more ammunition. He would have to make a choice.

Tommy took only minutes to assess the situation.

'Not enough, John. Maybe a few hours,' replied Tommy.

He did not disclose a number; he had no need to.

By now the Germans were more obvious. The platoon was indeed surrounded and looked to be outnumbered by four or five to one. Should he fight or surrender?

'What do you think, Tommy? It's hard for me to think properly.'

'I don't think we can win this one, John. It would be a slaughter. We could hold out for a few hours but by the looks and sounds of it...' replied Tommy.

John held his chin in his only good hand, his right, as if to think. There was no glory in surrender, but even less in death.

He then looked at the young fearful faces of his men. They would do what they were told; he knew that. A decision had to be made, and quickly.

'Put your weapons down. Show them a white handkerchief,' ordered John.

Tommy tied a white piece of cloth to the bayonet of a rifle and thrust it into the air.

Sixty or seventy Germans, all with weapons pointed at John's platoon, advanced towards him. When he reached John's position, a senior officer spoke directly to John, almost in perfect English.

'The war is over with for you and your men. Put your hands behind your heads.'

He had been fighting since late 1914 and this was how it was going to end for him, taken as a prisoner of war a few miles from Cambrais. It was not a hero's ending, but at least he and his men were alive. And they would have a story to tell.

* * *

Ada's last letter from John had been dated October 26th, over a month earlier. She usually wrote to him weekly, but he usually wrote back once every two weeks. They both used to write twice weekly in the early stages of the war, but the demands of home and the trenches were limiting. It was odd that she had not had a letter in November, and Ada was naturally worried. It was not like John to miss routine, whatever the circumstances of his situation.

A telegram arrived a few days before the end of November. It was the one communication that everyone dreaded. Ada knew what it was before even reading it. Handwritten on buff paper it was short and to the point.

Under the 'Post Office Telegraphs' printed information were the time and where the instructions were received, and the scarce details available:

'216 Lorne Street, Farnworth.

Regret to inform you Sergeant John Melia, British Army, reported missing.'

Stamped Farnworth November 28th, that was all the information she had. It was not even addressed to her.

Ada sank into the nearest chair, bewildered by the news. It told her nothing. Was he alive or was he dead? Had he been taken prisoner, or perhaps he was just lost, or even in hiding?

Half an hour after receiving the news, she left her own house and walked over to Mary's a few streets away. John's mother would have to be told, and it served no real purpose to delay. Mary's reaction was the same as most mothers. Although a practical woman she was now seventy years old and prone to mild melancholia. She was soon in tears.

'He's just missing, Mary. He might be alright. We just don't know what happened,' said Ada.

Mary was difficult to console. She had lost a husband and was in no mind to start losing her children. There had been enough death in the family already.

'It's too much. Austin will know what to do,' replied Mary.

Ada wrote a postcard to Austin and had posted it before the morning was over.

Two evenings later both Austin and Emma called in to see Ada to offer help.

'I don't know what you can do. Is there anyone in the army you can ask? Will there be any details? How can I find out if he is alive?' asked Ada.

Austin agreed to make enquiries but he knew that specific information would be hard to come by. He might not even find out exactly where his brother had been posted, such were the restrictions of censorship and military secrecy. They would just have to wait.

Christmas passed, and then spring. The news was hardly good, with the Germans having reached within a hundred and twenty kilometres of Paris, and the Spanish Flu epidemic now taking hold. By the end of May Ada had spent six anxious months without any news of John. That changed on June 21st.

Another morning knock on the door and another telegram.

'Happy inform you Sergeant John Melia, British Army, reported prisoner Altdamm'

'Further information Central Prisoner Committee, Thurloe Place, Kensington'

He was alive. It had taken seven months for the news to reach her, seven months of worry, stress, and anxiety, but she now knew he was alive. Even better, he was now out of the war.

* * *

John's hand was a mess.

Notwithstanding his medical condition there was still an attempt to interrogate him, but he really did know very little.

What he did know was already useless to them. The Cambrai offensive had significantly changed the situation. Any knowledge about positions and deployment was no longer relevant, several kilometres out of date. Soon realising this, he was taken to a field hospital in Le Cateau, close to the Belgian border, where he later considered his treatment very good.

But that was about to change.

Once the immediate medical needs had been attended to, John was discharged into a prisoner of war 'cage', a steel and barbed wire compound sited not far away. He was not there for long. Once rail transport had been organised, he was moved to Altdamm Internment Camp in the North of the German Empire, near the mouth of the River Oder. Built on sandy ground amidst pine woods, it was over a thousand kilometres from home. There was not much chance of a successful escape, but as prisoners they could still be difficult.

* * *

March 1918.

The flimsy wooden dormitories they had to sleep in, and virtually live in, were damp and dreary at the best of times. Nearly fifteen thousand men were encased in the camp, fed on a diet of cabbages and hard labour. It was inevitable that men would break from time to time.

'I won't.'

The fifty-nine other men assigned to John's sleeping accommodation froze in disbelief. Each knew what the punishment would be for disobeying any order issued by a prison guard. Their duties that day were much the same as they had been for several months. They were to work in the forests, typically moving trees that had been felled by German estate workers; internees were not allowed to handle equipment that might be used as weapons. The man, 'Johnson', had refused the order. Why he did, or why that day was not known. All that was known was that he refused, and that every one of his companions would pay the price.

Two other guards marched him off to what everyone believed would be a cell. What his treatment would be then was anyone's guess. The rest of the dormitory were compliant, as they were herded off to another part of the forest to undertake another day's work for Germany. It was not until they returned in the evening that they realised what the punishment would be. Instead of the usual rations of what passed for barley soup, a concoction mostly composed of cabbages, some rye bread, and a few vegetables, they were put on rations of bread and water. Not just for one day, but for five full days. Even at the best of times John and his colleagues hated the German bread, Kommissbrot. They called it black bread and would not have touched it had they any choice in the matter. To have nearly sixty men live on it for five days for the transgressions of one man felt more than unfair.

Johnson was only seen twice after that. They had moved him to another part of the camp, an area containing who they saw as the more difficult prisoners. And duties there were no less demanding, often more so, involving working in the sewers and more dangerous activities. John knew that to have any certainty of staying alive it was best not to fall foul of the German guards, especially with his left hand now almost useless. He knew that if he did break their rules, there would be little sympathy for a physical impairment. He just had to keep his head down.

* * *

'She's not at all well, Emma. With John away, I feel I really ought to be closer to Farnworth. I'm thinking of looking for a job there, or in Bolton,' said Austin.

Austin and Emma were at home in Middleton talking about Austin's mother, Mary. Thomas had joined the Royal Navy, and Edward had moved back home, getting some mechanical work in a local garage. Annie had no such adventures and was still working in the card room at Townley Mill.

'We should, Austin. You know I've wanted to move nearer to Sarah for years. We've said for a while that our next move will be our last, and that it should be to Farnworth, or Bolton,' replied Emma.

'I know, Emma. We did. I'll start to look for something. With most of the young men away I think the jobs will be there. And I have a lot of experience now,' said Austin.

'We could buy a house, Austin,' replied Emma.

'We could,' agreed Austin.

Several factors were now influencing Austin's decision. The increasingly brittle state of his mother's health, Emma's desire to be closer to her sister, and the need to help out John's family in Farnworth whenever he could. They had not heard anything more about John for months, and juggling the needs of travelling to Moston almost every day, and Farnworth weekly, was taking its toll. He needed to find work on the other side of Manchester.

Chapter 9

HOME

It took Austin little time to find a role but, as with many of the jobs he had taken, the opportunity appeared in a rather unorthodox way, at least to him. During the earlier part of his career much of his daily work involved 'getting his hands dirty'. It was the life of a junior engineer. If anything was amiss, or if there were technical repairs to undertake, he would roll up his sleeves and work directly on the machines. Age and experience brought with it seniority and changes in his duties. No longer was he expected to dismantle engines or grease their cogs and wheels. His role was now one of managers' meetings and the supervision of employees.

Although not a director of the mill, nor its manager or salesman, he would on occasion have need to visit the Royal Exchange in Manchester, the premier cotton trading floor in the world. There he would mix with other senior engineers, and sometimes represent the business on commercial matters. It was on one such visit in spring 1918 that he encountered Fred Whitehead, manager of the Dart and Denvale mills in Bolton.

Austin was always somewhat in awe of the Royal Exchange. Although he had visited it many times it was hard not to be impressed by its size, and it was in the process of being expanded still further. The four thousand four hundred square foot would have been nearly doubled in size had the war not intervened and delayed reconstruction. Before, or after, it would still remain the largest commercial trading floor in the world. He was in no doubt that the building was an architectural and engineering feat.

Plans for the new Royal Exchange included extensive basement dining facilities, a billiard room, bar, smoke room, and a post office. But until the war allowed those plans to come into fruition, the existing Exchange's more limited facilities were all that were available. More often than not business would be conducted within the myriad of restaurants that had sprung up in the building's vicinity. As something of a creature of habit, Austin had a tendency to use one particular establishment, having been taken there by Arthur Hadfield, a director of Moston Mill, a few years earlier.

Current plans were to increase the number of business rooms in the Royal Exchange to two hundred and fifty, although that would have to wait. Many mills had no fixed location on the trading floor, and would use private letter boxes for mail communications, or leave messages with the post room if they needed to be contacted.

Austin had left a message to say that he would be dining at the Kingston Restaurant on Mosley Street should anyone need to find him, although he did not expect to see anyone over lunch. His meeting with a number of other engineers was not until mid-afternoon and so he expected to be left undisturbed. It was therefore a surprise when two men appeared at his table just as he was finishing his coffee.

'Mr Melia? Mr Austin Melia?'

Edward looked up. He had been reading that day's copy of the Manchester Guardian.

'Yes. Can I be of service?' replied Austin. Both men were well dressed, a fact which put him on his guard.

'My name is Frederick Whitehead and this is Thomas Higham. Tom and I have some business today at the Exchange, but we do have another matter we would like to discuss with you. Would it be convenient to arrange a meeting, or perhaps even have a short conversation now?'

The two men had already got Austin's immediate attention. It had to be interesting if they were approaching him like this.

'I have a meeting at half past two. We could talk now,' replied Austin.

Fred Whitehead continued to lead the discussion, although Austin did feel that he recognised the other man. Three more coffees were ordered.

'You might have met Tom. He's well known on the lecture circuit hereabouts, the Mutual Improvement Committee.' suggested Fred Whitehead.

'I do recognise you. Excellent and informative lectures. I enjoyed them,' replied Austin who had turned to face the other man; he had indeed attended one or two of his lectures.

'Thank you. I've been impressed with yours as well. Which brings us to the reason why we are here. Do you mind if we call you Austin?' asked Thomas Higham.

Austin nodded.

'We are a little pressed for time, so I'll get straight to the reason for our little meeting. We have a proposition for you, Austin. Can we rely that you will keep this between ourselves before I say any more? said Fred Whitehead.

'Of course,' replied Austin, now fully intrigued.

'Thank you. We have a vacancy for a senior engineer at our Bolton mill, Dart Mill...'

Austin could already see where this was going.

'We also have a second mill in Bolton, Alexandra Mill, which would also be the responsibility of the person appointed. Before I go on, would such an opportunity be of interest to you?' said Fred Whitehead.

'How, er?' started Austin, avoiding an immediate answer.

'How do we know you? I attended one of your lectures last year in Manchester, Austin. It was a capital discussion we all had. You have probably forgotten,' interjected Thomas Higham.

'No, Mr Higham. I remember it well. I do recall it was on how making sure that if right steam pressures are set it can help save running costs. Yes, it was a good discussion. It probably had the best attendance of any I've done recently. Thank you. I would be quite interested. In fact, my wife and I have only recently had a discussion about moving back to Farnworth or Bolton. I'm from there you know,' replied Austin.

'No. I didn't know that. Even better. Perhaps we could arrange a meeting in Bolton to discuss the matter further. You would also need to meet Sir Amos Nelson as well. You might know of him?' said Fred Whitehead, posing it as more of a question.

'Yes, I have. Let me telephone your office and put something in the diary,' replied Austin.

'Of course,' said Fred Whitehead.

The impromptu meeting had lasted no more than twenty minutes, and Austin had essentially been offered a position. Should it result in a move to Bolton in the coming months Emma would be very pleased indeed.

* * *

Only a matter of weeks after the news of John's incarceration in a German internment camp had been conveyed to Ada, Austin was in Bolton negotiating to buy a house. They had chosen a stone fronted terraced house on Tonge Moor Road, only a short tram journey from Union Road, the road leading to Dart Mill. Alexandra Mill on Wolfenden Street, the other mill Austin would be responsible for, was a short walk from Dart Mill, should he want to negotiate the local footpaths and footbridges over the River Tonge.

Sir Amos Nelson, Austin's new employer, was the son of an overlooker. Like his father, he had worked his way up from the shop floor and knew exactly how the cotton business ticked. Grounded in Lancashire culture, he had a reputation for innovation and for being fair. He was also known as being against alcohol, and given the opportunity would have seen it abolished. Before accepting the job in Bolton, Austin undertook a bit of research. It was not difficult to find someone who either knew Sir Amos, or who knew of him, so by the time he had to provide an answer he felt he knew all he could. While both Austin and Emma wanted to move to Bolton, Moston Mill was a good position, and a wartime move might still be a big risk.

In addition to owning mills in Nelson, the Nelson family had interests in the Denvale Mill in Bolton, as well as the Dart and Alexandra. The Denvale was literally next door, a stone's throw away on Union Road. Dart Mill had been in operation since 1906 and was a larger mill than Moston, around a hundred and fifty-six thousand spindles; at least a third larger. The mill's engine was a McNaught build, a Rochdale company Austin was familiar with. Its triple expansion engine was of a similar type to the ones used in marine applications to power ships. The more he discovered the more attracted he was to the proposal. It looked like the answer both he and Emma had been looking for, and as had happened before, the opportunity came to him.

By August both he and Emma had settled in their new home in Bolton.

* * *

News of the Armistice rippled through Europe as fast as modern communications would allow. Many had heard even before the newspapers had printed the news. The mules in the Dart continued to work as the minutes counted down to eleven. On the stroke of the hour the sirens blared. Work suddenly stopped as pandemonium broke loose. Hundreds of workers spilled out on the Union Road to join others all shouting, cheering and singing with smiles on their faces as they marched in adventitious formation towards Bolton town centre.

Austin had decided to walk home to meet Emma, but he had no need. By the time he reached the entrance to the mill, Edward and Emma were both standing there, both eager to witness the spectacle that was developing, and join the celebration.

'It's everywhere,' said Edward.

'We passed hundreds, thousands even, on the way down. The trams were stuck as Tonge Moor Road was so full of people. The shops have shut as well. We walked down here,' added Emma.

'Every mill in Lancashire will have finished early today, probably the whole country. Let's make sure we stay together,' said Austin.

All three joined the multitude heading towards Victoria Square. When they reached Churchgate it became obvious that they would be lucky to get much further. The centre of the town was packed with celebrating townspeople. It was becoming difficult to move. But onward they pressed, determined to be as close to the centre of the occasion as they could reach.

'We'll never make it to the square,' said Austin.

He had to admit defeat. The mass of people was simply too dense, and some of them were starting to take advantage of the public houses which had opened their doors.

'It's getting rowdy, Emma. We'll make our way back. If the trams are running from Trinity Street, perhaps we should see Ada. I don't know what she must be thinking with John still in Germany,' said Austin.

'I'll stay in town,' said Edward, eager to stay in the thick of it.

By the middle of the afternoon the crowd was enormous. Every corner of Victoria Square and its annexes was filled with people, many carrying Union Jacks, shouting 'God Save the King', and singing the national anthem and other patriotic songs. One or two had attempted to create a scarecrow-like effigy of the Kaiser, before punching and stamping on it.

The tram to Farnworth was virtually empty, unlike the ones heading in towards Bolton. Smaller numbers on the street were encountered in Farnworth, but those that were there were no less enthusiastic than the people in Bolton. There was now no doubt that the scenes in Bolton were being repeated across every city, town and village in the country.

The back streets of Farnworth were mostly quiet. Those that intended to celebrate on the street had already left for Market Street, an impromptu meeting point. Fifteen minutes after arriving in Farnworth, Austin and Emma were knocking on the door of 216 Lorne Street, the plain red brick terraced house that had been Ada's home since almost the beginning of the war. Ada looked surprised but pleased to see them both.

'Come in.'

'Bolton is packed with people, and there are a few hundred in Farnworth as well, so far as we can see,' said Austin.

'Edna said most have gone into Bolton. I've got the little ones to look after,' replied Ada.

'There are too many people. I think it's better to do it with family, although we did walk in and have a look,' replied Emma.

'We couldn't get near Victoria Square,' added Austin.

'We wanted to see you. I'm thinking of John and how he might get back home,' said Emma.

'It's the first thing I thought of as soon as I heard the news,' said Ada.

'It could be a while,' said Austin.

'I know. But Edna said that in Leigh they let the German prisoners out of the compound. Just let them loose. No discipline. And you know, they just celebrated with everyone else in Leigh. I dearly hope the Germans are as good to John and our boys as well,' said Edna.

'News travels quickly,' remarked Austin.

'Edna's brother-in-law is a miner in Leigh. They let him finish his shift early and he saw what was happening as he walked past the internment camp. There were no guards. No one bothered. After he cleaned up, he came over to Farnworth with Edna's sister. That's how I know,' replied Edna.

'I wasn't doubting you, Ada. Everyone knew about the armistice before the newspapers were out,' said Austin.

'Can you help me with John, Austin?' said Ada.

'Of course. That's one of the reasons for coming. I'll telephone the Prisoner Committee in London from the mill tomorrow morning, though I think they will be busy. I'll get word to you as soon as I know anything. If we are lucky, he will be home before Christmas,' replied Austin.

'I just want to know he's safe,' said Ada.

'I know you do. I'll do my best,' replied Austin.

'Austin, why don't you go and get us some gin to celebrate. None of us drink very much but if we can't have one today, then when can we?' suggested Ada.

Austin smiled. One or two drinks would harm no one.

'I won't be long,' replied Austin before leaving.

* * *

News of the armistice took a couple of days to filter through to the prisoner of war camps in Germany. One of the methods the camp guards used to communicate with prisoners was through the use of a large bulletin board, updated daily. It usually contained details of new rules, instructions, punishments and anything else the Germans wanted to convey. It was as much a propaganda tool as a news board.

There was just one word in large letters emblazoned across it.

'Waffenstillstand'

A crowd had developed in front of the board.

'What does it mean?' asked one,

'Can someone translate?' asked another.

'Who speaks German?' said a third.

No one seemed able to decipher it.

After fifteen minutes of standing around and talking about it, the most senior rank in those held was summoned. Everyone knew that he could speak a little German, at least better than most present.

The small crowd parted as the officer walked to the front and read the sign.

'I think it's good news men, but I will question a guard,' said the officer.

'What does it mean, sir? asked several.

'I think it means the war is over,' replied the officer.

Ten minutes later the officer reappeared.

'It says armistice. A cease fire has been signed, an armistice,' announced the officer.

The group had multiplied to well over a hundred by this time, responding to the news with a loud cheer. Within half an hour the whole camp was aware.

'I'm going home,' thought John, as he digested the announcement.

* * *

Release was not immediate. Confusion reigned amongst the guards and former prisoners of war during the last couple of weeks of November. The Red Cross had been supporting prisoners with food packages were one source of information, but even they had no clear idea of how release would be administered, and when. To keep the spirits and morale up while waiting for some news, a theatrical party was organised and an orchestra. This helped but could only be a distraction for a short time. Every man wanted to go home.

Instructions were eventually received, and they were that everyone should stay where there were until transport could be organised. The gates were no longer locked, but the soldiers were still to follow orders. As a sergeant, John was assigned some temporary responsibility for some junior ranks. His role became one of keeping his men in the camp, while the former guards and sentries remained just as confused.

It was December 1st before John was released.

'You are going home. Arrangements have been made for you to be transported to the coast. You will be taken to Stettin, and from there to Copenhagen.'

An officer from outside had appeared at the camp two days earlier, and along with some subordinates had been organising the former prisoners into groups. John's group was not the first, but then neither would it be the last. The announcement from the captain had lifted the temperament of everyone listening.

'You embark the transport lorries at 01.00 hours.'

That was it. Two hours from now he would be on his way.

John believed Stettin to be only an hour or two from Altdamm. In his mind he was already thinking that he would be on board a ship by the evening, perhaps even on his way across the Baltic.

* * *

'They look like mines.'

A fellow traveller was pointing at some objects bobbing up and down amongst the waves.

'That's why we didn't leave last night. I spoke to one of the sailors. He said the Germans laid the mines in 1914 and that they will only sail in these waters during daylight. Some of them are tethered but others are free floating,' replied another.

John peered over the edge, nervously examining the strange objects, along with dozens of others. He dearly hoped that at this late stage the voyage would be without incident. The ship had just passed through the Swina River, and he hoped to be in Copenhagen the following day.

Arriving in Copenhagen on 3 December, John and his fellow former prisoners were met at Frihavn quayside by a Captain Davidsen, and a mix of British Army administrators, Red Cross, and Danish volunteers. They were then escorted by rail to a fully equipped Danish army camp that had been constructed during the war to help defend against the Germans. It was a relief to be there. Out of Germany and finally being treated like the soldiers they were. Any men requiring hospital treatment had already been identified onboard ship, and had either been transferred to a hospital in Copenhagen, or moved to a hospital ship. Though weakened due to his hand, John had been deemed fit to travel and was directed to the camp. There he was encouraged to clean up, and given fresh clothes and substantial meals.

The Danish had formed volunteer committees to entertain John and his fellow Tommies. Film shows, dancing, theatre, singing, and tours were organised to keep the returning soldiers occupied. Newspapers, books, and English tea was provided, and all were encouraged to write postcards and letters home. Unlike the long days in Altdamm, the time in Copenhagen passed very quickly, and five days after arriving at the Danish army camp he was on board another ship bound for Leith in Scotland.

* * *

The cold and damp December weather could not depress John's spirits as he emerged from the Moses Gate Railway Station. Home was five minutes away and he knew there would be a warm welcome. But then in those final few steps before reaching his front door he became hesitant; he actually felt nervous. In all of the more than four years he had been away, he had seen Ada and the children for only a few weeks, and nothing of her for nearly eighteen months. The warm welcome he had been thinking about only minutes earlier were suddenly shrouded in doubt. It made no sense but it was how he felt.

For a minute he stood at his own front door, hands clammy and stomach churning. He could hear voices inside, the children and visitors, neighbours perhaps? He had to go in. Grabbing the handle, he pushed the door open. The front room was full of people. He walked in.

'John!'

Ada rushed towards him, almost tripping over Elizabeth, now eight. She flung her arms around him in a tight hug.

Thomas, John's son, was next. He joined his mother in a hug, ignoring the manly convention of a handshake.

'You've grown,' said John.

'I'm thirteen now, Dad,' replied Thomas.

Elizabeth looked at her father a little suspiciously. She hardly recognised him, but could see her mother and brother's joy.

'Come here, Elizabeth. Give your father a hug,' said Ada.

Elizabeth complied, a little hesitant at first, but then seemed to enjoy it.

'And this is Edward. He's nearly five now. He'll have to get used to you, John. He's hardly seen you these past years,' said Ada, picking her son up.

Edward looked at his father then looked away.

'It will take a bit of time, John. But I know he will come round,' said Ada.

'I got your letter about Margaret, Ada. I'm sorry I could not be here,' said John, becoming emotional.

'It couldn't be helped, John,' replied Ada.

The mood in the room changed for a minute or two as the other guests waited for the subject to change. Margaret, John, and Ada's daughter had died while John was on the Western Front in 1917.

Austin and Emma had witnessed the welcome and decided to speak.

'We got your postcard, John. We knew you were coming back this evening but were not sure when. I've missed you,' said Austin, putting his hand out to shake.

'Thank you for helping out, Austin,' replied John.

Several neighbours had visited, bringing with them food and beer. They were not going to let the night pass without marking it. At eight, Austin and Emma decided to leave, realising that John had experienced a long day and that he needed some private time with Ada.

'We'll go, John and Ada, before the trams stop,' said Austin.

John nodded.

'Thank you again, Austin,' said John, putting out his right hand again.

'I should have asked about your other hand, John,' said Austin casting a quick look at his brother's deformed left hand.

'It's not so good, Austin. I don't know what I'll do about work,' replied John.

'Well, we'll have to see, John. They've sent you home but you're not officially demobilised yet. It's the same with our Thomas. We don't know when,' said Austin.

'I know. But the army won't want a cripple,' replied John.

'You aren't a cripple, John. You're a war hero. Let's worry about work when the time comes. I'll see what I can do if Potter's won't have you back. Though Potter is a good man from what I hear. He's done a lot for Bolton and Farnworth,' said Austin.

'I'll be seeing you then. Goodbye Emma,' replied John.

'You will, John. I'll see you right, John. I know others will as well,' said Austin.

Austin and Emma left John with Ada and two neighbours who were still talking.

'I hope they don't stay for too long, Emma,' said Austin.

'Let's hope,' replied Emma.

* * *

Thomas and his fellow ship stokers were told that Captain Bowden-Smith would be making an announcement during the morning.

He was on board the Carnarvon, generally regarded by the crew to be a formidable ship. A Devonshire class cruiser with ten guns, torpedo armaments, and a complement of six hundred and seventy-five, it had served in the Battle of the Falklands earlier in the war. However, it was the world of the engine and boiler room that Thomas was familiar with. He knew a little about engines as a result of being the son of a steam engineer, so when he was told during his training that the ship was powered by a triple expansion, four cylinder inverted surface condensing engine, he had a good idea what it meant, and how it worked. The engines, boilers and screw propellor were all made by Humphrys, Tennant & Co, a Detford based company well known for its maritime work. He was told they were the best engines a ship could have, so for most of the time he and the rest of the crew felt safe, at least with the engineering.

They were sailing somewhere in the Atlantic off the coast of Halifax, Nova Scotia. He was never sure exactly where they were. All he knew was that the ship had left Halifax on November 1st and was out on patrol, protecting the cargoes of British merchant ships bound for home. Great Britain needed food and supplies, and it was the ship's job to do the best they could to defend them from the German U boats which had sprung up everywhere. Hundreds of ships had already been sunk and thousands of lives lost.

It was unusual for the captain to call a ship-wide meeting involving all the ratings. There were rumours about what it might be, but no one was actually sure. They had taken a station at the head of a convoy a day earlier, but that had never been worth an announcement before. Excitement had started to mount, partly fear, but partly anticipation. Some had even claimed Germany had surrendered. Thomas chose to believe no one but the captain. He would wait, like most of the sensible ones, as he thought of his more respected companions.

At seven, chatter on the ship stopped as the captain began to speak. Despite the cold weather many of the crew were on deck, patiently waiting for what was to come.

'I can't hear him,' said Everard, one of Thomas's fellow stokers.

It was true. The captain was doing his best but the wind was picking up and some of his words were being carried away.

'Eleven.......Greenwich..........Germany........signed......
thirty days....,' shouted the captain.

A cheer from the front went up.

'What is it? What is it? Has Germany surrendered? We can't
hear. Sir! Sir!' Everard was insistent.

'It's an armistice. They've signed an armistice this morning,'
the standing crew jabbered and repeated the news.

'What does it mean?' asked Everard.

'It's over. The war's over. We might all be going home,' replied
a petty officer, standing within earshot to Thomas's left.

'No wonder they are cheering,' thought Thomas, the allure of
the Royal Navy already lost.

'Get back below deck.' It was a relief. Although the speech
had lasted a matter of minutes most were already cold and
anxious to return to the warm. Even the hot boiler room
seemed appealing in the face of November in the northern
Atlantic.

There was to be a service at eleven the following day, but that
was it for the celebrations. As far as captain and crew were
concerned, the war might be over but their duties were
certainly not.

With convoy obligations fulfilled, ten days later the ship was
entering the harbour at Devonport. By mid-afternoon it had
docked alongside the first wharf, and orders were issued to
prepare for coaling the following day. With over fifteen
hundred tons likely to be needed it was not a task that any of
the ratings looked forward to, but all understood its necessity.
It usually took a full day.

However, the talk below deck was of the war ending and going home. Some wondered why they were coaling and whether they were to return to sea. 'What was the point', some said. 'The war is over; there is no need,' said others. When most of them joined, it was typically for the duration of the war. Few were long timers; few wanted to stay and have a career in the Navy. Thomas knew that he would simply have to wait. It could be a few months, or it could be a year. The Navy would release him when it was ready.

Granted leave for Christmas, he was instructed to return in January to Devonport. But by the time he was back onboard ship, decisions had already been made. The vessel would not be put out to sea but was to be converted to a training facility for cadets. With the change of use many of the crew were no longer needed and, along with many of his companions, Thomas was demobilised on 9 February. His seventeen months service in the Royal Navy was at an end.

* * *

Emma picked up the postcard which had just dropped through her letterbox at their new home on Tonge Moor Road. Straight away she noticed that it had a Plymouth postmark. It was from Thomas.

'Ma, I'm being demobilised on Sunday morning. I'm coming home. Train gets in to Bolton at 8.45pm. Can't wait. Tom.'

Emma had to read it twice more to take it all in. Thomas was coming home for good. Both of her sons had survived war service. She was lucky, unlike a number of the mothers at St. Patrick's, the Catholic church she and Austin had been attending since coming to Bolton. Sunday was only four days away. There was not much time to organise a homecoming, and in some ways it felt awkward. So many other mothers had lost their sons.

She would have to discuss it with Austin.

* * *

The journey from Plymouth to Bolton was a long one. On boarding the familiar L&Y liveried Bolton bound train in Manchester, Thomas felt that he was already on home territory. It had been dark for over an hour by the time the train rolled into Bolton's Trinity Street Station. The train jerked to a stop as the engine brakes emitted a final squeal, and a jet of steam covered part of the platform. Trinity Street was quiet, although it was a Sunday night in winter. He was just a tram ride away now, a 'T' tram; he remembered from the two occasions he had been on leave. Thomas had to remind himself that it was Bolton that was now home and not Middleton, and that his mother and father had actually bought a house.

It took less than two minutes to reach the top of the wide stairs next to the booking hall.

'Thomas! Tom!'

His father was hard to miss, being one of only half a dozen people either booking tickets or waiting for arrivals.

'Dad.' Thomas acknowledged him.

'Tonight's special, Tom. Your ma insisted that I meet you and get the tram back home with you,' said Austin.

Thomas smiled. He was not a child anymore, but parents would be parents.

'Thank you. I'm glad to be home,' replied Thomas.

'There's one at nine. Did you have a good trip?' asked Austin.

'It was busy to Manchester. So many being demobilised. But quiet into Bolton,' replied Thomas, attempting to suppress a yawn.

'Tired? Your ma has prepared something, Tom. Try and stay awake,' pleaded Austin.

'Yes, Dad,' replied Thomas.

The tram journey was uneventful. Outside of the town centre Sunday evenings were always quiet, and a dark winter evening certainly did not help.

'I'm not sure what I'm going to do, Dad, now I'm out of the Navy. I think I've had my fill of stoking, but I just don't know,' said Thomas.

'There's plenty of time for that, Tom. You've not even got home yet. I can always find something at the Dart if you like. There are plenty of jobs around at the moment. Every mill in Lancashire seems to want to get fully back up and running. We'll talk about that later. Look. We're off at the next stop. I would have gone to the Royal Oak with you but I don't think your ma would have appreciated that,' replied Austin.

A bell rang on the tram, signifying that their Tonge Moor stop was imminent. Austin, Thomas, and another man disembarked. Two minutes later the tram shunted off, heading for its last stop, the Royal Oak terminus.

Emma had been waiting at the window and saw two of the men in her life leave the tram and cross over the road. She opened the front door just as Austin and Thomas arrived and flung her arms around Thomas.

'Ma, it's only been five weeks,' said Thomas.

'This is different, Tom. This is forever,' replied Emma.

'Tom.' That was unusual for his mother; it was usually Thomas.

'Ma.' Thomas could not think of anything else to say.

'Annie and I have prepared a meal and some cake. I know it's late but...' said Emma.

'I know, Ma,' replied Thomas.

'Edward said he would be back by nine. I don't know where he is,' said Emma.

Austin shook his head. 'It's becoming a habit, Emma. I'll have a word with him.'

The table was already set, and the smells of his mother's cooking permeated through all the ground floor rooms. Instead of electric lighting, candles had been lit; they barely illuminated the room but did give a sense of occasion. This was certainly different than the usual Sunday meal.

'Let's sit down. The meal is ready,' said Emma.

'What about Edward?' asked Annie.

'We can't wait. Who knows what time he will–'

'Appear. I'm here. I missed the tram. Sorry,' said Edward, who had suddenly appeared, bursting through the front door and into the dining area.

No one really believed him but no one wanted to argue either. After all it was Thomas's night.

Seated at the opposite end of the table to Austin, Emma scanned the faces of each family member, all of whom had waited for her to sit down. She rested her eyes on Austin who returned an admiring look. Emma was a picture of contentment.

'We should say grace and give thanks for the safe return of Edward and Thomas,' said Emma.

'Amen,' finished Austin.

'The future looks bright,' said Emma.

She hesitated.

'Let's eat.'

EPILOGUE

'Austin, are you asleep?' whispered Emma.

Austin grunted an acknowledgement.

The bedroom was dark except for a scintilla of light from a nearby street lamp penetrating the room through a gap in the closed curtains. Austin and Emma were both lying in bed waiting for drowsy wakefulness to slide into the relief of sleep. Austin's mind had suddenly been summoned from its dormant conscious state to conversational level by Emma's question.

'You know I love all three of them equally,' said Emma.

'I do know that, Emma. What's your point?' replied Austin.

'It's just Edward. And it's a lot of money,' said Emma

Austin knew exactly what Emma was thinking about.

'I know, but we did get the money back from the John Pilling business in Bradshaw. You were worried about it that time,' replied Austin.

'He's been repairing motor cars. This road haulage, lorries thing, is completely different. I know he learned to drive them at Chatham but this is a business. And if Thomas is involved, well, can they work together? You know what they were like at times when they were younger. Annie as well. We can't do for Thomas and Edward without Annie. That wouldn't be fair, would it?' said Emma.

'I'm up early, Emma. Can we talk about it some more tomorrow? replied Austin.

'They always seem to be around, Austin. This is the best time,' said Emma.

Austin yawned. This was a difficult conversation and, in his mind, not one for this time of night. Then again, when Emma had something on her mind it was difficult to argue. He knew she would be tossing and turning, and well, disturbing him if they could not come up with at least the rudiments of a solution. He sat up and reached over for the curtain, opening it slightly, to let in some more light from an outside street lamp.

'Alright. What have you in mind? I know you well enough to know you'll have something that you want to get off your chest.' said Austin.

Emma responded with the combination of an amused smirk and raised eyebrow.

'We need to keep control of it, not just give him, or should I say them, the money.'

'I don't have the time, Emma. You know how busy I am with the mills,' replied Austin.

'Remember, I was brought up in a slate business, Austin. I'll keep an eye on it. And we will call it Melias Lorries or something like that. I don't want Edward to think he owns it or controls it. Thomas, Edward and Annie will be partners,' said Emma.

'Edward won't like it,' replied Austin.

'He will if he wants our money to get it going,' said Emma.

'It's going to need day to day management. Somebody will have to be the boss,' replied Austin.

'We'll organise it so that each have responsibilities and meet on the important decisions. Don't you agree that we need to keep an eye on Edward, at least for now? Have you any better ideas, Austin?' said Emma.

Austin sighed. He needed to get some sleep and this was not helping.

'No, Emma. But I'll have a think about it,' replied Austin.

'Good. I think you will see it's for the best though,' said Emma.

Austin yawned again. Feeling the need to close the subject so that he could sleep, he decided to acquiesce with her thinking.

'Alright, Emma. Whatever you say. Don't call it lorries though. Transport or something,' replied Austin.

'Of course. We'll call it 'Austin Melia Transport'. I think they will understand that,' said Emma.

Closing the curtain, Austin lay back on his side of the bed, hoping that the trek back to an insouciant state of mind would be a short one.

'Let's sleep, Emma,' said Austin.

'I'm excited about it. It will be a family business,' whispered Emma, before laying her head down next to her husband.

ABOUT THE AUTHOR

Ged Melia is married with two adult children and lives on the West Pennine Moors, just outside the village of Edgworth in Lancashire. After a career in accountancy, general management and management consulting, Ged now spends his time writing, trading in collectable books and ephemera and working with a national charity. 'A Lancashire Story' is his second novel and is a prequel to his first, 'Family Business.'

9 781803 810102